BLACK SHEEP

DAVID ARCHER

A
NOAH WOLF
THRILLER

BLACK SHEEP

"I am a Wolf: It is in my nature to be kind, gentle and loving. But know this: When it comes to matters of protecting my friends, my family, and my heart. Do not trifle with me. For I'm also the most powerful and relentless creature you will ever know."

PROLOGUE

Noah Wolf packed his things while Neil and Marco prepared their own. The three of them spoke only when it was absolutely necessary, and usually in sentences of fewer than five words. Sarah's loss was weighing heavily on them all, and none of them, not even Marco, wanted to make it seem more real by talking about it.

There was a knock on the door and Neil turned to open it. Jenny was standing there, her own team behind her with their luggage.

"You guys about ready?" she asked. "I don't think I can stand this place much longer."

"Another minute," Noah said. "Our flight doesn't leave for a few hours, there's not exactly a rush to get to the airport. I was thinking about grabbing some lunch on the way."

Neil scoffed. "Geez," he said, "are you serious? Damn, Noah, even I can't think about food right now. Sarah's gone," he choked out, "doesn't that affect you at all?"

Noah looked at him, but his expression remained stoic. "There's a hole in my world," he said. He turned back to Jenny. "We'll be ready in five minutes. You guys can go on with the rental

1

car, we'll meet you at the airport and get some lunch at one of the restaurants there."

Jenny nodded and turned away without a word. The other three men followed her as Neil closed the door again. He stood there with his back to Noah for a moment, then released the doorknob and turned around.

"Look, Noah," he said haltingly, "I'm sorry about that. Maybe you don't feel things the way we do, but I know how important Sarah was to you. I shouldn't have said that, and I really do apologize."

"Let it go," Noah said. "We each have to deal with the reality in front of us. That's how life works, remember?"

They finished packing and went down to check out of the hotel, then Marco chose a taxi at random. The car was small, and the driver used a bungee cord to hold the trunk closed over their luggage as they got into it. A moment later, they were on the way to the airport.

Noah was in the front seat with Marco behind him, and Neil was behind the driver. He watched Noah as the car rolled along, noticing how the big man watched the city passing by. There was something in Noah's demeanor that Neil felt was different, but he couldn't put his finger on it.

* * * * *

Mr. Pak watched the Americans walk away, then turned to the monk.

"Did they believe you?" he asked.

The monk met his gaze. "The cold one recognized the locks of hair. Strewn among the ashes, they imply that we honored her according to our customs."

Pak nodded solemnly. "Agreed. I suspect that if you were doubted, both of us would soon be prepared for our own burials. The cold one, as you called him, is an American assassin, as is the woman. The lives of monks and businessmen would mean little to them."

He turned and left the temple, returning to the gym. There was no sign that the Americans had stopped there, so he went back into his office and relaxed. Lom, his most trusted man, stepped inside and bowed respectfully to him.

"They are gone," Pak said. "Prepare the girl for her journey. I want her out of the country before midnight."

Lom bowed once again and walked out of the room. Now in his fifties and showing the thinning that comes to an aging athlete, he had once been among the most respected of *Muay Thai* trainers. He passed through the parting sea of fighters and students that crowded the gym as he made his way to a door at the rear, then opened it and stepped through, descending the stairs into the basement. One of the many students who revered him, one of the many who hoped to earn a place in *Nay Thas* by his side, sat on a chair beside yet another door and rose as Lom approached. Without a word, he opened the door and let his Master step through it.

The girl lay on the mat that had been placed on the floor, curled up on her side. Her head turned as Lom entered the room, but she only groaned when she saw that it was him again. He had been the one who had seemed to buy her on the island, and it had been he who had taken charge of her on the boat, lifted her from it and carried her like a lifeless doll to whatever excuse for a doctor they used. The wizened physician had pronounced her alive, if somewhat bruised and with a mild concussion. She would live and could travel, and that was all that seemed to matter to these people.

"Can you stand?" Lom asked in perfect English.

"Screw you," the girl said. A hand went to her head and stroked what remained of her hair. It was less than an inch long, and the filth of the mat had turned it from blonde to a dirty gray.

"I do not wish to hurt you," Lom said. "If you will get up, I can see that you are fed and able to wash. You will be taking a journey this evening, and it is up to me to see that you are as comfortable as possible. I even have clean clothing for you."

She rolled onto her back and simply looked up at him for several seconds, then extended a hand. Lom stared warily into her eyes for a moment, then carefully reached out and took it in his own to help her to her feet.

She was not quite standing when she suddenly yanked him forward and threw a kick at his head, but he blocked it easily with an elbow, then caught her ankle in his hand. He had expected it, of course; she was a captured American agent and would be seeking any opportunity to gain the upper hand, even for a moment. Thrown off balance, she fell back onto the mat on her backside and his foot stopped barely short of crushing her throat.

"Men and women who have trained for years in *Muay Thai* are unable to successfully attack me," he said calmly. "Whatever training you have received, it will not be sufficient to allow you to overcome me. Please do not attempt it again, for I was speaking truth when I said I do not wish to hurt you."

She glared up at him, but when he pulled on her hand again she got to her feet. When he stepped aside and pointed toward the door, she shuffled slowly through it, favoring her right hip. The rip in the pants she was wearing allowed Lom to see the bruise that had spread on it, and he resolved to punish the fool who had damaged the girl. The entire party had been warned that she was of great value; there was no excuse for the condition she had been in when they had brought her to him. The old physician had said she suffered no permanent or serious injury, but valuable property must be handled with care. That fool would be an example to the rest, so that such problems could be avoided in the future.

He followed her out of the room and pointed to another door across the basement. "There is a bathroom in there, and I have already left some clothing in it for you. There is soap for your body and your hair, so that you may at least feel clean. Go and wash, and I will have food brought to you."

"I'm not hungry," she said. She limped toward the door and opened it, then stepped inside and pulled it closed behind her.

The man who had been guarding her raised an eyebrow at Lom, but said nothing. "Leave her alone," Lom said. "She is not to be disturbed as she bathes." He walked over to the bathroom door and slid a bolt into place, locking her in, before he turned and went back up the stairs.

Inside the bathroom, the girl heard the bolt slide home and then slowly began stripping off the filthy clothing she had worn since being taken from the prison. They stank, both from her sweat and the fact that she had been locked in a box with her own urine. She sat down naked on the toilet and made use of it, resenting the gratitude she felt for being allowed such a small touch of dignity.

When she was finished, she stood and stepped into the bathtub beside it. There was a curtain on a rod, and she pulled it across out of habit as she turned on the water and set it to be as hot as she could stand before pulling up the lever that would redirect it to the shower head. It came out cold at first, and she gasped, but then the hot water made it up the pipe and she let it flow over her head and down her body. The heat felt good.

After a moment, she pulled her head out from under the shower and looked around. There was a bar of soap and a small bottle on a shelf, and it wasn't long before she had scrubbed herself red. Once her body was clean, she used a handful of shampoo on the short remnants of her once-flowing blonde locks.

By the time she had rinsed herself off, the water was starting to cool. She turned it off and pulled back the curtain, found the towel that was hanging beside the tub, and rubbed herself dry. She tossed the towel onto the floor and stepped out onto it, then picked up the pair of jeans from the back of the toilet and slid into them before pulling the t-shirt over her head. They fit fairly well and were comfortable, despite the fact that she had no bra or panties.

She heard the bolt slide back, and then Lom opened the door just a crack. "Are you dressed?"

"Would it matter?" she asked. "Since when do animals like you have any respect for a woman's modesty?"

There was no answer. A second later, the door opened the rest of the way and she saw that he was holding a tray. There was a bowl on the tray, along with a bottle of some kind of juice.

"I brought the food anyway," he said. "As I told you, you will be going on a journey. I don't know how soon you will be able to eat again, so I suggest you take advantage of the opportunity now."

She glared at him, but then reached out and picked up the bowl. It was full of rice, with fish and pork and some sort of sauce mixed into it, and when she lifted a spoonful to her mouth she realized that she truly was hungry. Perhaps that was the reason it tasted so good. She'd read somewhere that hunger was the best sauce of all; it might have been true.

Lom turned and pointed, and she saw that he had set up a small table with a chair, so she carried the bowl over and sat down. She took another bite as he set the tray on the table, then looked up at him.

"So, where am I going?" she asked. "Somewhere close by? Some rich man's playground?"

"I'm afraid I cannot give that answer to you," Lom said. "I can only tell you that you will be leaving Thailand by boat. Someone has paid a very high price for you."

"For me? Then somebody is going to be disappointed. I'd rather die than become somebody's little sex toy, and not everyone has had the kind of training you have."

Lom's eyes narrowed as he looked at her. "Sex toy? I'm afraid you might soon prefer that fate to whatever awaits you. There may be many reasons behind your buyer's insistence on purchasing you, but I am quite certain that not one of them has anything to do with sex."

The girl looked at him askance. "Why not? Isn't that what you bastards do? Round up girls and sell them as sex slaves?"

"That is indeed a profitable business, but you have proven to be far more valuable than that. Are you truly surprised to find that there are those who will pay well for a captured American agent?"

She managed to keep the surprise out of her face, but her eyes gave it away. Despite her denials, she knew exactly what he was saying. "American agent? I'm just a girl who got busted for trying to buy some drugs."

Lom smiled at her. "Ms. Child, please do not think me stupid. We know exactly who you are, and who you work for."

She looked him in the eye for another second, then lowered her gaze to the bowl in front of her as she took another bite. "Boy, have you got the wrong girl. My name is Kayla Maguire, and I work for Dempsey's Department Store back in Omaha."

The smile didn't waver. "No. Your name is Sarah Child, and you are an agentF of the United States organization known as E & E. Your duties normally include being the driver for the American assassin whose code name is Camelot. We know this because the information was provided to us by a CIA informant who was involved in preparing the plan for your insertion into the prison, and it was quite costly."

Her eyes rose slowly back to his face, and he could see the defeat in them. She stared at him for almost a minute, then put another bite into her mouth. She picked up the bottle of juice and took a long drink from it, never letting her eyes move from his own.

"CIA sold me out?" she asked. "Who was it? Can you tell me?"

"I do not have that information. However, does it truly matter? The fact is that you have been compromised. As I understand it, your government will never acknowledge your existence. Should they ever admit that you and your compatriots were in Thailand to perpetrate an escape from our prison system, it would create an international incident, and could well be considered an act of war. Once you are captured, you become useless to them. Your only value now is in the information that can be extracted from you."

"Then you're still screwed," Sarah said. "As you pointed out, I'm just a driver. I don't exactly get briefed on any important state secrets."

"I'm certain you do not, but you know, at the very least, what your mission objective was, and I'm certain you know a great deal about the organization you work for and how it functions. I would naturally suppose that this is the information your buyer hopes to obtain. Considering how valuable such information seems to be, there is little doubt that those who bought you will stop at nothing to get it."

The fear in her eyes shone through for a moment before she could hide it, but then she put on a brave face. "I don't know that much," she said. "They can do their worst, but they're not going to get anything worth having."

Lom shrugged his shoulders. "That does not matter to me, of course. My duties only involve getting you ready for the journey. If you have finished eating, then I should be taking you to the docks."

"Keep your panties on," Sarah said, and she picked up the spoon again. "Like you said, I don't know when I'll get the chance to eat again." She shoved another bite into her mouth, then cocked her head to the left. "And just so you know, while my government might do nothing to try to get me back, that doesn't mean I won't be rescued. Remember that assassin, the one known as Camelot? His number one rule is that he never leaves anyone behind. I feel sorry for you when he finFds out I was here."

"I don't think I have anything to worry about," Lom said. "You see, he was here just an hour ago, and he was taken to the temple and shown evidence that you are dead. Our contact says he is already making preparations to return to the United States."

Sarah stopped chewing. "No," she said, "that's not possible."

ONE

The flight from Pattaya back to Denver took nearly a day and a half, with a total of four layovers along the way. It was already after ten PM when Noah and the rest were finally able to leave the airport and head back to Kirtland.

Jenny and her team had come back with them, but they had a van of their own waiting in long-term parking. By pure coincidence, it was parked only three spaces away from Neil's big Hummer, so they drove out of the parking lot and hit the highway together. Dave Lange drove the van, and kept it on Neil's tail until the Hummer peeled off the exit and onto the highway that would take it to Noah's house.

"What do you think will happen now?" Neil asked as he drove along the dark road. "Will there be a funeral, a memorial service?"

"Of course," Marco said. "Neverland never forgets her people. Sarah was one of its best, so you can be sure Allison is planning something big for her."

"Won't matter," Neil said, and there was a sniffle in it. "Sarah's gone, and it just won't be right to have someone else in her place. Especially not right after we lost Moose, y'know? She shouldn't have even been in that prison, they should've sent Jenny or someone like that in there. Not Sarah. She was just too—she was too nice, y'know what I mean?"

"Let it go, Neil," Noah said. "There's nothing you can do, and it wasn't your fault. You have to let it go or it'll eat you alive."

"Yeah, and that's from the man who can't even grieve over the woman who loved him. Forgive me, boss, if I don't think you're all that qualified to advise me on emotional matters, okay?"

"We all grieve in our own ways, Neil," Marco said, but Neil cut him off.

"Not him," he said. "Noah doesn't grieve at all. He doesn't even know how."

The kid shook himself, then, as if he was just hearing the things that were coming out of his own mouth. "Noah," he said, "man, I'm sorry, I didn't mean any of that..."

"Let it go, Neil," Noah said.

Noah and Jenny had both called in before leaving Thailand, and both were scheduled for debriefing the following morning, Noah at nine AM and Jenny at eleven. Noah climbed out of the Hummer and walked into his house without even saying goodbye to Neil and Marco. Marco got into his own car and drove away while Neil cut across the yard to park beside the trailer he rented from Noah.

Inside the house, Noah dropped his luggage and went into the bathroom. He took a quick shower, then walked into the bedroom and pulled the covers down on the bed and climbed into it. He set an alarm on his phone and closed his eyes, drifting to sleep only a few minutes later.

Noah Wolf dreamed only rarely, and most of his dreams

involved the afternoon his parents had died. That was the tragic event that had shaped the rest of his life by leaving him completely devoid of emotion. It was a rare form of PTSD known as histrionic affect disorder, but rather than cripple him, the condition had allowed him to form a code of ethics all his own, one that made him the incredibly efficient soldier and killer he had become.

On this particular night, however, he had a dream that was completely unrelated to that tragedy.

He was lying in bed, and suddenly felt Sarah's arms go around him. He turned his head to look at her and saw her face. It was bruised and bloodied, and the expression it wore was a pleading one.

"I'm not dead, Noah," she said in a hoarse whisper. "Don't leave me behind."

"I won't," he replied. "But I have to find the trail before I can come for you. I won't give up, I promise you. Stay strong, Sarah, and I'll find you."

She stared at him through bloodshot eyes for a moment, then shook her head. "No, you won't," she said, and then she was gone.

Noah awoke instantly and turned to look at her side of the bed. For the first time in many years, it took him almost an hour to get back to sleep.

When the alarm went off, Noah rose and dressed quickly, then made himself a cup of instant coffee and carried it to the Corvette. He started the car up and backed out of the drive, then hit the road toward Allison's office in the conference room.

He arrived ten minutes early, but Allison's secretary told him to go on in. Donald Jefferson was already there, just setting out the doughnuts, and Allison came in only a moment later.

"Report, Camelot," she said. "Tell me what the hell went wrong out there."

Noah had not shared his suspicions with anyone yet, and especially not over cell phones that were on two separate continents. When he had called in, he'd simply said that he would make a full report during his debriefing.

"Somebody sold Sarah out," he said. "I haven't figured out who yet, but I suspect it was someone on my team. While I don't believe Neil would ever betray her, I haven't ruled him out as a suspect. If it was one of mine, I'd have to put my suspicions on Marco."

Allison didn't seem surprised, but Donald Jefferson leaned forward. "Sold out to whom?"

"I have no information about that," Noah said. "While it may have been coincidental that Sarah was taken from the prison, the fact that she was in the possession of the *Nay Thas* and was then sold to someone before she was broken and trained tells me that the buyer had to have known something about who she really is. When I saw what was obviously lots of her hair scattered among ashes at the temple, I realized that she had not only been compromised, but was being turned over to someone for interrogation."

"And yet you did nothing about it before leaving Thailand," Allison said. "That sounds odd, Noah, especially for you."

"Pak involved the monks of the temple in the deception, so that tells me this is a lot bigger than just trying to cover up a girl sold into sexual slavery. While I might have gotten some information on where she was taken by torturing him, the people he surrounds himself with make it more likely that we all would have died in the attempt. I had to decide whether it was more important to attempt to retrieve her or to find out how she was compromised and identify the traitor, and I chose the latter. The security of E & E has to take precedence over the life of any particular agent. Once I know how this happened, I'm going to request permission to go back after her."

"Then you believe whoever has her was told who she is and who she works for?" Allison asked.

Noah nodded. "Logically, it's the only scenario that makes sense. I've gone over the mission repeatedly, and every member of both teams had at least one opportunity to make contact with someone, and that includes our people in Thailand."

Allison nodded back. "I agree with your conclusions," she said. "I've already got CIA working on our people over there, to see if any of them might have been compromised, but the reports thus far are clean. As for your team and Jenny's, I frankly find it hard to believe that any of them could have betrayed us this way, but I can't deny that I've seen it happen before. Agents who seem loyal and trustworthy may harbor feelings of resentment or dissatisfaction that lead them to betray teammates, organizations, even the country. At this point, no one is above suspicion." She looked him calmly in the eye. "That includes you, Noah."

Noah nodded. "Of course. I've been considering possible avenues of investigation, but I wanted to discuss all of this with you before making any recommendations."

Allison shook her head. "First, you made the statement a moment ago that every member of both teams had at least one chance to make contact and sell Sarah out. Explain."

"There are three logical possibilities." He held up one finger. "First, the people who took Sarah out of the prison may have known already who she was, and the roundup of girls may have been nothing but a smokescreen to hide the fact that they were after her in particular. If that were the case, then the most logical scenario would indicate someone from the E & E station in Bangkok, or it could be that either Marco or Neil made contact with a foreign agent and revealed that she was coming in. Marco was out of my sight twice before she got to the prison, and Neil is capable of making contact with anyone through his computers, possibly even right under my nose."

Noah held up a second finger. "The second possibility is that the roundup actually was coincidental, and that the unknown persons who took her were contacted after the fact. Marco and Neil are still possible suspects, but now we have added factors: Jenny and her team. Jenny spent several hours inside the prison posing as Sarah's sister, and it's possible she was compromised and gave up information to save herself, or sold it to benefit financially. David Lange went out with Neil to purchase some equipment, and could have made contact while he was out of Neil's sight. Randy Mitchell and Jim Marino also had opportunities to communicate with someone unobserved."

"Have any of them displayed what you would consider atypical behavior?" Jefferson asked.

"Nothing that I can specifically identify. Neil has acted perfectly normal for Neil, and while it's possible he could have done this, I personally find it inconceivable. Marco seems occasionally dissatisfied with my decisions, but he never offered me any argument and always obeyed my orders. Jenny's team is unfamiliar to me, but their behaviors were consistent from the moment I met them."

"What about the third possibility?" Allison asked.

"At Jenny's suggestion, we involved two women from the E & E station in Pattaya. It's entirely possible that one or both of them have some sort of contact with Pak and the *Nay Thas*. If so, the fact that an E & E agent had been captured in the roundup might have been too tempting an opportunity to pass up. That information would undoubtedly be extremely valuable."

Allison leaned back in her chair and looked at him. "I detest the thought that any of my people could have done something like this," she said, "but I can't find any flaws in your deductions. As I mentioned previously, I have CIA going over all of the communication and activity logs of our people over there, and they haven't found anything yet that could be a discrepancy. What do you recommend as the next step?"

"I considered suggesting polygraph tests, but most of the people in our line of work could probably beat one. What about a deception expert? From everything I've read, it's impossible to prevent the minute facial expressions and body language they watch for."

Allison frowned and ran a hand over her face. "It's difficult, but not impossible, and especially not for anyone with psychopathic or sociopathic tendencies. Unfortunately, the people best suited for this work display some of those. Donald and I have both been trained in deception detection, but we've been fooled in the past." She turned to Jefferson. "Donald? Any suggestions?"

Jefferson chewed his cheek for a couple of seconds, then nodded his head. "The thing to do is keep whoever betrayed us unbalanced. We've got the situation in Pyongyang that we need to deal with right away; it's complicated and dangerous, so my thought is to tell Jenny that Cinderella and Camelot work so well together that we've decided a joint operation between them is what we need for that mission. Put them back together and in the field again, with no time to rest, and give Noah a better chance to observe them."

"Then you're convinced Noah is not the one who sold Sarah out?"

"I don't think he could possibly have done it unless it somehow benefited the mission, and it certainly did not. As of this moment, Noah is the only one in this group that I trust completely."

"Good," Allison said. "We are agreed on that." She turned to Noah. "Noah, there are four CIA agents in North Korea who have been captured, and unfortunately they possess a great deal of knowledge regarding certain Top Secret plans that the president has authorized in dealing with the little madman who runs the country there. CIA says rescue is impossible, so they have requested immediate termination of all four in order to maintain National Security. We were about to brief Hercules on the mission today, but I'm going to accept Donald's recommendation. Because the mission will be difficult and dangerous, we're going to send you and Jenny and your people on this one."

"Yes, Ma'am," Noah said. "May I ask a question?"

"Go ahead."

"Sarah has been captured, and she also possesses secret information. Will she be sanctioned?"

Allison leaned forward and looked him in the eye. "How long do you think she can hold out under interrogation?"

"Sarah is tougher than she thinks she is," Noah said. "She's loyal to the organization, but she'll regard any demand to give up information about our organization as being forced to betray me as well as E & E. Combined, both of those factors will keep her from any betrayal until she's subjected to enough pain to make her willing to die to escape it. Once that happens, the thought of dying will mean she won't have to face any of us if she betrays us, so she can give up something in the hope of getting what she wants, which at that point will be death. Depending on the level of torture, we could be talking anywhere from three days to a week."

Allison paused for a second then went on. "The most damaging information she could give up would involve the secret areas around Kirtland, and perhaps a few of our proprietary procedures or some of the inventions Wally's kids come up with. The world intelligence community already suspects that we exist, and neither my name nor Donald's is any secret in those circles. She might compromise your team, but we could simply switch up identities again and put you right back in the field." She leaned back and put her elbows on the arms of the chair, steepling her fingers in front of her face. "Noah, I won't authorize a sanction on Sarah. I don't think she knows enough to do us any real harm, and frankly, I want her back. That means you've got no more than a week to identify the traitor *and* find out where Sarah has been taken. I'm going to authorize unlimited resources for you on these two missions."

She sat forward again. "Go home. Tell Neil and Marco that you're being briefed on an urgent new mission at one o'clock this afternoon, and will be flying out tonight. I'll explain that to Jenny during her debrief this morning, so you'll all be here at one."

"Yes, Ma'am," Noah said, as he rose and started toward the door.

"Noah?" Allison said.

He stopped and turned to face her. "Yes?"

"When you identify the traitor," she said, "your orders are to terminate with extreme prejudice."

Noah nodded once. "Yes, Ma'am," he said. He walked out the

door and was on the way home a few minutes later. As he drove, he took his phone out of his pocket and called Neil.

"Mmpf," the boy said, trying to rouse himself from sleep. "Wassup?"

"Emergency mission," Noah said. "Get yourself awake and head over to the house. We've got an emergency briefing at one, and we're going to be flying out tonight."

"What?" Neil sputtered, and Noah heard Lacey's voice in the background asking what was wrong. "We just got in!"

"As I said, it's an emergency mission. I'll call Marco now, so he'll know to make the briefing. And just so you know, Team Cinderella is going with us on this one. The Dragon Lady likes the way we work together."

"Oh, God," Neil mumbled. "Jenny scares the crap out of me. That woman is just plain evil." He let out a long sigh. "Okay, boss, whatever you say. I'm getting up."

Noah ended the call and punched the icon for Marco. Unlike Neil, Marco was already awake.

"Hey, boss," he said. "To what do I owe the pleasure?"

"We've got an emergency mission," Noah said. "Briefing at one o'clock."

"Geez, already? Doesn't that break some kind of rule, sending us out again this quick?"

"The Dragon Lady thinks it's necessary, and she makes the rules. See you at the briefing."

"You got it," Marco said, and then the line went dead.

Noah drove on to his house, deep in thought. No matter how many times he went over what he remembered of the snafu'd mission, he couldn't make the facts line up enough to identify a particular traitor. Until he had some idea of who had sold Sarah out, it was going to be hard to find any leads on where she'd been taken, unless he retraced his steps and went back to Pattaya.

The problem was that trying to find out anything from Pak would still be likely to result in a bloodbath, and Noah couldn't go after Sarah if he was dead.

* * * * *

Sarah was driven to the dock in the back of a van with no windows, but it wouldn't have mattered if she had been able to see out. She didn't know anything about the area, and had no way to signal anyone. If Lom had been correct, there was no one to signal in any case.

At first, when Lom had told her that Noah was leaving her behind, she had refused to believe it. Later, however, it dawned on her that if he truly believed she was dead, his logical mind would see no reason to remain. He would go home, and go on with his life without her.

That was the hardest part for her, the knowledge that he wouldn't even grieve for her loss. It wasn't his fault, she knew that, but still…

When they arrived at the dock, she was quickly taken out of the van and hustled onto a large motor yacht. The boat was big enough for her to think of it more as a ship, but she only saw its stern. She was hustled down a flight of stairs and pushed into a room. She heard the door lock as soon as it was closed.

She seemed to be in a stateroom, a nice one with its own en-suite head. She had only showered a short time earlier, and she remembered what Noah had always told her about resting whenever she could, so she lay down on the bed and tried to relax.

Her mind was racing, though. Just the thought of someone betraying her, someone she had worked with and trusted, was more than she could take, but if it was anyone close to her, she was convinced it had to have been Marco. Noah would never do such a thing, and it was impossible to even entertain the thought that Neil might.

Of course, there were other possibilities. The local station chief was going to be aware of their mission, and who knew how many others? That thought made her feel a little better, at least; perhaps it wasn't someone she knew, but a perfect stranger who had done this to her.

The huge diesel engines started up and the big vessel moved away from the dock. Wherever she was going, she was on the way. Between the vibration of the engines and the rocking motion, Sarah's thoughts finally wound down and she drifted off to sleep.

She woke suddenly and found herself in her own bed, with Noah, and the relief that it had all been only a dream washed over her like a wave fifty feet high. She rolled over and wrapped her arms around him, and he turned his face toward her.

It wasn't Noah! The man she had wrapped her arms around was Lom, and he was laughing as he saw her pulling back. "Where is he?" she screamed at the thin old man, but he only laughed harder.

She tried to get up out of bed, but the sheets and blankets were tangling around her, pulling her back down, and then they were wrapping themselves around her face so that it was hard to breathe...

TWO

Jenny Lance walked into Allison's meeting room precisely on time, and sat in the same chair Noah had used earlier. Allison smiled at her as she took her own.

"Report, Cinderella," Allison said.

"My team and I arrived in Hanoi on schedule, and I made contact with the target that evening. His reputation as a ladies' man proved to be quite accurate, so I had dyed my hair blonde and dressed in the youthful styles he seemed to like. He invited me to a party and I agreed, then pretended to be drunk when it was time to leave. He took me to his home, and as soon as I was sure that we were alone, I cut his throat, disemboweled him, then removed his penis and put it in his mouth. I then signaled my team for pickup and returned to my hotel."

"Perfectly executed, as always," Allison said. "You'll be interested to know that his associates in the heroin trade are all accusing one another of the killing. The bit with his pecker was a nice touch; two of his partners were known to have done exactly that with American soldiers during the Vietnam War. There is so much infighting in the organization now that it will probably be defunct within a few months. Good job."

Jenny smiled at her. "I enjoyed it," she said. "Of course, as we were preparing to leave Hanoi the next morning, I got the call telling us to join Camelot in Bangkok. You remember that when you told me the situation, I suggested I pose as the sister, and that seemed to work fairly well. As I anticipated, the prison officials notified the *Nay Thas*, and they attempted to abduct me as well. My team worked with Camelot and his to extract me, and we were able to ascertain that Sarah and the other girl were taken to *Khram Yai*, an island in Pattaya Bay. We all went together to Pattaya and I contacted Maggie Lightner, our station chief there, and arranged for her and another woman from her staff to accompany us on a rented yacht. While most of us stayed on the yacht or played in the water around it, Camelot and Marco swam to the island to reconnoiter. They were able to confirm the presence of the two girls, so we returned to Pattaya and planned a night attack. The whiz kid, Neil, came up with an electric boat that was almost silent and we used it to reach the island in the dark, and were able to retrieve the other girl, but Sarah had already been taken away. I interrogated a few of the men from the island and was told that she had been sold to a man named Pak, but did not seem to be breathing when she was taken, so we returned to Pattaya. Neil located Pak, so the next day, after making sure the girl we rescued was sent back to the states, we paid him a visit. I posed as a fight promoter to get access to him, then explained that we were really looking for the girl he had bought from the island. He informed us that she was deceased, and we were taken to the temple where locals' funerals and cremations take place. A monk there confirmed his story verbally, and we were shown a place in a flower garden where the monk said her ashes had been scattered. He also said that in order to honor her, they had cut off locks of her hair and spread them with her ashes. Camelot confirmed that he recognized the hair, and that he accepted their story. We returned to our hotel and made arrangements to leave the country."

Allison smiled at her again. "Concise and to the point. Now, give me your opinions."

"There's something not right about the whole mission," Jenny said. "First off, it seems awfully funny that we send an agent into a prison to set up the rescue of another inmate there, and then both of them are kidnapped out of it by known slave traders. Strikes me as an awfully big coincidence, you know? Then there's the fact that Sarah got sold to Pak, but the other girl didn't. If he was into pretty Americans, I'd expect him to want them both. I can definitely tell you that he lit up when he saw me; the man had a bulge in his pants the whole time I was near him. He didn't go to that island looking for sex toys, he was looking for Sarah."

Allison narrowed her eyes as she looked at the young woman in front of her. "And your conclusions?"

"Someone involved with Pak found out that Sarah was an American agent. That tells me that somebody on our side sold her out. After watching Camelot, I can't believe he would do it, so I suspect it was one of the two men with him. There are other possibilities, of course, including the possibility it was someone on my own team, but I don't think so. Also, after watching Camelot in action, I'm fairly certain that he has also figured this out. If I'm right, then I'm probably his number one suspect. After all, I spent a lot of time inside that prison demanding answers. From his point of view, I had the best possible chance to sell or trade the information that Sarah was one of ours."

"That's very astute," Allison said. "You are correct in that Noah came to the same conclusions, and even mentioned your time in the prison as being a good opportunity, but he does not suspect you above anyone else. Have you shared these opinions with your team?"

"No," Jenny said. "As I said, there is at least a slim possibility that one of my guys decided to capitalize on the chance to make some big money. God only knows how much somebody like Pak would pay to get his hands on an American secret agent, but there is no doubt he'd know how to turn a profit from her."

"I agree," Allison said. "Anything else?"

"The girl isn't dead. And Camelot knows that, too."

"Why do you say that?" Jefferson asked. "Both."

Jenny turned her face toward him. "If she was actually dead, Pak wouldn't have bothered trying to convince us, he'd simply have dropped her body somewhere it would be found. That way, there wouldn't be any doubt. The fact that we were taken to the funeral temple and shown ashes and hair means that he wants us to give up on her, but he still intends to make a profit. He couldn't do that if she was dead." She shrugged. "As for why I think Camelot knows it? That guy has a mind like a computer, he can see things nobody else would. There is no way he wouldn't figure out exactly what I just said, and he probably even saw things I missed that confirm it for him."

Allison watched her face while she was speaking, and sat in silence for a moment after she finished.

"Once again," she said, "you are correct. Camelot is aware that Sarah is alive, but he could not see any reasonable path to being able to retrieve her at that time. His mind, more like a computer than you can imagine, led him to the conclusion that identifying her betrayer was of paramount importance to our organization, and probably the only chance he has to get whatever intelligence it will take to get her back alive. Like you, he considers our local people in Thailand as suspects, but I keep them on a much tighter leash than any other agency does, and it's virtually impossible for one of them to have done this. CIA has gone over each of them with a fine-tooth comb for the last nineteen hours, and we've found nothing to indicate that any of them has made any improper contacts."

"So that means the traitor is either on his team or mine," Jenny said. "If it turns out to be one of my guys, I want the pleasure of killing him."

"I suspect you'd have to beat Camelot to it." She looked at Jefferson. "Donald?"

"Jenny's smart, but she's not as smart as Noah. If she were the one who had betrayed Sarah, she wouldn't have shared her suspicions with us so readily. Also, I observe that every time she mentions Pak, her eyes contract slightly and the corners of her mouth turn down for a split second. Together, those micro-expressions indicate that she is controlling feelings of anger, disgust. If she had secretly profited from whatever deal he made to get his hands on Sarah, that little sign of anger wouldn't be there; I'd expect to see something more like satisfaction, or pleasure."

"I agree," Allison said. "Jenny, I'm sending your team back out with Camelot on another mission, today. Have your team here at one o'clock for briefing. This is a very serious and important mission, so I expect it to be carried out successfully, but the real reason for teaming the two of you up is to identify the traitor. Camelot will have lead on this mission, and you'll all be subject to his orders."

She leaned forward and clasped her hands together on her knees, looking Jenny straight in the eye. "You will not share your suspicions with any of your team. I'll let Noah know that we consider you eliminated as a suspect, but be certain that you don't even discuss it with him if there's any possibility of being overheard."

Jenny smiled brightly. "Okay. See you at one o'clock."

She got up and walked out of the room, still smiling, but by the time she got to the elevators the smile had vanished. Unlike Noah, Jenny was a creature of emotions, and the strong suspicion that one of the men she had worked with during this last mission had betrayed one of their own had her blood boiling. Before she reached the parking garage in the basement, Jenny had already figured out how she wanted to kill the traitor if he could be identified.

She got into her classic '65 Mustang and took out her phone. It took her only a moment to text all three of the men on her team.

Emergency mission. We are going out with Camelot again, woo hoo. Briefing room at one o'clock.

Jim Marino was the first one to call her, as she pulled out of the underground garage. "Jenny? What gives?"

"I told you, emergency mission," she replied. "Something big, but I don't know any details yet. Boss lady says she wants us and Noah on this one, so it must be pretty serious. Why? You got some kind of vacation plans?"

"Nah," he said, "but I was hoping for at least a little bit of a break. They don't usually send us out again so soon after a mission. You're right, it must be something pretty hot."

"Yeah, that's what I said. Gotta go, Randy's beeping in." She hit the flash button and smiled into the phone. "Randy, baby! Ready to get back in the saddle?"

"I guess so," Randy said. "Any idea where we're headed?"

"You know the old lady won't give me any advance details. I'll find out when you do, at the briefing. One o'clock, you got that?"

"Yeah, I got it," he said. "Okay, I'll be there."

"See you then, stud." She ended the call and waited, but it didn't ring again. Instead, she got a text back from Dave saying he'd be at the briefing on time.

Jenny drove straight to her house on McKinley Street and pulled the Mustang into her garage. She hit the button to close the garage door, then sat in the car until it was down and the inside lights came on. It was an old habit she had gotten into, never getting out of the car until the door was closed. It lowered the risk of being targeted if a sniper was watching for her return.

When the lights came on, she got out and walked into the house through the steel door she had installed between it and the garage, then turned immediately to the right and went down the stairs into the basement. Jenny had a room set up down there as a home theater, with a projection TV set that put the picture on a ten-foot-wide screen. Sometimes she invited friends over for movie parties, and it was a lot like having her own theater all to herself. She even had a popcorn machine and soda fountain installed, so it would be even more like the real movie-house experience.

She dropped into one of the couches that were set up as seating, picked up the remote and started scanning through movies. There was an incredible selection, all saved digitally on a massive Seagate hard drive. All she had to do was choose, and the movie would be on the screen before she could put down the remote.

She chose one of her favorite horror films. When the rage started to build up inside her, watching extremely realistic scenes of cruelty and murder was the only thing that could damp it down and put her back in a good mood. That was usually enough for a short while, and then she'd get to go out on another mission.

Sure was a good thing they didn't deduct points for when she went overboard, but Allison had told her point blank that she could indulge herself all she wanted, as long as she only killed the target and any necessary collaterals. That was fine with Jenny; she only really got off when she knew her victim really deserved it, anyway.

THREE

Noah Wolf was a logical strategist. He examined every detail he could learn about a mission before it began and developed a mission plan that allowed him to take every possible advantage of advance knowledge. He made every effort to deduce and include factors that might go wrong, so that he could simply take them in stride and continue.

Jenny Lance, on the other hand, preferred to go into a mission and evaluate it from the inside. Since the vast majority of her targets were totally and viciously male, her petite, athletic figure and angelic face were almost always enough to let her get close to them. Once she accomplished that, determining how, where and when to make the kill was easy for her.

Jenny was classified as a high-functioning sociopath. She had always been manipulative, and with an IQ of nearly 140, she had always been the girl who could get whatever she wanted. Unfortunately, her relationships had suffered because she had a tendency to use people like pawns and then discard them when she was finished. She could be a charmer when she wanted, and could instantly adapt herself to any social situation. With those abilities, it was easy for her to get just about anyone to do whatever she wanted at the time.

The only person she had ever felt truly close to had been her sister, Leanne. Jenny was the elder by four years, and while she had occasionally used Leanne as she did others, she spent more time protecting her baby sister from their abusive father and apathetic mother. When she graduated high school and left for college in Florida, she spent at least an hour every night on the phone with Leanne.

Then, just after beginning her sophomore year at FSU, Jenny got the phone call that would change her life forever. Leanne had been found dead during a trip with her mother to New York City, the victim of rape and strangulation. The police suspected a sixteen-year-old boy of the crime, but more than a dozen of his friends smugly swore that he had been with them when it happened. They were all members of the same gang, and the suspect became a full member immediately after Leanne's death. Investigators were convinced that the rape and murder had been part of his initiation, but without conclusive evidence there was nothing they could do.

Jenny dropped out of college and went to New York. Her name at the time had been Genevieve Spears, and her search for a job led her to audition for a part in a soap opera, which she got. It was a small part, but her innate acting ability got her noticed by TV critics and magazines. Had she chosen, she probably could have worked her way into some form of stardom.

It was all part of her camouflage, however. Jenny had decided that her sister's death would be avenged, at first only planning to try to bring the killer to justice. When she found out that her sister's life had been the price of admission to a gang, however, she decided that a more permanent solution was needed.

Jenny had once seen a movie that left an impression on her. Val Kilmer played a prison inmate who was serving multiple life sentences because he murdered sixteen people. His reasoning was that one of them had murdered his wife and daughter in cold blood, and so he killed that individual along with his entire family, in order to remove their seed from the gene pool.

For more than two months, Jenny carefully stalked then-seventeen-year-old Shaundel Sanders. Watching him carefully, never exposing herself, she saw his sadistic and cavalier attitude toward girls, which convinced her that the police had been correct. Once, she overheard him joking with his brothers about "that little white bitch I wasted." It was at that moment that Jenny decided to emulate Kilmer's character. She would eliminate things like Shaundel from the gene pool of the human race, by killing not only him but his entire family.

Four more months passed as Jenny, in various disguises, carefully studied Shaundel's family, which seemed to consist only of himself, his three brothers and their parents. She observed each of them, determined to figure out the best way to get close enough to kill them all. She had watched their movements throughout the day, knew their habits and even those of their neighbors. The little four-flat building they lived in had only two other tenants, a couple who owned a bakery and always left for work at three o'clock in the morning. The two flats on the ground floor were empty, and the windows and doors boarded over.

She struck just after dawn. One of the brothers, Michael, had a habit of coming in as the sun came up, and Jenny was on the street where she knew he would see her. The sight of a pretty little white girl was all it took to catch Michael's attention, and as she'd expected, he instantly began to flirt. Jenny batted her eyes and blushed, pretending to be flattered, and then accepted when he told her he was an artist and wanted to paint a picture of her.

As he took her arm and walked her toward his apartment building, he told her about his brothers and how he was sure they would all love to meet her. Still smiling, she told him she thought that would be great, so when they made it up the stairs to his apartment, he told her to have a seat on the sofa while he woke them up and got his easel and paints.

It took almost 20 minutes for him to get all three of his brothers, including Shaundel, to roll out of bed and come meet "his new ho," and Jenny sat patiently as she was introduced to first one, then another and finally the youngest. Their parents, Michael told her, were still sleeping but would be up soon. She could meet them then.

Jenny had smiled sweetly at all three of the boys, then asked if they would mind if she smoked. When they laughed and told her to go ahead, she opened her big purse and reached inside. Instead of cigarettes, however, she pulled out a nine-millimeter pistol.

Three months of almost daily practice at a gun club in Jersey paid off. Jenny didn't need to aim; each bullet went where she pointed the gun, and she saved Shaundel for last. He had watched in shock as she fired three times in less than two seconds, blowing the brains out of all three of his brothers before turning the gun to him.

"Remember the 'little white bitch?' The one you raped and murdered so you could join the Purple Bloods? That was my little sister."

Shaundel had fallen off of the sofa onto the floor and was crying as he tried to crawl backward away from her. "I din do shit to no white girl, bitch, why you doin' this? Who da hell is you?"

The terror in his face and voice sent a thrill down Jenny's spine, and she suddenly broke into a huge smile. "Who is I?" she asked. "I am death, you asshole," she said, the last words he ever heard. Her single bullet wiped him out of existence as it pushed his brain out the back of his skull, leaving his face with what almost looked like a third eye.

Provided you didn't look too closely.

She turned toward the door Michael had pointed to when he said his parents were sleeping. It was time to make sure there couldn't be any more like these, but suddenly she heard shouting from the apartment next door.

"Police comin'," she heard a man call out, "I done call nine one one, they comin'!" She cursed softly, frustrated that the neighbors had apparently not left for work at their usual time. For a brief moment she considered adding them to her list, but then she chided herself. They'd had nothing to do with her sister's death, she knew, and she was only here for vengeance.

The bedroom door opened and a woman looked out, saw Jenny and slammed it shut. An instant later she heard hysterical screaming from inside that room, so she raised the gun and emptied its clip through the door, then turned and left the apartment. She ran down the stairs, shoving the empty gun back into her purse as she did so, and emerged onto the sidewalk just as a squad car slid to a stop in front of her.

Two officers leapt out with guns drawn and ordered her to freeze. She looked at them and began to sob, crying about someone going crazy upstairs with a gun, but one of the officers pushed her against the wall and yanked her purse away. When he dropped it on the sidewalk it fell over, and the pistol spilled out.

More police arrived and Jenny was arrested on three counts of murder and two of attempted murder. Neither of the parents had been hit, and when Jenny learned that fact during her interrogation, she looked at the detective across from her and said, "I should have waited until they woke up, I guess."

Everyone who knew her was shocked, and the tabloids and TV magazines spread the story around the world. Jenny was convicted on all counts and sentenced to life in prison without the possibility of parole, which she later referred to as "a long-term death sentence."

Two months after her sentencing, it was reported that Genevieve Spears had committed suicide in her prison cell. Two days later, Jennifer Lance arrived at Neverland.

Every recruit Allison came up with had to pass an interview with Doctor Parker before entering training. If the candidate failed, the note that Parker gave them at the end of the interview would simply say, "Pass." When that note was shown to one of the senior officers of the organization, that single word would be a death sentence. The candidate would be taken out to a remote location behind the training facility, where a single shot to the head would bring their short Second Life to an end.

"Allison said you were a fox," Parker said to her as she entered his office. "Nice of her to send me something to look at once in a while."

Jenny's eyebrows went up at his comment. "I'll bet you say that to all the girls," she said.

"Only the pretty ones," Parker said. "Sit down and shut up. You don't say a word unless I ask you a question."

Jenny sat in the chair in front of his desk. "Okay," she said.

"*Bzzzzzzzzzzzz!*" Parker spat out. "I hadn't asked a question. Mess up again and I'll reject you."

Jenny said nothing, but the ghost of a smile appeared on her lips. Parker looked at her for a couple of seconds, then slipped on a pair of reading glasses and glanced down at some notes on his desk.

"Says here you murdered four people in revenge for the killing of your sister," he said. He took off the glasses and looked up at her. "How did it make you feel afterward?"

"Horny as hell," Jenny said. When Parker just stared at her for a moment, she shrugged. "Well, you asked."

"And later? After you were arrested and locked up?"

Jenny pursed her lips and thought for a moment. "I kept going over it and over it, again and again in my mind. I was a little bit nervous before I pulled the trigger on the first one, but then all of a sudden I felt like—I felt this wave of pleasure go through me, and when I shot the second one it got more intense. The third one took it up a couple more notches, but that last one, the one who actually killed my sister? I had a freaking orgasm. When I was reliving it in my cell, I realized that this was something I really, really enjoyed and wanted to do again."

"Hmpf," Parker said. "Psychiatrist at the jail talked to you several times and decided you're a sociopath."

"High-functioning sociopath, actually," Jenny said. "Oh, I'm sorry, wasn't that a question?"

"Close enough for that time." He put on the glasses again and glanced at his desk, then looked over them at Jenny. "According to the psychiatrist, you also display tendencies of sadistic psychopathy. That would refer to your becoming aroused and gratified by violence. However, he notes that you display a well-developed sense of right and wrong. How would you respond to that?"

Jenny's face displayed a brief expression that Parker took as a form of shrug. "Well, I think it was wrong of that bastard to kill my sister just so he could join a gang, and while it may have been legally wrong to blow his brains out, it felt right to me at the time." She winked at him. "On the other hand, I didn't kill the neighbor who called the cops on me, so I guess that should count for something."

"We compiled a history on you," Parker said, "going back all the way through elementary school. There are notations in your school records indicating that you had a tendency to be disrespectful of others, but there are no recorded instances of violence. Did you ever become violent as a child?"

"I got into a couple of minor fights," Jenny said, "but I never actually set out to hurt anyone. Is that what you're asking?"

"Close enough. What about in your adolescence, were you ever aroused by scenes of violence in movies or books, or by witnessing someone being hurt or injured?"

Jenny smiled. "Yeah. I can remember, I was probably, oh, maybe fifteen or sixteen when I saw this movie where this family of crazy people were all into being killers. There was some pretty graphic death scenes in it, and it got me really turned on. But I never thought about it like, I wanted to be doing the killing, that never occurred to me until this happened. That's kind of interesting, now that I think about it; I wonder why it didn't?"

"Yes, I wonder," Parker said. He sat forward and took off his glasses, folded his hands on his desk, then looked Jenny in the eye. "How do you feel about what we do?"

"I guess—from what I was told, this outfit kills people who need to be killed. Considering my own situation, that strikes me as making a lot of sense. Some people just don't deserve to live, and if it makes the world a better place to take them out of it then somebody needs to do it. That lady who came to see me said she thought this might be the best place for me, and if it means I get to have a life again *and* get my rocks off, I'm all for it."

The conversation went on a while longer, but in the end, Parker approved Jenny for training as an assassin. Her training program had been a few months longer and much more intense than Noah's, since she didn't have his military background, but she finally went on her first mission only two months after Genevieve Spears's twentieth birthday.

FOUR

Three days. It's been three days since they loaded me onto the boat. Three days, don't forget that.

Of course, it was hard to tell for sure. Sarah was counting days by the number of times she'd been fed, because there were no windows in the room she was held in. The boat had run at high speed once they got away from the shoreline some distance, and the ride had been rather rough as it bounced over the choppy waves, but it hadn't been a long one. A couple of hours out, the boat came to a stop and it wasn't long after that before Sarah heard the *whomp-whomp* of a large helicopter. It had settled onto a platform on the topmost deck and two men had come and dragged Sarah out of the room and up the stairs.

She was shoved into a rear seat and strapped in, and the helicopter lifted off. Two men sat facing her, and both of them were not only armed, they had the look of men who hoped that the person they were guarding would be stupid enough to try to escape.

Sarah wasn't stupid. A couple of hours later it landed on a beach and she was dragged out again, then hustled into an amphibious airplane that had been run up onto the beach and strapped into a seat once more. Tweedledum and Tweedledee took their seats around her, and then the two huge engines high overhead started up. The big seaplane moved backward until it was afloat, then turned and bounced faster and faster across the waves until it managed to catch the air and rise into flight.

She slept on that flight, but had no idea for how long. One of the flight crew woke her at some point and gave her a plastic bag that contained slices of dried meat, along with a bottle of water. She ate and tried to go back to sleep, but was still awake when the plane landed a few hours later.

She was blindfolded, this time, before they took her off the plane. The two men took hold of her arms as they walked her down a ramp and pushed her into a car. She could hear a number of sounds she associated with the military—the sound of many people marching together, as well as the distant sound of gunfire and helicopters and aircraft passing overhead.

Those sounds finally fell behind them, and it wasn't long before she could tell they were in heavy traffic. The ride lasted almost an hour, and then she was unceremoniously dragged from the car and walked into a building, then down a flight of stairs. She was taken into a cool room and then the blindfold was removed.

That's where she had been ever since. The room contained a cot, a table and a single chair, as well as a covered bucket that was obviously intended for use as a toilet. As soon as the men escorting her left the room, she took advantage of the last item.

Since then, she had only seen the man who brought her meals and took the bucket away for cleaning once a day. She admitted to herself that she had not been mistreated, but the fact that she was a prisoner was not lost on her. From what Lom had said, she knew that she would be interrogated at some point; her guess was that the interrogator had yet to arrive.

The worst part was the torment of her own thoughts. Lom had told her that Noah believed she was dead, and had left Thailand. A part of her couldn't believe he would leave her behind, but if they had truly convinced him that she had died, his logical mind would decide there was no reason to stay.

The only problem with that was convincing herself that he would accept her death without seeing her body. That would be out of character for Noah; it just wouldn't fit with the way his brain worked. And if that was the case, then she had no choice but to believe that he suspected what had happened and was already working on a plan to get her back.

Yes, that was the Noah she knew. Unfortunately, there was no way for her to know what that plan might be. Until he found her—and she was certain that he would—Sarah was on her own.

The most recent meal she had eaten was one she thought of as breakfast: boiled rice in sweetened milk. That had been a few hours earlier, and she was anticipating the arrival of lunch in another hour or so, but then she heard the key in the lock on the door and hastily sat up on the cot. A man she didn't recognize opened the door and looked at her.

Sarah looked him over, as well. He was a few inches taller than her own five foot two, and she got the impression that he was not as young as he appeared. He looked to be in his mid-twenties, but something in his eyes made her add about ten years to her guess. His hair was black and neatly combed, and he was dressed casually in black slacks, a white shirt and a light brown jacket.

"Hello," he said in English. "Have you been treated well?"

"Other than being locked up like a prisoner? I guess okay."

The man smiled. "My name is Chung," the man said. "It is my hope that you and I shall become friends. Would you care to take a walk with me?"

Sarah looked at him for a moment and considered whether cooperation might be advisable, and decided that it was. "Sure," she said. "Where we going?"

"Only for a walk," Chung said. "I thought perhaps you might enjoy being outside for a little while. The air is fresh and the sun is shining, a very pleasant day."

Sarah stood and walked slowly toward the door. When Chung stepped back and motioned for her to come on out, she saw that he was alone. She knew, however, that there were other men in the building, so she didn't want to give them a reason to beat the snot out of her just yet. Better to accept the friendliness while it lasted; it might give her a chance to learn the layout of the building. She would need that if she got any chance to escape.

She stepped out of the room and waited quietly while he shut the door, then fell into step beside him as he started along the hallway toward the stairs. The overhead lights were not bright, but she could see light streaming down from the floor above.

"I apologize for taking so long to get here," Chung said. "I was actually supposed to arrive the night before last, but you have created something of an uproar. Your capture marks the first time my country has ever been able to confirm that your organization truly exists. For that reason, there are many in my government who wished to advise me on just how to deal with you." He smiled at her. "You should be happy to know that I have little respect for most of them, and will not be taking their suggestions. You and I will get along much better that way."

Sarah turned her head and glanced at him as they ascended the stairs. "Everyone I've met so far keeps asking me about this organization," she said. "I tried to tell them all I don't know—"

"Ms. Child," Chung said, "I have heard the recording that was made when you informed your captor that he should fear this Camelot, the assassin you work with. You cannot lie to me, not if we are to be friends. And I truly do want that. If I am unable to gain your cooperation, those others I spoke of will send someone else to do what I choose not to. Torture is unpleasant, but in skilled hands it is extremely effective in obtaining information."

Sarah stayed quiet as they emerged from the stairs, and continued to walk beside him as he led her through another hallway. They came to a door, and a guard standing beside it quickly opened it for them. Sarah looked through it and saw what looked like a quite lovely garden, full of flowers and trees. Chung extended a hand to invite her to step out first, then followed her when she did so.

"As you can see," he said, "this is an enclosed courtyard. As this is an official government building, there are guards stationed all around it. Escape is out of the question, I'm afraid, so please do not consider trying."

Sarah shrugged as they walked along, her sandals making flopping noises with every step. "I get the impression I'm in China," she said. "Considering I know absolutely nothing about China, trying to escape probably wouldn't get me anywhere, anyway."

Chung beamed at her. "That is a wise decision. You are correct in your assumption; we are actually not far from the city of Hong Kong."

"Figures," Sarah said. "That's one of the places I always wanted to visit. Somehow, I don't think you're going to let me go there for a holiday, though, are you?"

"If you are cooperative, I think I could arrange something. Of course, I would have to accompany you, and there would be others along to ensure that you did not try to get away."

At least in Hong Kong, she thought, *I might have a chance to make contact with an American, maybe a tourist or even the US Embassy.* "What kind of cooperation are we talking about? It's not like I have any important secrets or anything."

"We have found that employees of American organizations often know far more than they believe they do," Chung said. "I have a number of questions I would like to ask, and if you provide the answers we need, I can assure you that you can have a long and happy life here. If your cooperation is complete and genuine, you might even earn the freedom to live as a welcome guest in our country."

"And if I don't," she said, stopping and turning to face him, "you turn me over to the Chinese inquisition, right?"

Chung made a grimace and shrugged. "Unfortunately, that would be likely. As I told you, there are those who believe that my approach has little chance of success. If it were up to them, you would already be suffering. I truly hope to avoid that, but it will, in the end, be up to you."

Sarah crossed her arms and looked down at her feet. "So, give me an idea what kind of questions you want me to answer."

He laughed softly. "Americans are always in such a hurry," he said. "Can we not simply enjoy the beauty around us for now? There will be more than enough time for questions after we move you to your new room this afternoon."

"New room?" Sarah asked.

"I was actually intending to save it for a surprise, but that is not the first time my mouth has given me away. Yes, I have ordered a room prepared for you on the second floor. You will find it much more comfortable than the one you're in now. There is even a television, or if you prefer to read, I can see that you are given books and magazines."

Sarah allowed herself to give him a small smile. "TV would be good," she said. "Anything is better than the boredom of just being locked in by myself." She narrowed her eyes at him. "Of course, that's part of the psychological conditioning, isn't it? Boredom is a form of torture in itself, right? Now you come along, and like a hero of some kind you're going to rescue me from that boredom. That's supposed to make me feel indebted to you, so that I'll want to cooperate when you ask me to." She leaned her head toward him with a small grin. "Sorry, I was just reminding myself of the class we took on psychological conditioning. The section on dehumanization was really interesting."

Chung gently touched her on the shoulder. "All of that is true," he said, "which is precisely why I have decided to bring that sort of thing to an end. Ms. Child, I am not one who believes that torture is necessary in this world. Your country and mine are not at war, though there are many who believe we should be, among both our peoples. Your associates perform a necessary service in the world, but we have learned that the great Sun Tzu was correct."

"Keep your friends close, and your enemies closer? That Sun Tzu?"

"Indeed. Your E & E is an organization of our friend in the West, the United States of America. We simply wish to know whether our country has anything to be concerned about with them."

"That's a question I couldn't answer," Sarah said. "I don't know anything about politics or policies or how everything is run. All I am is a driver, the girl who has to get my boss to where he's going, and then get him out again. The closest I ever come to knowing what's going on is when he tells me where to drop him and when to pick him up."

"You see?" Chung said with another smile. "That was being cooperative. You have shared with me a truth about the work you do. In return, I shall let you decide what we have for dinner. The kitchen here can prepare almost any kind of meal. Tell me what you would like to have, and that shall be our dinner for tonight."

Sarah deliberately let her face brighten. "Really? I mean, anything I want?"

"You will find that I am always going to be honest with you. Yes, really. Anything you wish."

Sarah puckered her lips and narrowed her eyes, comically appearing to be deep in thought. "Hmmm, I gotta think this through. Anything I want…Okay, I've got it. How about we have spaghetti and meatballs, with Parmesan cheese? Can your kitchen do that?"

Chung laughed with delight. "Of course," he said. He leaned toward her as if imparting a secret. "You know, there are those who still believe that spaghetti was originally based on Chinese noodles."

Sarah rolled her eyes. "There's also people who believe the American moon landings were a big hoax." She turned her expression serious. "Mr. Chung," she said, "what makes me so important? What do you really expect to learn from me?"

Chung's smile remained bright. "Sarah—may I call you Sarah?" She nodded permission. "Sarah, the truth is that we do not know what we expect to learn. However, my government has spent much of the last decade in trying to curtail American spying in our country, even to the point of eliminating our own countrymen who were suspected of selling secrets to the West. Now we have discovered confirmation of numerous bits of intelligence indicating that the Americans practice political and economic assassination. Your organization was created in the middle of your former president's first term, and yet it has taken us all this time merely to confirm its existence. Do you find it surprising that we wish to learn everything we can about that organization?"

"No, I guess not," Sarah said. "But I don't really think you're going to learn that much from me. I mean, I'm not gonna roll over and tell you anything I think I shouldn't, but I'm sure those people you were talking about will get tired of waiting for you to charm it out of me. Sooner or later, you'll be gone and I'll face the Inquisition. I'm not stupid enough to think they won't break me, but even then I don't know anything important. It'll all be a waste of time and effort."

The Chinaman's smile slowly faded away. "I do not care about wasting time," he said. "I do not, however, wish to waste the beautiful woman before me."

Sarah rolled her eyes. "Oh, so now I get the charming side, right? The flirtatious hero, coming to rescue the damsel in distress. I know it might seem like I'm pretty dumb, but even I can see through that one. You're not here because you want to be, any more than I am. You're here because it's your job to try to get answers out of me, so don't bother paying me compliments and flirting with me. It won't get you anywhere, and I really would rather not insult you."

Chung smiled at her. "Sarah," he said softly. "Do you not believe that a man can find a woman attractive, even if they have opposing political views? There have been many epics written about such ill-fated romances; perhaps you and I might be another one?"

Sarah grinned at him. "Nice to meet an optimist," she said, "but forget it. Ain't gonna happen, Chung, not in a million years!"

FIVE

Neil had been awake and dressed by the time Noah got home, so he came walking over as soon as the Corvette pulled in. Noah got out of the car and stood beside it waiting for him, and then the two of them went into the house.

"Have a seat at the table," Noah said as they entered the kitchen. "I'll make coffee."

"No, let me," Neil said. "You don't do it the way Sarah does..." The boy's face suddenly looked crestfallen. "Anyway, you make it too strong." He picked up the pot from the coffee maker and filled it with water at the sink.

Noah stepped aside and took a seat at the table, watching Neil work. When he turned to pour the water into the machine, Noah saw the tear that was sliding down his cheek, and then decided that what he was seeing was grief, rather than any sign of guilt.

"Neil," he said, "Sarah is alive."

Coffee grounds spilled across the counter as Neil dropped the container and spun to face him. "What?" he demanded. "Did they find her? Is she okay? How do you..."

"I knew it before we left Thailand," Noah said, "but there was no hope of trying to rescue her at that moment. The only possible source of information would have been Pak, and he was too well protected. There was no chance we were going to catch him alone in the near future, so I chose to let him believe that I accepted his story of her death."

Neil's eyes were wide as he stared at Noah. "But we've got to go," he said loudly, "we got to go back and find her. Noah, we can't go out on a new mission when she's—"

"Neil, she was betrayed. Someone, either one of my team or Jenny's, or possibly one of the E & E people in Thailand, revealed to someone that Sarah is one of ours. That's the only logical reason for Pak to try to convince us she was dead. They know exactly what they've got, and I'm sure they plan to try to get any information they can out of her."

"And that makes it even more important we go back," Neil said. "God, Noah, you know Sarah, she'd never be able to handle being tortured for information."

"Sarah's a lot stronger than you think, Neil, but at the moment we have no intel at all. The most logical move at the moment is to figure out who sold her out, and who they talked to. I don't think it was Pak, I think he was a middleman that was called in to handle getting her to whoever wanted her so badly. Allison's got CIA working on the people in Thailand to see if one of them has made any improper contact lately, but they don't think it's likely. If it was one of them, she might have been betrayed even before she was taken to the prison, but it seems more likely she was sold out after she was taken by the *Nay Thas*, and it's more than a possibility that it was one of the people who were with us at the time. That means it was either Marco, Jenny, or one of her team."

Neil stared at him for a moment, then turned around and

continued making the coffee before cleaning up the spill. It wasn't until he was finished that he turned back to face Noah.

"When we figure it out," he said, "I want to be the one to kill him."

One of Noah's eyebrows lifted slightly. "Him? You're assuming it's not Jenny?"

"Huh-uh," Neil said. "Jenny's an evil bitch, but not that way. You heard her, she gets her thrills out of killing people. Whoever did this probably did it for money, and Jenny wouldn't care about that. She wouldn't risk losing the only possible job that lets her indulge her desire to be a serial killer and covers her back while she does it."

"Who do you think it was?" Noah asked bluntly.

Neil closed his eyes. "My very first thought would be Marco," he said, "but I'm smart enough to know that's because I resent him taking Moose's place. It could be him, but I can't point to any kind of evidence that makes me think so. I know it wasn't you or me, and I'm sure it wasn't Jenny, but I don't know her guys well enough to even make a guess about them. I got along okay with all of them, but me and Jim probably hit it off best. We speak the same language, you know?"

Noah nodded his head. "I agree. I saw nothing that lets me point to one of them as a suspect. This is the reason Allison is sending us out together again, to give me the chance to try to figure out which one of them might have done it, if it was any of them." He looked Neil in the eye. "Once we know that, I'm going to make certain he tells us everything he knows."

"I'm just worried about Sarah. Noah, she's pretty tough in some ways, but I don't know how long she could hold out under torture."

"She'll hold out for a while, if for no other reason than to protect me and you as long as she could; she truly cares about us, Neil. Sooner or later, though, she's going to break. Allison doesn't think she knows anything that would be devastating, but we still need to get her back as quickly as possible. Interrogation can do some pretty severe damage to the mind, as well as the body."

Neil rubbed his hands on his face. "So, we have to go out on a mission with people we can't trust. Wouldn't it be easier to just take the whole bunch of them and put a gun to their heads? Talk or die, that sort of thing?"

"The problem with that is that they're all going to swear they know nothing about it, and there's no way to know which one of them is lying."

"Yeah. I bet Jenny could find out, if we could trust her. I've never seen anybody get off on torturing people the way she does."

"Same issue, we can't be sure of the results. The even bigger problem with torture is that it can make people admit to things they didn't do, just to stop the pain. That's why Jenny tortured one man while appealing to the other to save him. In this case, whoever did this probably doesn't care if somebody else is being skinned alive. Sooner or later, the person she's torturing will admit to anything she wants just to make it stop."

"And then the real culprit gets off scot-free. Yeah, I get it." He turned and looked at the coffee maker, saw that it was more than half-full and pulled the pot away. He poured two cups and set it back on the machine, then carried the steaming mugs to the table.

"You wouldn't tell me about this if you thought it could have been me," Neil said as he sat down. "I guess I should thank you for that."

Noah cocked his head to one side and looked at the kid. "I

spent my whole life studying other people's emotions, so that I could pretend to have some of my own. When you accidentally mentioned Sarah a while ago, you had the same expression of grief that I saw when Moose died. I told Allison earlier that I couldn't believe you would have done this, but that cinched it for me. That's when I decided to let you know what's going on."

Neil wiped another tear away and busied himself adding sugar to his coffee for a moment. "So," he said when he finished, "do you know anything about this mission?"

Noah nodded. "We're going to North Korea. There are four CIA agents who have been captured there, and the Company says they can't be rescued. We have to kill them so they can't give up any secrets. And before you ask, Allison says she will not sanction a termination on Sarah. That's why she mentioned that Sarah doesn't know enough to do any real harm to the country."

Neil chewed his bottom lip for a moment. "North Korea? Can Americans even get into that country?"

"I'm pretty sure they have some kind of tourism that Americans take advantage of, probably something that lets them watch every move they make. There have been news stories about American tourists being arrested over there, sometimes for the most ridiculous reasons, so this certainly isn't going to be an easy one. We'll find out more about the mission and how we're supposed to accomplish it at the briefing."

Neil took a deep breath, as if trying to steady his emotions. "And in the middle of all that, we're supposed to play a very dangerous game of Clue, figure out who among us is a traitor, right? Damn, I'm sure glad the Dragon Lady isn't handing us a difficult job."

"People tend to reveal themselves under stress," Noah said.

"The whole point of sending our two teams on this mission is to put whoever did this under a lot of stress, and then I'll apply even more to see if we can force him to make a mistake that gives him away. I'll probably need your help with that."

Neil's eyes had been on his coffee cup, but he suddenly looked up at Noah. "Anything you want," he said. "Anything at all. You figure out who it is and want me to pull the trigger, I'll do it without even blinking."

"I know," Noah said.

The two of them sat and talked, stopping twice to refill their coffee cups. They were going over possible scenarios, ruses they might employ to try to identify the traitor in their midst, when Noah's phone rang.

"Hello," he said.

"It's Allison," his boss said unnecessarily. "We've just spoken with Jenny, and both Donald and I came to the conclusion that she can be trusted. She had deduced the same things that you had, that Sarah is alive and that she had been betrayed by one of our own. Latest report from the CIA says they can find nothing to implicate any of our people over there, so if it's an inside job, then I'm afraid it's down to your men or hers."

"I brought Neil in on this," Noah said. "I'm convinced he had no part in it, so we're going over ways we might trick the culprit into revealing himself."

"Very good," Allison said. "You can use Jenny as you need to, as well. Just make sure no one other than Neil hears anything the two of you talk about."

"Will do. Briefing still at one?"

"Yes." The line went dead.

Noah slipped his phone back into his pocket and looked at the kid across from him. "Jenny's in the clear," he said. "Once we leave the house, we don't discuss any of this where anyone else can hear it."

"Deal," Neil said.

"Good. Why don't we go grab some lunch? Unless it's too early for you to eat."

"Ow! Stop twisting my arm!" The joke was lost on Noah, so Neil rolled his eyes. "Yeah, let's go eat."

Even with the passenger seat in the Corvette slid all the way back, Neil couldn't quite straighten his legs out, but he didn't complain as they rode into town. A new restaurant, Colorado Charlie's, had recently opened only a few blocks from the main offices and the team had tried it before they left for Thailand. The food had been good, so Noah headed toward it.

When Neil realized where they were going, he looked at Noah and said, "Do we gotta? I mean, that's the last place we ate with..."

Noah glanced over at him, and then made the next right turn. There was an Applebee's a couple of blocks over, so Noah went there, instead.

They had just gotten inside and were waiting to be seated when Noah's phone rang. "Hello?"

"It's Jenny," he heard. "Allison talk to you yet?"

"Yes. I understand you and I are on the same page."

"You bet your ass we are. How well do you know your guys? Do you think it could have been one of them?"

"It wasn't Neil," Noah said. "He and I have talked it over and I'm certain it wasn't him. Marco is new with us, a replacement for Moose, so he's a lesser-known quantity."

"Yeah, he's at the top of my list, at the moment. No particular reason other than the fact he's the new guy, but I've had all three of my boys for almost two years, now. I know them, Noah, and I have a real hard time believing any of them could have done this."

"I understand, but people have been turned in the past, people you'd never believe it could happen to. Listen, Neil and I are about to have lunch at Applebee's. Would you like to come and join us?"

"Yeah, that sounds good. Applebee's? I can be there in fifteen. Get me a sweet tea."

"Okay, we'll try to get us a table where we can talk a little bit. See you when you get here." He turned to Neil. "Jenny is going to come and join us."

Neil shivered. "That's like sitting down to eat with Death! It's hard to get the image of what she did to that guy out of my mind, and I don't even try to imagine what happened on the island. I'm just glad you left me at the boat."

"Yes," Noah said without looking over at him. "I thought you might be."

SIX

They were early enough that the lunch rush had not yet begun, so Noah asked for the booth that was farthest away from where most people were sitting. The hostess smiled and put on a hip-wiggling display as she led them to it, and a waitress appeared instantly to take their drink orders. Noah told her that a third person was coming, then ordered a beer for himself and Jenny's sweet tea. Neil asked for lemonade, and the girl hurried away to fetch them.

Jenny arrived just as the drinks did, and slid into the seat beside Noah. "Hey, whiz kid," she said to Neil. "How you holding up?"

"I was fine 'til you got here," he said with a smirk, but then he grinned at her. "I'm just kidding. I'm okay, I guess, but I won't be right until we get Sarah back."

"Then that's what we gotta do." She picked up a menu and began looking it over. "If it was one of my guys," she said without looking at Noah, "I'd have to say Randy would be the most likely one. I've been thinking it over, and I can recall a few times he seemed to go off the reservation. Disappear for a little while, know what I mean?"

Noah raised an eyebrow. "He disappears on the job?"

Jenny nodded. "Every now and then, just for a short time. I've always chalked it up to him being the impulsive sort. Give you an example, there's been a couple of times when he disappeared and it turned out he was in a bookstore. He loves to read, he's always got a couple of books with him, but if we're out long enough that he finishes them, he'll go find another one. Another time, while I was still playing up to my target and he was supposed to be watching me from the street, he decided I had everything under control and went two blocks away to grab a sandwich."

"And you've never reported this?"

"Didn't see a need," she said. "He's always been right there if I actually needed him, and that time he went for the sandwich was no big deal, I did have it under control. On the other hand, that's the only time he ever wandered off when we were active. Usually it happens when we're just staying in character, waiting for an opportunity for me to get close to the target."

Noah considered what she had said. "He's the only one that ever gets out of your sight?"

"Well, no, the others go out on errands and stuff, but he's the only one that ever does it spontaneously. That's why it occurs to me that he might, and I said might, have made contact with someone somewhere along the line."

The waitress returned and took their orders, then hustled away. Jenny took a sip of her tea before turning back to Noah.

"The thing is, Noah," she said, "if one of my guys was going to sell someone out, why hasn't it been me? Or you, for that matter? One of us would have been a lot more valuable than your transportation specialist, don't you think?"

Noah thought about it. "I see your point," he said, "but are you ever alone? It might be difficult to get one of us into a position where we could be taken. I'm thinking this was just an opportunity. Sarah was trapped in that prison, so if it was Marco, he could have called somebody and let them know she was vulnerable, there. They call in the *Nay Thas*, she gets snatched away and then picked up from them. Or the *Nay Thas* roundup was purely coincidental after all, but then she's even more vulnerable in the hands of slave traders. The traitor lets his contact know, and they use whatever resources they've got to reach out to them. Pak gets sent in to buy her, then he hears that we wiped out the camp on the island and comes up with his scheme to convince us she's dead. In that case, it could be any of them, or any of the station people; could even be someone we've never heard of, someone who learned Sarah was there and saw a chance to make a score."

Jenny shrugged. "Good point. She was an easy sale. They'd have to send a squad to take you or me, and even then the chance of taking one of us alive would be pretty slim."

They continued to discuss the situation until their food arrived, but by then the place was beginning to get busier. A couple of businessmen sat down in a booth close to them, so they switched their conversation to more mundane things.

By the time they finished eating, it was almost half past twelve, so Noah suggested they go on to the briefing room. "We can hang out there until the others arrive," he said. Jenny agreed, so Noah paid the tab on the way out and they got into their cars and drove to the office building.

Allison's secretary had gone to lunch, so they bypassed her desk and let themselves into the conference room. Allison was already there, and so was Don Jefferson. They both looked up as the trio entered, but neither of them smiled.

"You're early," Jefferson said.

"We just had lunch a couple blocks away," Noah said, "so I thought we'd come on down. The rest of the guys should be here on schedule, but only we three know what's really going on."

"Then I've got something for you," Allison said. "One of the analysts over at Langley ran across a report she thought we ought to see. It seems a source in China has heard that his people have acquired something that confirms the existence of E & E."

"They got Sarah," Noah said.

"Has to be," Allison replied. "That's all we've got, no indication of where she might be or anything else, but at least it's something."

"At least she's alive," Neil said.

"It only means she was alive when the source heard about it," Noah told him. "The Chinese are notorious for their interrogation techniques. She isn't going to last long in their hands."

"I agree," said Allison. "You're going to have to work fast. However, I'm not convinced that it was one of your men or Jenny's who put her in this position, so you've got to determine that quickly, then figure out which one and interrogate him as soon as possible. If not, then we need to find out who the hell else it could be, and then you've got to interrogate that individual. That's the only way we can see any chance of finding her before it's too late, and failure is not an option."

"And we've still got to carry out the actual mission, right?" Jenny asked.

"Absolutely. This mission genuinely is of critical importance, so it has to be completed. I'm briefing both of your teams at one, but we are also briefing Team Hercules at three. Hercules will be sent in after you, as backup. That way, if you determine the identity of the traitor before the mission is completed, they can take it over. You can head for China and they can terminate the captured agents."

The three of them sat down on one of the couches and Jenny leaned toward Allison. "Can you give us any kind of heads up on the mission?"

"I've already shared part of it with Noah," Allison said. "There are four CIA people who have been captured by the North Koreans. They were in the country to get information on North Korean ballistic missile tests, because they seem to have developed a missile that could conceivably reach the continental US. The problem is that these people know some things we can't afford to have revealed, and Langley says there is no hope of getting them out. They're to be terminated as quickly as possible, regardless of any collateral damage."

"How are we supposed to get to them? Do we even know where they're being held?"

"Yes. One of the satellites had eyes on them when they were captured, and analysis was able to determine where they were taken. They're still in the same place, and if it changes, we will know and can tell you. We don't have any people of our own in North Korea, but CIA and NSA both have local operatives. Arrangements are already being made for weapons and explosives, but you have to determine the most effective means of accomplishing the mission."

Neil shook his head. "I knew we'd end up on one of these sooner or later," he said, "but I hate the thought we have to kill some of our own people. That just sucks."

"It does," Allison said, "but sometimes it's necessary for the security of our country. These agents were fully aware that it could come to this when they went in. Each of them accepted that risk, and is willing to die to protect our country and its secrets."

"Officially, Noah," Donald Jefferson interjected, "there is to be no attempt at rescue. Even if it appears a rescue could be accomplished, the decision has been made that we can't take the risk. If you were to try and fail, you may not be able to terminate these agents before they could be recaptured, and then they'd have you, as well. You're to just go in and terminate, then get out of the country."

"Understood," said Noah.

"With that being said, however," Allison said, "I'm personally authorizing a change to the plan if Noah believes the rescue is feasible. Noah, it's got to be on you to make the decision, nobody else."

"I understand. I'll base it only on my evaluation of the situation after recon."

Allison turned to Jenny. "As I said before, Jenny, Team Cinderella will be under Camelot's orders for the duration of this mission. Any problem with that?"

"No problem," Jenny echoed. "Is there any kind of game plan worked out yet?"

"I'm afraid not," Jefferson said. "There's no possibility of subterfuge. This is going to have to be a stealth mission, which is why you are authorized any level of collateral damage. The building they are housed in is a civilian structure in an industrial area of Pyongyang, a concrete structure on the edge of a cement plant. It's a long, low building with only one level, but CIA suspects there may be sub-levels underneath. Satellite reconnaissance has photographed military vehicles going to and from the building at different times, and there are armed patrols around it. We'll show you photos during the actual briefing."

A sudden tap on the doorframe made them all look around. Marco stood there looking in, and Jefferson waved him inside.

"Thought I'd come on up and see if there's any doughnuts left," he said. He glanced over at the empty table on the side of the room. "I guess Neil got to them before I could."

"Very funny," Neil said.

Marco came and sat down on the couch across from them, just as another sound announced the arrival of Jenny's crew. Jim, Randy and Dave came in and joined them, with Jim and Randy pulling chairs away from the conference table to sit in.

"Now that we're all here," said Allison, "we can get down to the actual briefing. Donald?"

Jefferson tapped a tablet that was in his lap and the screen behind him lit up. The first image showed four people: three women and one man.

"The people you see on the screen behind me are agents of the CIA. They were in North Korea posing as consultants on an engineering project and the plan was for them to meet up with some of the agency's local sources in order to receive and retrieve data relating to the recent ballistic missile testing that's been all over the news. The agency has reason to believe that the DPRK has developed a missile capable of reaching anywhere in the continental US with a nuclear warhead. These agents were sent in to collect and retrieve that missile's blueprints and specifications."

He tapped the tablet again and the image changed to an overhead view of a city street, zoomed in so close that they could see a car surrounded by armed men pointing guns at it.

"The day before yesterday," Jefferson went on, "all four of them were arrested on spying charges and taken into custody." Another tap and the image changed to a long, narrow building seen from above. "They were brought to this building in the Sunan-guyok Industrial District. It sits on the back edge of Pyongyang's largest cement plant, but it appears to be used primarily as a secret military facility. Military vehicles and troops can be seen around the building at times, and it is suspected that the single-story building is camouflage for a larger underground structure. Your targets are almost certainly being held somewhere under that building."

The image disappeared and Allison leaned forward. "We have no intelligence regarding the interior of that building or its sub-levels. For that reason, it's almost certainly going to be necessary for you and your teams to infiltrate the building itself, and that means that you cannot have a public presence in the country. Because of that, you'll be flying into Incheon International Airport, which is on an island just off the coast at Incheon, South Korea. You will be met there by some of the CIA's local operatives, South Korean nationals in the employ of the agency. They'll take you to the north coast of the island, where a small submarine will be waiting. It will take you across the border into North Korea, where more local operatives will be waiting with a truck to smuggle you into Pyongyang. There is a CIA safe house that is uncompromised less than two miles from the cement facility, and that's where you'll be taken. Once your mission is complete, the locals will transport you back to the sub, which will take you directly back to Incheon. The plane will be waiting to get you out of the country as quickly as possible."

"Any questions?" Allison asked.

"I have one," Jenny said, actually raising her hand as if she were in school. "I get the impression this is going to be more like a commando raid than anything else, am I right?"

"That will be up to Noah to determine," Allison replied. "He has command on this mission. Because of its importance and its unusual nature compared to what we usually do, I feel it's best to have his detachment running the show. You will all be under his orders."

"Yep, I understood that," Jenny said. "For something like this, I want that computer brain making the decisions, and his combat experience running point."

"Exactly. Should anything happen to Noah, you'll take charge. Remember that the mission is paramount. With the risk that critical secrets could be revealed, I have to tell you that I expect the mission to be completed regardless of the cost to yourselves or your teams."

"Hell, Allie, isn't that always the way it is?"

Both teams got up and started to leave, but Allison called Noah back for a moment. The two of them spoke quietly, and then Allison put something small in the palm of Noah's hand. He slid it into his pocket and followed the rest of them out the door.

SEVEN

Noah, Jenny and their teams were given identity kits and told to go directly to R&D, where luggage containing clothing for each of them was waiting. They could study the back stories on their mission identities while on the flight, but their personal identification, cell phones and jewelry were all to be left with Donald Jefferson. Once they left R&D, they would then go to the Kirtland airfield and board a Gulfstream IV that would take them directly to San Francisco International Airport.

At the R&D facility, after they picked up the tightly packed duffel bags that were prepared for them, Noah asked to speak to Wally for a moment. The clerk who had given them the bags smiled and called through a walkie talkie, and Wally appeared with a big smile a moment later.

"Noah!" Wally said as he grabbed his hand. "Man, I heard about Sarah, I'm so sorry."

"Thanks," Noah said, "but we're in a rush, and I need something you let me use once before."

"No problem," Wally said, "just tell me what it is." The two of them walked off together while the others carried the bags out to their cars. When Noah returned, they all headed for the airfield together. The Gulfstream was waiting as promised, and they were led aboard and seated quickly. A field crewman loaded their luggage and the plane was closed up and the engines started. Fifteen minutes later, they were in the air and climbing, destination San Fran.

When they reached the Bay, the plane was led directly into a hangar, where they were led down the boarding stairs and then into a special cargo container that had been fitted with seats, a bathroom and a small galley.

"This is what we call a special delivery cabin," said the CIA operative who showed them into it. "We have an agreement with various airfreight carriers to use these, but it's not always feasible. South Korea, luckily, is one country that accepts our freight seals, so once we close the doors and put the seal on, no one will tamper with it until it gets to our people there. It's got its own power supply, air supply and everything else, and there's enough food for several days. Eat what you want, there's plenty more where that came from."

Noah looked around and nodded. "Enough seats for a dozen," he said. "This is slick."

The CIA man grinned. "Glad you approve," he said. "Wanna sit down and put on your seat belt, please?"

They all sat down and strapped in, and then the crew closed it up, the latches making a loud thump as each one caught and snapped into place. There were a few minutes while they waited for the seal to be applied, and then a lift truck carried it to a waiting FedEx 777 that was headed for Incheon.

"Randy," Jenny said once the container was sealed, "got an extra book with you? This is going to be a long, boring flight."

"I got a couple of Terry Pratchett's books," Randy replied. "I got *Hogfather* and *Monstrous Regiment*. Which one you want?"

"Hell, I don't care, just toss me one."

Ten minutes after the container was fastened down in the plane, the big jet engines began to scream and they felt themselves moving. It took a few minutes to taxi out to the runway, and then they felt the thrust kick in as the plane launched itself into the air.

This leg of the trip would take about nine hours, they'd been told, and the seats that had been mounted in the container were designed to recline so they could sleep on the way. Noah kicked his seat back as far as it would go while the plane was still climbing, and it wasn't long before the rest of them followed his example. They woke off and on during the flight, especially when they had some rough turbulence over the Pacific, and ate some of the frozen meals a couple of times, so all of them felt fairly well fed and rested by the time they landed at 5:15 AM Seoul time.

The container they were in was offloaded within minutes of landing, and they felt it being trundled away on the lift truck. The ride seemed to take a few minutes, and when it came to a stop the door was opened quickly.

"Come on, come on," a couple of young Korean men said to them. "We gotta get you going now, you come on!"

A stepladder had been set up in front of the door, and Noah was the first one to step out and climb down. They were less than twenty feet from the shore, on a roadway that appeared to circumnavigate the entire island. The sun had not yet made it over the horizon, but Noah could just make out a dark shape bobbing in the waves a short distance from shore. An inflatable boat was waiting for them at the water's edge, and they quickly loaded their duffels and climbed inside.

The two young men pushed the boat into the water and then hopped in, and one of them turned on a pair of electric outboard motors. The boat moved silently out onto the water toward the submarine, and then the bow slid right up over it.

The sub was black and almost flat on top. The hatch stood open right beside where the boat had ridden up onto it, and they were able to step over the side of the boat and onto the solid surface, then grip the hatch and climb down a short ladder. Another young man inside quietly urged them all to move toward the back of the chamber they found themselves in.

Once they were all inside, the boat was pulled the rest of the way onto the sub, deflated and quickly rolled up. The electric motors and batteries were lowered through the hatch, and then were followed by the boat itself. It was made of thin, rubberized nylon, and had rolled up into a package that was less than eighteen inches in diameter and not over three feet long. The two men who had brought them from shore climbed down the ladder and the hatch was sealed above them. It was only then that a few small LED lights came on.

"Which one of you is in charge?" one of them asked, and Noah raised a finger in the dim light. "Okay, here is what is happening. We will take you past the border and drop you on the shore about ten miles past. Our associates from that side will pick you up and take you to Pyongyang."

"How will they know where to find us?" Noah asked.

The young man smiled. "Because we do this every week," he replied. "We take people in and bring people out, sometimes every morning for three or four days. Our submarine is made of fiberglass and rubber, not easily detected by sonar, and our associates are never noticed because they are doing their jobs. They work on the farms, and several times a day they drive the trucks to and from Pyongyang. They know exactly where to find you, don't worry."

Noah nodded and leaned back against the bulkhead he was sitting beside. Neil leaned a little closer to him. "Did he just say this thing is made of fiberglass?"

"They're not that uncommon," Randy Mitchell said softly. "They call them smugglers' subs. Drug smugglers use them in the Gulf of Mexico to bring dope up from South America. Very hard to spot, but they travel along at about three knots, just barely deep enough not to leave a wake behind them on the surface."

Neil looked at him for a moment, then closed his eyes and leaned his head against his arms, which were propped on his knees. Except for a low whirring sound that must've been the electric motors, the interior of the vessel was almost completely silent.

"Wish it had portholes," Jenny whispered. "I'll bet there's some beautiful fish out there."

"Probably," Noah said, "but even this little bit of light might show up on the surface if it did. For what they're doing, it's better to run dark and silent."

Slipping past North Korean border security and naval patrols required the little submarine to swing out to the west a couple of miles before cutting back to the north, then turning east again to reach the shoreline. The entire voyage took nearly five hours at such a low speed, and all of them were delighted to get out of the vessel when it finally broke the surface.

A small but effective periscope was raised, scanning the shoreline. There was no sign of anyone observing, so the hatch was opened and the inflatable boat quickly carried up the ladder. An electric air pump was passed up, and five minutes later Noah and the others were told it was time to disembark.

As quietly as they could, they climbed up the ladder and onto the boat, each of them carrying the small duffels they had been provided, and slipped into the boat as it lay atop the hull. Two of the men expertly pushed it off and jumped in, and one of them took the tiller. The motors came to life as the submarine hatch closed, and the vessel sank beneath the surface before they had gone twenty yards.

The next fifteen minutes were nerve-racking, as they were completely exposed on the open water. The nearer they got to shore, however, the less it became likely that anyone would spot them bobbing across the waves. The boat ran up onto a muddy shoreline, and both teams quickly got out and made their way to the undercut bank.

"Wait until you hear a diesel motor stop just above you," said the man who had stayed in the bow. "That will be your ride into Pyongyang. When you are ready to return, they will bring you back to this place and we will watch for you each day at this time. Good fortune to you."

He pushed the boat out into the water and jumped in, and the two of them were gone.

The teams waited less than twenty minutes before the sound of the diesel engine could be heard approaching, and when it stopped almost directly above them, Noah stood and peeked over the bank. An enclosed truck stood on a gravel roadway that ran along the shore just above the bank, and two men were standing beside it sharing a cigarette. One of them spotted Noah's face and reached up to open a door on the side of the cargo compartment, then looked at Noah and nodded.

"That's our ride," Noah said, and then he was up and over the bank. The rest followed, jogging low until they got to the truck and then hopping inside. The door closed and left them in darkness, but it was easy to find places to sit behind what appeared to be hanging bales of produce. A moment after the door was closed, the truck began moving again.

This leg of their journey took another ninety minutes, and the truck seemed to stop often. Each time, the teams prepared themselves for discovery, but the doors never opened. The truck would start moving again, and the whole thing would be repeated a few minutes later.

"Stop signs," Neil muttered, "or maybe traffic lights."

"Long as that's all it is, I'm happy," Marco said.

Finally, the truck drove slowly along for several minutes and then came to a stop. They heard the cab doors open and close, and then the side door swung away to let the midday sunlight come in. One of the men looked inside and smiled.

"This where you go," he said. "Safe house. We come back every day this time, see when you ready to leave."

Once again, Noah led the way and hopped out of the truck. The "safe house" appeared to be a run-down shack surrounded by several small gardens and a number of chickens scratching at the ground. A young Korean woman stood in the doorway of the shack, motioning for them to hurry inside, so they did so.

She closed the door as the truck drove away and turned to look at them. "I am Soo Mi. You already know who I work for, so we don't need to go into that. Follow me and I'll show you where you can rest for a while. You're probably exhausted." They followed her through the little shack to what appeared to be a kitchen, with a tiny gas stove and an ancient refrigerator sitting next to a sink with a pair of ancient faucets. She turned one of the knobs on the stove and lit the burner with a match, then grabbed it and swung it aside.

"The knob controls the locking mechanism," she said. "Nobody would ever think of that, because they'd smell the gas when they turn it."

"Isn't that cute?" Randy asked. He looked at Soo Mi and grinned flirtatiously. "Almost as cute as you."

The girl grinned back, and didn't even object when Randy crowded in close to her, obviously grabbing her butt for a second. While this might be considered some form of sexual harassment in other situations, men and women in the assassination business tend to have a cavalier attitude about such things. Should the opportunity arise, the two of them might act on the obviously mutual interest, but they also knew that the mission had to come first. Soo Mi just rolled her eyes and pointed down, where a hole had opened up under where the stove normally sat.

A ladder led down into a cellar, and she went down it first and turned on a light. When the others had followed, she showed them a set of wooden shelves, and how to press on a particular bolt head to make it swing away and reveal a door into another room. She led them inside and they were surprised to find what looked like a nicely furnished hidden apartment with a small kitchen much nicer than the one upstairs. There were two other rooms that each held four bunks, and a smaller one that had a single full-sized bed.

"I call dibs on the bed," Jenny said quickly.

Soo Mi smiled at her. "If they don't give it to you, let me know. I'll kick their butts."

"Oh, deary, don't worry," Jenny replied with a saucy grin. "They all know better than to mess with me."

"Okay." She pointed to a panel on the wall beside where they had entered. "That's an intercom that reaches upstairs to me. If you need something, push the red button and wait for me to answer.

That button makes the lights upstairs flicker, and that signals me that you need to talk to me. The yellow button opens the door we came in through, and there's a rope hanging beside the ladder. Pull that rope, and you can push the stove out of the way without turning on the burner."

She turned and indicated the refrigerator and cabinets. "I keep that pretty well stocked, so you should be able to find plenty to eat. There's also some soft drinks and coffee, can't do without those."

She pointed one more time, at a very small door that stood beside the sink. "Bathroom is in there, and it's small, but the shower has great pressure and hot water. Don't worry about making noise, unless you plan to sing opera or something. This whole thing is pretty soundproof, but nothing is perfect." She pointed at some boxes that were sitting against one wall. "Weapons and explosives. The big box holds seven IWI Tavors, each with six 30-round magazines. The smaller one has a dozen grenades and six blocks of C4 with radio-controlled detonators and a trigger transmitter. Oh, and there's a couple of Colt .45's upstairs that I can spare, and I've got a couple mags for each of those." She looked around at them. "Any questions?"

Jenny raised her hand again. "I got one. I'm just wondering how you learned to speak English so clearly?"

"Oh, that's easy," Soo Mi said with a smile. "I grew up in Bakersfield. My grandparents moved away from here during the Korean War, and settled in California. When I was recruited by the CIA, it was specifically to come back to my family's homeland and run this place for them." She made a happy little face. "But you no worry, I do good Korean accent, too. Even speak language, learn from grandparents."

Jenny squealed with delight and clapped her hands. "Oh, that was so cute," she said.

Neil looked at Noah and rolled his eyes. "Boss," he said softly, so only Noah could hear, "please tell me we're not gonna be stuck with this woman for good."

"Noting to worry about on that score," Noah said just as softly. "Allison says she's almost as good as we are at getting the mission done, so she wants to get her back out on her own as soon as possible. If it hadn't been for the screw-up in Bangkok, we'd probably never have worked with her at all."

"Then that's two reasons I've got for wanting to kill whoever did this to Sarah!"

EIGHT

The spaghetti had been absolutely fantastic. Who would have ever believed that Chinese cooks could turn out such wonderful Italian food? The Parmesan cheese had been some of the best she had ever tasted, the sauce had been awesome, and the garlic bread —there just weren't words.

Chung had been her only dinner companion, which she had expected. He was indeed one of the most charming men she had ever met, but she didn't let herself forget that it was only a role he was sent to play. His job was to try to woo her to the point that she would be willing to tell him what he wanted to know, but she was determined not to let that happen. While some people considered China to be one of the U.S.'s allies, Sarah wasn't the political sort and didn't really care. What mattered to her was that anything she said might end up harming Noah or Neil. As for Marco, she was privately convinced he had to have been the one to sell her out. If she could finagle her way into a chance to relieve him of his manhood, she was fairly sure she'd be more than willing to do it. She might even be willing to seduce him, at least as far as getting his pants down. After that, it'd be all up to the knife.

The new room she'd been assigned was also pretty wonderful. A big, fluffy bed, a TV with satellite service, so she could actually find channels she could understand, chairs that she could be comfortable in, its own bathroom—one of the nicest jail cells she could ever imagine, but there was no doubt that's what it was. Two soldiers stood guard outside her door, and there were four of them on the ground outside her windows. If she tried to leave, Chung had warned her, they had orders to take her alive. Unfortunately, that didn't mean unhurt. The guards were experts at aiming for the legs, he'd explained.

Still, she'd had the best night's sleep she'd gotten since the whole mission began. She had looked in the closet and dresser and found clothing that was close enough to her size, including a very comfortable nightgown. She had run herself a bath and soaked in it until it got cold, then crawled in under the big comforter on the bed and was shortly dreaming.

The dream wasn't disturbing, but she found herself lying next to Noah. She had wrapped her arms around him the way she always did, and felt his hand clasp hers, pulling her arm tighter. That was something she always loved when he did it, but it was only when he was sleeping. She enjoyed the feeling for the fleeting moment it lasted before the dream faded out.

Sarah had awakened refreshed and taken care of morning necessities before slipping on a dress and a new pair of sandals. It was only a few minutes later that Chung knocked on her door, and he smiled appreciatively when he saw her.

"My goodness," he said, "but you do look lovely this morning. Compared to you, I look like I fell out of bed and landed in a pile of my dirty laundry."

Sarah gave him a sarcastic grin. "Very funny," he said. "You look like you're dressed for a business meeting or something. Why the suit and tie? Going somewhere today?"

Chung's eyes went wide, and he looked down at himself before turning back to her. "Is this not the way a man should dress if he expects to be in the company of a lovely young lady? Or have all of my American etiquette books become outdated?"

"Okay, now I know you're pulling my leg," Sarah said. "Nobody would use an etiquette book today, they'd just look things up on the Internet. And if you did that, you'd find out that the only time a guy gets dressed up for a girl is if he's taking her out on some kind of fancy date, like to a restaurant or something. Not just to hang out and interrogate her."

Chung couldn't keep the smile off his face. "Why is it that you see through me so easily? Is that something you were trained in? Psychology, perhaps?"

Sarah just shook her head. "Okay, so what are we doing today? What devious plan have you come up with to try to get information out of me that I have no intention of revealing, even if I know it?"

"Well, I thought we might begin with breakfast, if that's all right with you." He stepped aside and extended his elbow. "Would you care to accompany me to the dining room?"

Sarah rolled her eyes, but tucked a hand inside his elbow and let him lead her to the dining room once again. A pair of Chinese girls, different ones from those who had served them the night before, placed bowls of rice and cream before them both, and Sarah found it delicious.

They chatted about simple things while they ate, such as what kinds of movies Sarah liked to watch, and her choices in music and reading. The conversation was pleasant. Sarah knew that it would become more serious at some point, and that no matter how charming he might be, Chung was still an interrogator. Sooner or later, if she failed to give him what he wanted, he would be forced to resort to less pleasant tactics.

When breakfast was over, Chung invited her to walk in the courtyard again. They strolled around for a few minutes, and then sat on a lovely wooden bench. There, in a Chinese garden, Sarah found herself wishing that Noah was with her.

"Will you tell me your thoughts?" Chung asked.

Sarah looked at him with a sad smile. "I was just thinking of my fiancé," she said. "He probably thinks I'm dead."

Chung's face looked sad. "I am very sorry about that," he said. "Unfortunately, that is beyond my control. And yet, I am surprised that someone employed as you are pursues a romantic relationship. Does he know what you do?"

She started to say that of course he did, but caught herself. "No," she said, turning to look at a tree in a different direction from his face. "He knows I travel a lot, but that's all. Under circumstances like these, the plan is to let him think I was kidnapped by some local gangsters or something like that. That way, if I turn up alive, we can always say I got lucky."

Chung was silent for a moment, then touched her shoulder. "Is it difficult? To have such a relationship, when you must keep so many secrets?"

The answer came easily to her, because she had wondered about that back when she had first been recruited. How would someone like her have a relationship, if it was with someone who didn't know about E & E?

"Well, he knows I work for the government, but he thinks I'm just kind of a messenger. When we started dating, I had to explain to him that I wasn't allowed to talk about what I do, and he said that didn't matter. It wasn't my job he wanted to date, anyway."

"Ah," Chung said. "That sounds very wise."

Sarah turned and looked at him. "What about you? Are you married? Got a girlfriend?"

He shook his head. "Unfortunately, the position I hold does not allow me to have any personal entanglements. It is considered to be a security risk, since a foreign agent might use someone I care for against me. To help you understand, imagine that your fiancé was in our custody. If one of my advisers were to threaten him if you did not answer a question, would you not feel the need to protect him?"

Sarah let her face go cold. "Is that some kind of threat?"

Chung's eyes were suddenly wide as he tried to portray the picture of innocence. "Oh, no, no, no," he said. "I was merely trying to illustrate the reason why I am not allowed to have a girlfriend or wife. I can assure you that we know nothing about your personal life, or who your fiancé might be. In fact, I give you my solemn promise that I will never even reveal that you have mentioned him. He will have nothing to fear, I promise you."

"But aren't you required to report what we talk about? I wouldn't want you to get into trouble."

Slowly, he let himself smile again. "There is no reason to worry about me," he said. "I have been given considerable autonomy in dealing with you. If you share something with me that I believe should not be reported, I have the authority to keep it secret, between us."

Sarah nodded. "A way to build my trust in you, right?" She

slowly smiled at him. "You are definitely a charmer, I'll give you that. The thing is, Chung, I really don't think I know anything that's going to be important enough to keep your—what did you call them, advisers?—from deciding to use whatever kind of torture techniques are popular with them these days." She turned and looked across the courtyard again. "One of the first things they explain to you when you take a job like mine is that if you're ever captured, you are almost certainly going to die. You and I both know that's what's going to happen to me, in the long run."

She felt his fingers gently touch the back of her hand as it lay on her thigh. "Sarah," he said softly, "here is something you may believe. I do not wish to see you tortured, and so I shall do all that I can to prevent that from happening. For as long as I can, I will contrive to keep you with me."

She looked at him again, and this time he saw the doubt in her face. "Chung, why would you do that? The only thing that could do is blow up in your face, and then mine. Yes, you're very charming, but I am not interested in living my life inside these walls. Sooner or later, you'll have to let me go, and then other men will do whatever they think it takes to break me. That's how this game works, remember?"

"But, Sarah," he replied, "the important thing to remember about a game is that it has rules. Rules can be used to strengthen your own position, or to weaken those of your opponent. Fortunately for you," he said, giving her a conspiratorial grin, "I am one of those who write the rules."

Sarah looked at him for just a moment, then suddenly burst out laughing. "Oh, my goodness," she said as she caught her breath. "Chung, if you weren't holding me prisoner you'd be almost likable."

The Chinaman offered her a broad smile. "That is possibly one of the nicest things anyone has ever said about me. Let us hope that I shall only continue to become more so."

Her laughter subsided and faded away. "Well, letting me go would be a step in the right direction."

"I'm certain it would, but I'm afraid it is not within my power to do so. You and I, Sarah, are much alike. We both work for a government, and we are both subject to orders we may not always wish to follow. We perform the task set before us, and we cannot imagine failing to do so. If it were not for the fact that my government considers yours to be deceitful and cunning, you and I would not be having these conversations."

Sarah shrugged her shoulders. "I guess you're right," she said. "So where does that leave us?"

Chung let out a long, slow sigh. "Sarah, today I must begin asking you questions, and report to those above me what you say. This does not mean I will reveal everything; as I said a moment ago, some things I will keep between us."

"Yeah, I figured that was coming. So, what happens when I refuse to answer? Is that when the friendliness ends?"

"I suggest we simply start with some easy questions. If you do not answer one of them, I will simply move to another. This way, you can choose what you wish to tell me."

Sarah gave him a humorous but knowing look. "And the more questions I answer, the easier answering them becomes." She suddenly grinned. "I'll tell you what," she said. "You can ask anything you want to know about me personally, and unless I feel that it's going to endanger anyone I care about, I'll answer."

Chung bowed his head to her. "I accept," he said. "And my

first question would be a very simple one. Would you tell me how old you are, Sarah?"

She shrugged again. "Don't see any harm in that," she said. "I'm twenty-two."

"Twenty-two," Chung mused. "I would've thought you were a bit younger than that. Simply judging from your appearance, I had taken you for only twenty, perhaps even nineteen."

Sarah chuckled. "Flattery isn't going to get you anywhere with me," she said. "How about you? I figure you're about thirty-five, am I right?"

Both of his eyebrows shot upward. "I am only twenty-nine," he said. "It appears that while you look younger than your true age, I must look older."

"No, not really," Sarah said quickly. "There's a look in your eyes that made me think you were older. Like maybe you've seen too many things you didn't really want to see. I've seen that look before in people who work for their government."

Nodding, Chung said, "And this is probably true. I began my career in the Army when I was quite young, and displayed a propensity for intelligence work. I was transferred to the Ministry of State Security, where I spent four years as a field agent, then two more years as an attaché in our embassy to the United States. It was for that position that I was taught to speak English, but afterward I was placed in our counterintelligence division and trained as an interrogator." He looked at her with a slight grin. "My next question is also an easy one. How did you come to be in this type of work?"

Sarah considered whether or not to answer for a moment, then decided it was safe. "I was raised by my dad, who was a car thief. By the time I was fourteen I could drive anything, and better than most professional drivers, so that's when he started taking me out to steal them. We got caught when I was nineteen, and I was offered this job instead of a prison sentence."

"So you are truly nothing more than a driver?"

"That's what it says on my job description."

"And yet, you were sent into Bangkok prison for some reason. What was the purpose of placing you there?"

"Sorry, buddy," Sarah said. "That's one of those questions I'm not going to answer."

Chung smiled. "Very well, I'll leave that alone. For now."

NINE

Noah, Neil and Marco had taken one of the bunk rooms, and Jim, Randy and Dave took the other. While Jenny went into the bathroom to shower, the men decided to catch some rest while they had the opportunity. Neil hopped onto the bunk over Noah's, stretched out on his back, and was asleep only a moment later.

Marco was sitting on the other bottom bunk, and he suddenly grinned and pointed at Neil's feet, which were hanging in the air almost a foot from the end of the bunk.

"You know that's got to be uncomfortable," he said, and Noah nodded.

"Most likely, but I'm sure he's used to it."

"Yeah, probably." Marco looked back at Noah. "Hey, boss?"

"Yes?"

"Is there something going on that I don't know about?"

Noah looked him in the eye. "What makes you ask that?"

"I've been watching you and Jenny," Marco said, "and it looks to me like y'all are watching the rest of us pretty close. Like maybe you two know something the rest of us don't. Anything I need to worry about?"

"Not as long as you do your job right," Noah said. "Is there something bothering you?"

Marco chewed the inside of his left cheek for a couple of seconds. "Matter of fact, there is, but I've been reluctant to say anything. Permission to speak freely?"

"Go ahead."

"Okay. It's that whole mess that happened in Thailand. I can't for the life of me figure out how it could be some big coincidence that Sarah got snatched out of that prison, can you? If the guys who took her were really looking for sex slaves, wouldn't you think they'd go after locals, especially the younger ones? Why would they grab American girls?"

"Western girls have been abducted into the sex trade before," Noah said. "You heard the local guys, this happens every now and then at the prison."

"Yeah, I heard that," Marco said, "it's just the timing that throws me. What are the odds, you reckon, that Sarah would get there on the very day these goons show up to do their girl shopping?"

"Marco, what are you trying to say? Are you implying that someone knew Sarah wasn't who she claimed to be?"

"Well, hell, Noah," Marcus said. "I just can't wrap my head around the idea that this is all some big coincidence. I mean, didn't it strike you as odd?"

"That thought had crossed my mind," Noah replied. "The problem is that I can't put my finger on who could have slipped up and allowed anyone to know about her. Any thoughts on that?"

"Only ones that come to mind would be that Darrell and his

people. They live there, and sometimes they work with the local intelligence folks. Could be they've gotten pretty friendly, or at least that's a possibility." He chewed his cheek again for a moment. "There's another thing that's bugging me, too. I can't help wondering if maybe Sarah's still alive and that whole thing about showing us her hair in the ashes and all that was just a smokescreen."

Noah looked into his eyes. "I've also considered that possibility," he said. "Another possibility is that the way she was taken out of the prison really was coincidental, but then someone found out just who they had. There's pretty much no doubt in my mind that somebody knows she's an American agent. Whoever was behind her abduction is after information. If she's still alive, and I personally think she is, then we need to find out who it was that betrayed her."

"Damn straight," Marco said. "But if it was after they took her, then it could be somebody on Jenny's team, maybe even Jenny herself. Ever thought about that?"

"I've considered it. Of course, it could also be someone on mine." He let his eyes bore into Marco's.

Surprisingly, Marco only nodded his head. "Which naturally makes me the number one suspect. I already kinda figured that might be a possibility." He made a point of making eye contact. "For what it's worth, boss, I ain't the kind could ever do that. If I say you can count on me, then you damn well can. I don't betray the people I work with."

Noah looked at him for another moment before speaking. "Okay," he said. "I'll take you at your word unless you show me something different. Don't say anything to the others about this."

Marco nodded. "Stays between you and me." He turned and

lay down on the bunk, folding his hands under his head. Noah did likewise a few minutes later.

Several hours passed, and Noah was awakened by the sound of someone moving around in the large outer room. He got up and opened the door to see Jenny going through the cabinets. She turned and looked at him, smiled and said, "I think Soo Mi must really like chicken. There's probably five of them in the freezer. I found some canned potatoes and carrots in the cabinet. How would you feel about chicken stew for dinner?"

Noah nodded, then walked into the bathroom. When he came back a couple of minutes later, she had filled a deep pan with water and put it on the stove. She dropped in an entire frozen chicken and turned the burner up as high as it would go.

"It'll take that an hour to boil down to the point I can get the bones out, then I'll add the veggies and flour. It'll be ready in about ninety minutes, I'd say."

The other men had roused themselves and come out of the bunk rooms, flopping down on the sofas and chairs. "Anybody know what time it is?" Randy asked, and Jim looked at a wristwatch he was wearing.

"Almost 6:00, local time," he said. "Noah, have you worked on a mission plan yet?"

"No. I want to go over to where the agents are being held tonight, do some reconnaissance. Marco, Randy, you're with me on that."

Both men grunted agreement, and Noah pushed the button on the intercom to let Soo Mi know he wanted to talk to her. Jenny glanced at him with an eyebrow slightly raised, but didn't say anything, and the intercom came to life a moment later.

"Yes?" Soo Mi said.

"This is Noah. Is it safe to come up for a moment?"

"Sure. Give me a minute to open up."

Noah pushed the shelving unit out of the way and stepped out into the cellar, then closed it behind him. Soo Mi swung the stove aside and Noah climbed up the ladder. As soon as he was up in the kitchen, she pushed the stove back into place and turned off the burner.

"What can I do for you?" Soo Mi asked.

"I'm taking a couple of men with me when it gets dark to recon the holding facility. You mentioned a couple of handguns?"

"Yep, Colt 1911's." She opened a cabinet door and took out a box that had once contained crackers, then passed it to Noah. He opened it and withdrew the two pistols, setting them on her table, and then took out four additional magazines and a box of bullets.

With practiced ease, he stripped one of them down and saw that it was in excellent condition, then turned back to Soo Mi. "Are you particularly fond of these guns?" he asked.

Her face registered surprise, but she shook her head. "Not really," she said. "They actually got left here by mistake about a month ago. I'm in deep cover, I don't normally carry. Why?"

"Because I can't guarantee they'll be coming back." He reassembled the weapon and then repeated the process with the other one. When he was finished, he loaded all six magazines and slid two of them into the pistols.

Soo Mi watched him carefully, but didn't ask any questions. He picked up the guns and the additional magazines, then went back down to the cellar and handed them to Randy and Marco.

"It should be dark by the time we finish eating," he said. "I want to head out as soon after dark as we can. It's about two miles to where they're being held, and I've got the GPS coordinates plugged into my phone. We shouldn't have any trouble finding it."

"So, this is just recon?" Marco asked. "We're not going to try a strike tonight?"

"Not at this point. If we find a way into the building, we'll come back for the others and try to make the strike after midnight. If there is no other option, we'll use the explosives, but I'd prefer not to."

Marco held up the .45. "Only two guns? What about you, boss?"

"I prefer to be unarmed for a recon like this, because it forces me to do all I can to avoid being detected. I'll have the two of you to cover me, but you'll stay back while I check out the building. If I'm caught, I want them to think I'm alone."

Marco grunted, but didn't say anything else. Noah took out his iPhone and glanced at it, then looked around the room until he spotted an electrical outlet. Over it, someone had written "110 V," but it looked nothing like a conventional outlet in the United States. Instead of having two flat, rectangular holes, it had two perfectly round ones. He went into the bunk room and pulled a power adapter out of his bag, then plugged his phone charger into that before plugging the adapter into the wall outlet.

Dinner was finally ready and Jenny had managed to find bowls and spoons. She dipped a bowl out for herself, then told the men to help themselves. Noah got himself a bowl and sat down beside her on the sofa to eat.

"You sure about doing it this way?" Jenny asked softly. "Taking those two, I mean?"

Noah nodded. "I'm sure. It'll be fine."

Jenny rocked her head from side to side in surrender. "You're the boss," she said. "You won't try to do this all on your own, will you?"

"No. The mission comes first, and it has a much better chance of success if we all go in together. This is just a scouting mission, trying to find out a few things."

"Okay, then. We'll be ready when you get back."

Noah nodded, still shoveling food into his mouth. "Good. The sooner we get this job done, the better."

"I hear ya," Jenny said.

They finished eating, then changed into all-black clothing, and Noah checked in with Soo Mi via the intercom. She confirmed that it was dark out and moved the stove so the three men could climb up the ladder.

"You're going east," she said, "so you want to go out the back door. There are only a few little farms around here, so no one will notice if you keep to the fields. The building you're looking for is about two miles away, and is currently being guarded by de-perk Army troops."

"De-perk?" Marco asked.

"DPRK," Soo Mi said. "Democratic Peoples Republic of Korea. De-perk." She looked at Noah. "Camelot—look, I know who you are, and I know what you do. The thing is, those people —I knew them, you know? I was their liaison officer with Langley. I understand what you have to do, but do me a favor. Try not to let them suffer."

Noah caught the slip, but only nodded once. "I understand," he said.

The three men slipped out the back door and started walking quickly in the direction she had indicated. Noah had his iPhone set to give him GPS directions through an earplug, but it simply told him to continue the way he was going. On foot, the GPS said, the trip should take about fifteen minutes.

The safe house was about two-and-a-half miles northwest of Pyongyang, and their destination was roughly two miles to its west. As Soo Mi had said, most of the area was occupied by small family farms, and they were able to make their way through fields of cabbages, potatoes and tomatoes, being careful not to damage the crops any more than what was unavoidable. A half-moon hanging low in the sky cast barely enough light, but they were essentially invisible as they made their way across the countryside.

When Noah stopped at one point to scan the terrain ahead of them, Marco stepped close. "You brought me and Randy," he whispered. "We must be your prime suspects, huh?"

Randy caught up with them then, so Noah didn't bother to reply. After looking over the fields in front of them, he simply started walking again. Marco and Randy followed, side-by-side.

"Something going on?" Randy asked Marco in a soft whisper.

"Just trying to get the job done," Marco replied. "Like the man said, we're just here to cover his back."

They reached the industrial area only a few minutes later, and the building they were looking for was clearly visible. Noah had found a small stand of trees a couple of hundred yards away, and had chosen it for his staging area.

"All right," he said, "you guys stay put here. I'm going to go and see what I can find out. Watch closely, because if I'm caught or killed, you've got to go back and tell Jenny it's on her, now." He crouched low and moved swiftly across the open ground, and was lost to their sight by the time he'd gone fifty yards.

Noah moved to within 100 feet of the building and then dropped to the ground. He lay perfectly still for several minutes, watching the back side of the building and looking for any signs of motion. Any shadow that crossed his line of sight would probably mean a guard, but after more than ten minutes, he had seen nothing.

He stayed on the ground and low-crawled slowly the rest of the way, constantly watching and listening for any approaching soldiers. He reached the wall of the building without incident, then rose once more to a crouching position.

As far as he could tell, there were no windows on that side of the building at all, but he had spotted at least three doors. Staying low, he moved quickly to the first one and put his ear against it. There was no sound coming through it, so he reached into a pocket and took out the special item he had gotten from Wally.

It was the iPhone, but when Noah entered a security code and tapped an icon that looked like a windowpane, the screen lit up gray. Noah held it up close to the door, and a ghostly image of the room beyond appeared. This was the backscatter radiation viewer they had once used on a mission that took them to Russia, and it allowed him to see through walls as if he had x-ray vision.

On the screen, Noah could see two desks with computers sitting on them, but there was no one in the room. He scanned the edges of the door with the viewer, looking for contacts that would indicate the door had an alarm attached to it, but found none. He did, however, discover that the door was dead-bolted from the inside. There was no keyhole on the outside, so he wouldn't be able to pick the lock.

He turned off the viewer and moved to the next door. This one was apparently the guardroom, because he saw five men sitting on a couple of sofas. Each of them looked like a skeleton wrapped in plastic, and each was holding an assault rifle.

He moved quickly to the third door on that side of the building and turned the viewer on again. This door led into a storage room, and he could see boxes on shelves. There was another door on the far side that he assumed would lead into a hallway. He checked the outer door and found that it was also dead-bolted, as well as alarmed.

Noah turned off the viewer and slipped it back into his pocket, then moved to the end of the building and looked carefully around it. There was no one in sight, so he turned the corner and slipped toward the front side of the building. Another quick glance around that corner showed him two guards standing watch near one of the doors on that side, so he turned around and started back.

He stopped suddenly, when he realized that he had passed a window on the end of the building without even noticing it. He stopped and looked at it, but it was covered on the inside by heavy curtains. The viewer came out of his pocket once more and he turned it on, then looked through the curtains with it.

A ghostly, skeletal figure was pacing around in the middle of the room, holding something up to its ear. Whoever it was seemed to be making a phone call, but Noah couldn't hear anything. He turned off the viewer and slipped back around the corner, heading back to where he had first approached the building. He had just reached the middle door when it suddenly opened and two of the soldiers stepped outside, looking frantically around.

And the only thing they saw was Noah.

TEN

Noah was too close to avoid being seen, but not close enough to strike before they could react. One of them spotted him instantly and leveled his rifle at Noah's face, and then the other followed suit, calling to the others inside as he did so. A moment later, Noah was surrounded by five men, all aiming automatic rifles at him.

He put his hands on his head and stepped inside when the man who seemed to be in charge motioned with his rifle. The rest of them followed him in, and then two of them handed off their rifles and wrestled him to the floor. His hands were yanked behind his back and quickly secured with plastic bands. As soon as that was done, he was searched and his pockets gone through. His captors removed the iPhone, and then he was picked up and thrown onto one of the sofas.

The man in charge said something to one of the others, and he took off down the hall. He was back only a moment later, with another man in civilian clothes in tow. This one looked at Noah for a moment, then knelt down in front of him.

"You are American?" he asked in English.

Noah shrugged at him and grinned. "Yeah," he said. "I was

with the tour group yesterday, and we went to look at some farms, but I guess I wandered off and got lost. I found my way back to town, I was just trying to find someplace I could make a phone call. Saw some lights in your building, here, and thought I'd knock on the door, but these guys stuck their guns in my face before I could even try."

The man grinned at him, but it looked more like a snarl. "You are a spy," he said. "How many more of you there are?"

Noah shook his head. "No, seriously, man, I'm telling you straight. Let me call my tour guide, he can tell you."

"Do not attempt to lie to me," the man said. "Do you think we do not have sources of information? You arrive here with no identification, no passport. If you are tourist, you must keep your passport with you at all times, all tourists know this. You are a spy."

The English-speaking man stood up and looked at the soldier who had been giving orders. He said something in the local language, and two men suddenly grabbed Noah and hustled him through the door into the hallway. He was taken toward the other end of the building, but then a door was opened and he was suddenly going down some stairs.

At the bottom, his escorts yanked him to the right and into yet another hallway. He was taken several yards, and then shoved through another door that was ordered open by two men who were standing guard. He stumbled into the room as the door was slammed behind him, and then realized that he wasn't alone.

There were four Americans in the room, three women and a man, all sitting on the floor and leaning against the walls. Noah had found his targets.

"Looks like you made a mess of things," the man said. "Assuming you're one of ours, that is."

Noah held up a finger and looked around carefully. The room was completely bare, nothing but concrete walls, floor and even ceiling. There was no sign of any type of listening devices or cameras, but Noah dropped his voice to a nearly silent whisper as the man got to his feet.

"I am. I was doing recon on the building when I stumbled right into a couple of the soldiers guarding the place." He shrugged his shoulders. "Hopefully, my partners saw what happened and got away."

The man stood and Noah saw that he was unbound. "What's your name?" the fellow asked.

"Noah," Noah said. "You?"

"I'm Dale, Dale Jackson." He pointed at the women. "This is Chrissy Smith, Shirley Stubblefield and Liz Tyler." He looked back at Noah and narrowed his eyes. "Considering the fact that we're under Protocol 15, I'm guessing you weren't sent here on a rescue mission, am I right?"

Noah looked him in the eye for a second, then shook his head. "I'm afraid not," he said. "I'm E & E, and my orders were to terminate all of you before you could be broken."

Dale nodded. "Yeah, we expected as much. The ironic thing is that nobody has even tried any real interrogation, at least not yet. We've been asked a few questions, but no one's attempted to force any real information out of us."

Noah's eyebrows lowered. "Any idea why not? Langley seems to think you would have all been on the rack by now."

Dale scoffed at that. "Of course they do," he said. "That's Protocol 15. Any operative who's captured is automatically presumed compromised." He shook his head. "That makes it easy to get rid of inconvenient people."

Noah looked at him and his left eyebrow went up. "What do you mean by that?"

"It means we were set up," Shirley said. "Our covers were solid, we were here as advisers on some engineering projects, and there's been nothing that could have burned us. Somebody sold us out, and Protocol 15 lets them clean up the mess and get away with it."

Noah looked at her for a long moment, then turned to Dale. "Do you all believe that?"

Dale ran a hand through his hair and exhaled sharply. "Yeah, we've talked it over. It's the only thing that makes any sense. We made contact with our source, got the information we were sent for and gave him data he could use to hamper their missile development, but we weren't arrested until several days later. Our work was already done, and our liaison was arranging for us to go home. We had what we'd come for, but these clowns, they haven't even asked us about anything connected to it. The way they've been treating us, they seem to think we were only trying to steal agricultural secrets. I don't think I've ever even heard of anything this stupid."

Noah looked at him, then looked at the three women. "None of you have been interrogated about your actual mission?"

"Not unless you count questions about how many tons of potatoes we grow each year," Shirley said. "It's like Dale told you, they act like we've been trying to learn how to farm over here."

Noah thought about it for a few moments, then frowned. "Have you answered them?"

"Yeah," Shirley said, "I said we grow a hell of a lot of potatoes. What else am I gonna say?"

Noah nodded slowly. "Acclimatization and disorientation," he said. "I read about this not long ago, it's a new interrogation technique. Ask a lot of extremely confusing questions that don't seem important, and keep doing it until you get any kind of answers. Apparently, once you start answering questions, it reduces your resistance to answering more sensitive ones. It's harder to hold back information you don't want to give up."

"That's not new," Dale said, "our people have been using that for forty years, but we didn't ask questions about farming. To get someone loosened up, you just ask them simple questions about themselves. It's supposed to break down the wall we all put up between us and whoever we perceive to be the enemy. If we feel ourselves becoming familiar with the interrogator, it's hard to think of him as someone you should oppose."

Noah nodded again. "Yes, I'm familiar with that, too," he said. "This is a little bit different, though, because it's designed to not only get you accustomed to answering, but also to keep you confused. Do some of the questions seem completely ridiculous?"

Chrissy nodded her head. "Yeah, they do," she said. "They asked me yesterday if I knew the difference between an orange and an orange. Like, what the hell kind of question was that? When I said I didn't know what they meant, they kept asking it over and over again."

"Confusion impact," Noah said. "If you can sufficiently confuse someone, the mind is disoriented and can't figure out what to do, so it will seize on the very first sensible thought it's given. I've seen demonstrations of it; you can literally walk up to someone on the street, start spewing gibberish at them until they are obviously confused, and then if you tell them to do something they'll do it without even thinking. I watched a man talk to a woman for a minute and a half and make no sense whatsoever, but then he suddenly told her to give him her purse and she did, without realizing it. He turned around and walked away with it, and she just stood there completely unaware of what happened. Lucky for her, it was just a demonstration and he brought it back a minute later, but she still hadn't realized that it was gone."

"I've seen that, too," Liz said. "Some kind of instant hypnosis thing, there's videos about it on YouTube. It's really amazing. In one of them, somebody answers a payphone and hears a lot of really confusing things, but then the caller says 'go to sleep' and he just slumps down to the ground, out cold."

Dale was looking at her as she spoke, but then he turned his eyes back to Noah. "Are you telling me we may have already answered the real questions, without even knowing it?"

Noah shrugged. "Highly unlikely," he said. "From what I've read, you might not be able to stop yourself from answering, but you'd ultimately remember it if you had. I'm more concerned about how and why you would have been sold out. Any ideas?"

Dale seemed to hesitate, but Chrissy spoke up. "The Company has something rotten inside it," she said. "Nobody's really talking about it, but it seems like China has gotten its hooks into us somehow. An awful lot of classified information is being leaked to them, and since they share a border with North Korea, that makes anything going on here pretty important to them. Our best guess is that whoever's working with them from inside our offices is feeding them all kinds of stuff about American activities in the peripheral countries."

"Which means," Dale added, "that any activities we're involved in that affect China's neighbors equals something they'll pay a lot of money for. One of the top guys I know at Langley thinks the mole is compromising a lot of missions for the sake of money. As for our situation, I get the impression the Ministry of State Security here was told about us by the Chinese. I understand the language fairly well; a couple of the guards were talking about the fact that we might be going to China, but that's all I've heard."

Noah looked at him for a long moment, then nodded his head. "One of my team members was sold out in Thailand last week, but I've been suspecting the people I was working directly with. Now I'm wondering if there might be a connection to your problem."

"If you are actually E & E," Liz said, "I'd bet on it. There's been a lot of buzz and chatter the last year or so that China is trying to identify an E & E primary, code name Camelot. If your guy could possibly know anything about that one, he'd be worth a fortune."

"But don't write off your own suspicions, yet," Shirley said. "Like in our case, the only one who could have passed on the info about where to arrest us was our liaison, a deep cover agent who lives on a small farm outside Pyongyang. The mole might have told China we were here, but no one back at Langley had any information about where we were staying over here. Information isolation; no one but the local liaison knew that, so it couldn't accidentally be intercepted in phone or computer chatter."

Noah stared at her for a moment, his mind racing with sudden possibilities. *If the Chinese are after me, why didn't the mole give me up instead of Sarah?* Noah wondered, but the logical answer was the same one he and Jenny had come to. *It was a moment of opportunity. CIA probably provided the intel on the prison, and would have known we were sending in a female operative, even if they didn't know why. If the mole somehow learned it was my team, then all he had to do was alert his contacts to snatch American girls. The prison would have told them who the newest one was, and they probably took the Ingersoll girl to make it look more coincidental.*

But what about information isolation? That was a standard protocol for top secret missions, so the actual date and time of her insertion into the prison wouldn't be available back in the States. If the Chinese were behind the abduction, and I'm almost certain now that they were, then there was still someone else involved, someone who was involved with the actual mission.

It was just like these folks. Soo Mi was their liaison; only she could have given the local State Security ops the intel on where to arrest them. She may have also tipped these folks that I was coming, because it seemed they were looking for something when they came out and found me. And then there's the fact that she knew I was Camelot. Only E&E personnel should know that, not CIA. I should have seen it then.

And Jenny and the others are back there with her, even now!

He turned his back and wiggled his fingers. "Do you have any way to take these zip strips off me?"

Dale leaned over and looked at Noah's hands, then turned around and picked up what looked like the lid of a tin can. "Yeah, turn around."

Noah felt Dale working on the plastic with the edge of the lid. It took a couple of minutes, using the edge of the lid like a saw. A moment later his hands were free, though one of the strips was still around his right wrist.

"It suddenly occurs to me," Dale said, "that cutting you loose might have been a mistake. Are you going to carry out your orders?"

Noah looked him in the eye. "Not yet," he said. "I was told bluntly not to attempt to rescue any of you, on CIA orders, but my own boss gave me leeway on it and the situation changed the minute I was captured. The rest of the team I was with will be working on how to complete the mission, but now I'm on the inside with you. If I can figure a way to escape and time it for when they come, it might be possible for us all to get out alive." He flexed his wrists, working the circulation back into them. "Considering what you just told me, I want to bring you back alive if I possibly can. But if I can't..."

Dale searched his face for any sign that he was lying, and seemed to relax. "If you can't get us out alive, then you have to do what you have to do."

"I'm afraid so. Let's cross that bridge if we come to it, all right? What can you tell me about the security setup here?"

Dale looked around as if he could see through the walls, then turned back to Noah. "There's usually between fifteen and twenty soldiers around, and I would imagine that half of them are sleeping right now. Then there's Colonel Song; he's in command here, but he doesn't wear a uniform. As far as I know, he's the only one who speaks English properly, though there are a couple of women who come now and then, and they speak some."

"Okay. I saw the guard room upstairs. Are there more down here?"

Dale pointed back the direction Noah had come from. "Two doors down, that's their bunk room. How many guards did you see up and about?"

"About nine. There were two standing guard outside, two outside your door and five more in the guard room when I was caught."

"Then there are probably about that many more catching some Z's right now. Other than them and the Colonel, there's occasionally a few other men around, usually only during the day. I doubt there's anybody else here tonight."

"Well, Song is probably the man they brought in to speak English to me. He didn't buy it when I tried to tell him I was a lost tourist."

Dale simply stared at him, but the three women laughed derisively. "Well, he wouldn't, would he? Would you?"

"Of course not," Noah said, "but I would naturally expect someone to try it. Giving him what he expected me to say was the easiest way I could think of to get myself thrown in with you."

Dale scoffed. "What made you think they'd throw you in here? They could have tossed you in an entirely different room."

"Possible, but unlikely. A limited number of soldiers to use for guard duty indicates that whoever was in command would probably keep any prisoners together. It was just bad luck that the guards stepped outside while I was snooping around, but once I was captured it made sense to just let them bring me to you."

"Well, you certainly took a risk," Dale said. "It was always possible they'd just assume you were trying to find out what happened to us, and shoot you for snooping around. They seem to think this place is pretty important."

"Actually, I didn't think it was that big a risk. If I'd made it back without being seen, I would have simply followed the mission outline and done what I was sent for, but the moment I was caught, I had to rethink the whole thing. I know the rest of my team won't shy away, so that meant I might have a small chance of rescue if I could get myself close to you. It worked."

Dale's eyes bounced from Noah's face to the floor and back. "Look, if it comes down to it," he said quietly, "get the women out. Leave me behind if you have to, or kill me, if it helps you to save them, all right?"

"I'm not planning to leave any of you behind," Noah replied, "not if I can avoid it. You need to tell Langley what you know about the mole, and I need to see that Soo Mi doesn't get to betray anyone else."

Dale looked up sharply. "You know Soo Mi?" he asked. "Damn, man, that's probably how you got caught!"

Noah nodded. "That's a possibility I've been considering," he said. "The guards who caught me came out looking for something, so it's possible they were tipped off. And if Soo Mi is aware of the Chinese interest in Camelot, it's even more likely, and I'll let you read between the lines on that."

Dale glanced over at the women who were still seated, then motioned for Noah to follow him to the far side of the room. They kept their backs turned, and Dale lowered his voice to a whisper.

"Do you really think there's a chance you can get us out of here alive?"

Noah looked him in the eye. "I'm not going to lie to you," he said. "If it looks like we can't get out of here together, I'm not going to let you be retaken. My team will come sometime between now and morning, and if I can help them from the inside then there's a chance we can take this place down and then get you out of here. Can any of you fight?"

"We all had basic hand-to-hand training, and we can all handle a gun if you can get any."

Nodding, Noah said, "All right. The next question is how do we get the guards outside the door to come in here?"

"They won't," Dale said. "Somebody will bring us breakfast in the morning, but those two always stand back and keep their guns aimed at the doorway. Their job is to keep us in here, and I guess they take it pretty seriously."

"Their job isn't to keep you in, it's to make sure Song doesn't lose you, and there's a difference. What we need to do is make them think they failed."

Dale looked confused. "And how do you plan to do that?"

"Where's that can lid you used as a cutter?"

ELEVEN

"He's coming back," Marco whispered. Beside him, Randy nodded as they watched Noah come back around the corner of the building. He was moving swiftly and staying low, making his way back to the point that was closest to the little stand of trees.

A thin vertical line of light appeared suddenly, and instantly swelled into a rectangle as one of the doors on the back of the building swung open. Noah was less than twenty feet away when two soldiers stepped out, and one of them spotted him instantly. The muzzle of his gun snapped up instantly to center itself on his face, and the other one matched it a second later.

"Oh, shit," Marco hissed. "This ain't good." He gripped the pistol in his hand tightly and tensed himself to rise, but Randy put a hand on his shoulder.

"Stay down," Randy whispered. "We've got orders, remember? He's caught, so we got to go back and tell Jenny to take over."

Marco huffed, but stayed put. They watched as more guards came out of the building, weapons waving in every direction, but then Noah was hustled inside and the door slammed shut. They held their position for a minute, but when no other guards came out to start searching the area, Marco looked at Randy again.

"You're right, bro," he said. "Let's head back."

Despite the dim light, it wasn't difficult to retrace their steps. When they got back to the safe house, a light tap on the back door was enough to rouse Soo Mi. She let the men in and sent them down the ladder, then followed them to learn what was going on.

"It may have been just dumb luck," Marco said, "but I'm not really sure." He sighed. "Noah was captured. He was running recon on the building when some soldiers stepped outside all of a sudden, like. Thing is, I'd swear they knew he was there when they came out, and they grabbed him in a hurry and dragged him inside. Last thing he told us before he went in was to come back and say it's on you, Jenny, if he got caught, so that's what we did."

"Son-of-a-bitch," Jenny cursed. "Dammit, I like Noah, and I don't like very many people!" She crossed her arms and paced around the room for a moment, then turned back to Marco and Randy. "Okay, did you hear any gunshots?"

"No," Randy said. "They drug him inside, and the last I saw of him before the door closed was him getting pushed down on the floor. Looked like they were going to search him, but I don't think they were going to kill him." He shrugged, then glanced for a second at Soo Mi before turning back to Jenny.

"Good, that means we've got an asset inside the building. With any luck, they might have tossed him right in with the targets. If it were me, I'd probably enlist their help in creating a diversion when we go in." She turned to Jim Marino. "Break out the gear," she said. "Rifles for everybody, but we take the grenades and C4, too."

While Jim, with Neil helping, started passing out guns and grenades, Jenny turned back to Marco and Randy. "How many doors on the building? How many windows?"

"There were only three doors on the side we could see," Marco said, "no windows." He was standing slightly behind Randy, and suddenly wiggled his eyebrows and flicked his eyes at Randy and Soo Mi. Jenny raised her own eyebrows in a silly face, then relaxed them. It was enough to tell him she'd gotten the message he was trying to convey.

Soo Mi spoke up. "I've seen pictures of that building," she said. "Your guys would have been looking at the back, but there is one window on each end and only one door and half a dozen windows on the front. The building is made of concrete blocks, but the cavities were filled with concrete as well, so it's pretty solid."

"Okay, thanks," Jenny said, keeping her face bland. "Any idea on the interior layout?"

Soo Mi shook her head. "No, sorry."

Jenny continued pacing for a moment, then suddenly stopped and looked around at the men. "Okay, we're going to blow the three doors on the back of the building, then move in in teams of two each. Randy, you're with me. Marco, you take the whiz kid, and that leaves Jim and Dave. This is going to be a wipeout, we take out anyone in uniform and any other opposition we run into. Everybody keep your ears open, because Noah's gonna be trying to work with us from the inside once he hears the explosions, and I'd like very much to bring him out of this alive."

"Damn right," Neil said. "We've got to get him back!"

"And we will," Jenny said emphatically. "Chill out, whiz kid." She took the mini assault rifle Jim held out to her. "Everybody ready? Let's do it!"

Soo Mi went up the ladder first, then confirmed that everything was clear, and the rest boiled out like bees from a disturbed hive. It was dark in the old farmhouse, but that only made it easier to see through the windows. After checking to be sure there was no visible activity, Jenny nodded once and Randy opened the door.

Randy and Marco went out first, and then the rest of the men followed. As soon as all of them were outside, Jenny spun away from the door and grabbed Soo Mi by the throat, pressing her face up close to the Korean girl's own.

"I'm gonna say this one time," she whispered. "I know you're a traitor, and I can't stand a traitor. I've got two questions for you, bitch. Answer me fast and you might live through this."

Soo Mi's eyes were wide as they could be, but she shook her head. "I'm not—"

"Wrong answer," Jenny said. "Next one costs you your life. Who on my team is working with you to sell us out? Remember, a wrong answer and you die right now!"

Soo Mi licked her lips quickly, then lowered her eyes. "It's Mitchell," she said. "He passed me the code name, Camelot, and the Chinese are screaming to get their hands on him."

Jenny nodded. "One more answer and you're home free. How do you call for us to be picked up and extracted?"

Soo Mi slowly pointed toward a cell phone lying on the kitchen table. Jenny glanced at it, then whispered, "Call it in now. Tell them two hours, pick us up here. Tell them we'll be hot and that there will be no further communication tonight." Soo Mi stared at her, and Jenny grinned. "You don't think I'm going to leave you conscious, do you? Let you tip them off? Now, do it!"

Soo Mi picked up the phone and dialed a number. She spoke in broken English. "Ai, you get truck for eggs? Ai, eggs all ready, but I very tired, very tired. You come get eggs, two hour, okay?

Okay, two hour! I sleep now!"

She ended the call and looked at Jenny. "That's it. Eggs is the code for a pickup, they'll be here in two hours. No problems, I promise." Her eyes were still wide and tears were brimming over.

Jenny smiled at her. "Good girl," she said. "And I said you'd live through this, right? Well, I lied."

Soo Mi gasped and tensed, but Jenny spun the girl around and pulled her to the center of the room, holding her by her hair. The knife came from under her left arm, where she always kept it, and she thrust it forcefully into the small gap between the top cervical vertebra and the base of Soo Mi's skull, then let the body fall where it stood. She reached down and drew the knife back out, wiped off the small amount of blood on the dead girl's clothing, then slid it back into its sheath. A moment later, she had the body under covers in Soo Mi's bed, and then slipped out the door.

"I had Soo Mi arrange for our ride out in two hours," she said as she caught up to the men outside. "It's all set."

They moved out, still careful to watch for any possible observers, but still moving along fairly quickly. It took them slightly more than fifteen minutes to reach the point where they could see the building, and they were surprised to find no sign of any extra guard activity on its outside. Randy and Marco led them to the stand of trees where they had watched and waited, and they all settled in to catch a moment's rest before the action began.

"Okay," Jenny said after giving them time to catch their breath. "Those look like standard steel doors, so let's go for the hinges and the doorknobs. Wrap C4 around each, and when it all goes off the doors will go flying. Ready? Let's go."

Jenny and Randy headed straight for the center door, and Dave and Jim took the one to its left, so Marco and Neil went to the right. They moved quickly, crouching low, and stopped just before making contact with the wall.

Marco pulled the C4 out of his pockets and broke it up, packing it around all three of the hinges on his door and then wrapping the rest around the doorknob. The detonator was set up with contact wires, so he stuck it into the putty on the doorknob to hold it in place and ran wires from it to each glob of the explosive. He looked up toward Jenny and held up a thumb, then took Neil twenty feet further down the wall. They crouched down on the ground beside the wall, with their backs to the door and covering their heads with their hands.

Jenny had the trigger, and as soon as she saw that Jim and Dave were also ready, she took Randy to the midpoint between her door and theirs, and they also crouched down and covered their ears.

Suddenly, a muffled screaming, several voices at once, could be heard coming from a lower level, and Jenny knew it had to be Noah's doing. She grinned maniacally and dropped a thumb on the button.

The three blasts went off simultaneously and the doors flew dozens of feet away from the building. All six of them jumped instantly to their feet and ran toward the doors, then rushed inside. Jenny had taken the center door, the guard room, but the blast wave from the explosion had rendered the four men inside unconscious. She snatched open the inner door to the hallway, then she and Randy each thrust their heads out to look in both directions, yanking them back instantly.

"Looks clear," Randy said, and Jenny nodded. She jumped through the door, deliberately placing herself against the far wall in the hallway and facing to the right, as Randy stepped out and faced left.

Jim and Dave appeared at their end of the hallway, just as two men burst out of the doorway that led to the stairs. Dave's Tavor burped twice and they both fell, but voices could be heard shouting behind them. Both men put themselves against the wall and began moving toward the stairwell door.

At the other end of the building, Marco and Neil had rushed into the store room. There was no one inside, so they opened the inner door and looked out into the hallway. Jenny and Randy were already there, and a moment later they saw Dave and Jim. They started to look behind them just as the two soldiers came out of the stairwell, then spun as the sound of Dave's gun caught them off guard.

Marco and Neil had each raised their weapons, but didn't fire when they saw both men fall. Marco took a step toward Jenny, but Neil suddenly realized that he had glimpsed a door at the other end of the hall, and turned instinctively.

Sure enough, the door was only about fifteen feet away, in the short wall that made the end of the hallway. Neil took a step toward it and then froze as he saw the knob turning slowly. His Tavor came up instantly, so that it was aimed directly at the center of the door when it suddenly flew open.

Colonel Song stood there, dressed in gray slacks and a T-shirt, but incongruously without shoes or socks. He was holding a pistol in his hand, but he lowered it slowly when he realized there was a gun pointed at him.

Neil stared at him for a moment, then motioned quickly with the barrel of the gun for the man to get down. "Get down," he shouted, "drop the gun and get down now!"

Song stood where he was and looked at Neil for a moment, but then Marco spun and added his own gun to the number of weapons aimed in his face. "All right," Song said, then scowled and slowly knelt down. He laid the pistol on the floor beside his feet and then stretched himself out onto the floor with his hands behind his head.

Marco quickly stepped over him and checked the room he had come from, but there was no one else there. He snatched up the pistol and tucked it into his waistband, then grabbed Song by his collar and hoisted him to his feet. "How many downstairs?" he demanded, and then they heard gunfire from down below.

* * * * *

Noah had taken the can lid and looked at it closely, then folded a third of it over and knelt down. He rubbed the remaining edge on the concrete floor, putting the best edge on it that he could manage under the circumstances. "We're going to put on a little act shortly," he said. "Those guards are supposed to keep you in, but they're also supposed to keep you safe. When I give the signal, I want all of you to start screaming. Unless those guys are really stupid, it will dawn on them that something bad happening to you will mean something bad happening to them. As soon as they come charging in here, I'll take them out, but I want to give my team time to get here first. That should take about another forty minutes, so be ready."

The three women continued to sit by the wall, but they were watching him intently. Dale knelt down beside him.

"You want those guys to think you're killing us, right?" Dale asked.

"That's the idea," Noah said. "It'll have to happen fast, so I hope nobody is squeamish."

They looked down at the can lid. "You can only cut one throat at a time," he said. "By the time you get the first one done, the other one is going to be ready to blow you away."

"I don't plan to give him the chance. As soon as they're both in the room, I'm going to land on them hard, and I'll worry about cutting them then. If I missed one or he gets away, it's going to be up to you to get him down. Understood?"

Dale nodded, and Noah kept working the edge. He kept rotating the lid as he shaved it across the concrete, tiny bits of metal glittering onto the floor.

Noah's internal clock had been ticking off minutes and seconds since he had been grabbed, and he was making educated guesses about what Jenny and the others were doing. Unless something went terribly wrong, Marco and Randy would lead the rest of them back to the stand of trees they had watched from, and Noah had no doubt Jenny was planning to blow open the doors on the building. That would mean they split into three pairs, coming in through all three doors on the back of the building. With any luck, they would capture the first floor easily. All that would remain were the soldiers in the sub level, and Noah hoped to take at least some of them out before they could put up any serious resistance.

When he judged that it had been something close to an hour since his capture, he positioned himself behind the door and nodded to the others. All three women began screaming at once, and Dale let out a bellow that sounded like rage. They kept it up, and it was only a dozen seconds later when a key rattled in the lock and the door flew open.

The two guards rushed in, and then stared in surprise at the four people who were sitting on the floor and screaming. The scene was so ridiculous that it confused them, but before they could recover the ability to think, Noah grabbed both of them and spun them around, then took them down to the floor.

At that moment, a terrific explosion seemed to take place above them, but they didn't have time to worry about it. Dale leapt up and pushed the door shut, then jumped on the soldiers as well, as Noah yanked back first one man's head and dragged the makeshift blade across his throat, and then reached for the other one. It was over in less than thirty seconds, as the severed carotid and jugular drained the blood from their brains and took them into a sleep they would never awaken from.

TWELVE

They heard the chatter of gunfire upstairs, but it was muffled. Noah snatched up one of the assault rifles the guards had been carrying and pulled the door open, as Dale grabbed the other and stepped in behind him. A quick look around into the hallway showed Noah several soldiers huddled there, apparently focusing their attention on the stairs. He stepped out and flicked the assault rifle's selector to full auto, then squeezed the trigger and sprayed thirty rounds into them.

Dale swung out and added his own fire to the fusillade, taking the soldiers so by surprise that not one of them managed to return fire. Dale checked the bunk room and found it empty, while Noah dropped his rifle and ran through the hallway, snatched up another from one of the fallen soldiers and looked into the stairwell. One man was halfway up, but he was looking back at Noah with eyes full of terror. When he saw Noah pointing the rifle at him, he quickly dropped his own and thrust his hands into the air, but Noah put a single bullet between his eyes.

"Jenny?" Noah shouted.

"Noah?" Jenny yelled back. "Is that you?"

"Yes. We're all secure down here, how about you?"

"Secure, one prisoner. It's safe to come up."

Noah turned to Dale and told him to fetch the women, then made his way up the stairs. Jenny and her men were gathered where the stairs exited into the hallway, and he saw Marco and Neil coming toward them with Song.

"The targets?" Jenny asked.

"They're alive and coming up. We're taking them with us."

Jenny's eyes went wide as she looked up at him, but she didn't argue. "Okay. What about our captive, here?"

Noah looked at Song. "This is Colonel Song, the interrogator. I don't know how much he's actually learned from his captives, but I don't think it was anything important. I'll fill you in later, but there is a lot more to this situation that we were led to believe. As for the Colonel, here, the question is whether he's valuable enough to try to take with us, or if we should terminate him and leave him here." He turned to Dale, who was just coming up the stairs behind him. "Any thoughts on that?"

Dale looked at Song and scowled. "I know he's supposed to be some kind of bigwig in their intelligence," he said. "Might be a feather in your cap if you bring him in, your call."

Noah turned to the Korean. "I can put a bullet in your head, or you can go with us without resistance. Which way would you have it?"

Song glared at him for only a couple of seconds, then lowered his eyes. "I will not resist," he said.

"See that you don't, because I can kill you just as quickly in the field as I can here. Where's my phone?"

Song pointed with his chin at the guard room, and Noah

followed as Marco walked him into it. "It is in the top drawer of the desk," Song said. Noah walked across the room and yanked the door open, then picked up the iPhone and shoved it into his pocket once more.

"All right, let's go," Noah said. "The explosions are going to bring somebody pretty soon, and we want to be as far away as possible before they get here. Randy, lead out. Marco, you take our guests and follow him, and the rest of us will be behind you. He tries anything, don't hesitate to put a bullet in his brain."

"Be my pleasure, boss," Marco said. He slung the little rifle over his shoulder and pulled out the pistol Song had dropped. It had a large sound suppressor attached to it, and he waved it in front of the Colonel's face. "Won't even be noisy, now will it?" He poked Song in the back with it, and then he and the Colonel followed Randy out the door. Neil was next, followed by Dale and the women, and then Jim and Dave.

Noah kept Jenny back until the others were a few yards ahead. "I found out something interesting," he said. "The CIA has a mole who's been selling information to the Chinese, information related to US activities in its neighboring countries, and their liaison here, Soo Mi, was involved in selling these agents out. She might also have been the reason I was caught, because she knew I was Camelot."

"Yeah, it was her," Jenny said, "but not without help. Seems I was right about Randy. He told her who you were, and she dropped the dime to her contact with China or whoever, which is why they were waiting for you when you got here. She's dead, by the way."

"Okay," Noah said without missing a beat, "but it seems that China has been trying to get particular information about me,

Camelot. The mole might very well be connected to what happened to Sarah. CIA would've been involved in planning that mission, so the mole could have found out Sarah was the Camelot trans officer."

"Unlikely. Allie doesn't share that intel easily. She says she doesn't want anyone out there trying to influence her teams, so the less they know, the better."

"So the mole compromised Randy, you think? If he's the one who sold out Sarah, then it had to have been after she was taken from the prison, rather than before."

Jenny scowled. "Not necessarily," she said. "Remember I told you he had a habit of disappearing now and then? I was thinking about it, and one of those times was the day she was snatched. We were all done, and getting ready to fly out the next morning, and Randy sort of went for a stroll. I didn't think anything of it at the time, because I was used to it, but with all I know now, I have to figure he might have gotten a message. I know he's been turned and is working with the CIA mole, so it all fits together."

"Then we need to interrogate him now," Noah said. "Find out if he knows where she was taken."

"No, we need to get our asses out of hostile territory, first," Jenny replied, "and check in with Neverland. The thing that bothers me is, if the Company knew it had a mole, why the hell weren't we told?"

"That's for Allison to figure out. It just strikes me that if the mole used Randy to sell Sarah out, then she's almost certainly in China."

"Yeah," Jenny grumbled, "which only leaves the question of how the hell we find her and get her out!"

"Yeah, but I've got another hunch on that."

Noah had been correct about the explosions bringing attention, and they heard a number of sirens approaching the cement plant behind them. They hurried along as quickly as they could, and made it back to the safe house in just over thirteen minutes.

"We've got about thirty minutes before our pickup," Jenny said to Noah as they gathered in the yard behind the shack. "Let's get down in the hidey-hole."

"Good idea," Noah said, and lit the burner on the stove, then moved it aside.

Randy looked around. "Uh, where's Soo Mi?" he asked.

"Catching some sleep," Jenny said. "You can flirt with her later, when our ride gets here. Let's get downstairs."

Randy looked over toward the curtained area that was Soo Mi's bedroom, and it was obvious he was getting nervous, but he climbed down the ladder after Marco, Neil and the rescued agents. Noah went down next, and Jenny, Dave and Jim followed.

Randy walked into the big room and stood in its center, and something in his face said he knew he was caught out. Noah leveled his assault rifle at him, and said, "Put the gun down slowly, Randy. Soo Mi gave you up, we know you told her who I was and to let the Chinese know."

Randy let his Tavor slide down his arm on the strap and clatter onto the floor. "It isn't like that," he said. "I didn't..."

"Don't bother, Randy," Jenny said. "Just tell us the truth, now, okay? Where is Sarah?"

Randy bit his bottom lip and ran his hands over his face, the sheer terror of his predicament showing in his eyes. "Jenny, I..."

"Oh, come on, Randy," Jenny said. "Do I need to torture it out of you? Soo Mi owned right up, she didn't even try to lie to me more than once. Don't make me rip it out of you, man, please?"

There is an old phrase that is often used in stories to describe when someone has reached the point of accepting defeat: His countenance fell. At that moment, Randy Mitchell's face would have served as a dictionary definition of that phrase.

"I don't know where she is," he said. "I was only told to see that a certain man found out about her being in the prison and that she worked for Team Camelot, and someone else would do the rest. I swear that's all I know."

"Who did you contact?" Noah asked. "I want the name."

"It was a guy who works for that fight promoter, Pak," Randy said. "His name was Lom, but that's all I know." He finally looked up at Noah. "This isn't what you think, Noah. It wasn't for money or anything like that. Somebody knows who I used to be, and they've got my little sisters. If I don't do what they want, they'll kill them."

"Why didn't you come to me?" Jenny asked him. "We could have handled this without you becoming a traitor, Randy. I woulda helped you, you know that. I woulda killed the bastards for you!"

"They said if I told you or anyone else, they'd know and kill Cindy and Meri. The girls are all my mother has, now, since they all think I'm dead. What else was I supposed to do?"

Jenny almost got to him, but Noah caught her in time. "Randy, you're going back to the states with these agents," he said, "and you're going to tell our people everything you know about this person. Jenny, you're going to escort him back and see that Allison gets him, while my team goes back to Thailand. If Lom works for Pak, I'll find him."

"Okay," Jenny said. "And, Randy, for what it's worth, the person controlling you is a CIA mole. When we find out who it is, I promise you I'm going to beg for the mission to kill him." She turned to Dave Lange. "You and Jim keep him covered. I don't want him getting away or making any fuss. If he tries to draw attention, kill him."

Dave swallowed hard, but nodded. "Yes, Ma'am," he said.

"Time for our ride pretty soon," Noah said. "Everyone get a drink or something to eat if you need it, because we don't know when we'll get another chance. We're taking the weapons with us, just in case we need them. Marco, you keep an eye on Randy as well. Soon as everyone is ready, let's go upstairs and wait for the truck."

They didn't have to wait long. It showed up, running without headlights, less than five minutes after they got upstairs again, and Noah hustled everyone out the door and into it as fast as he could.

The driver stopped him just before he climbed in with them. "You have too many? More people?"

Noah nodded. "Yes. The captured agents, we were able to rescue them." The man smiled and clapped Noah on the shoulder. "Good job, good job," he said. "I tell your people in Seoul! Get in, get in, we go!"

The truck pulled out quickly with its lights off, and Noah saw that the driver was wearing night vision gear. They went a couple of miles, and then the driver stopped, took off the starlight goggles and turned on the headlights before going again.

The drive lasted more than two hours, and one of the men explained to Noah that they had gone around the western edge of the city completely. They were now about four miles southwest of Pyongyang, but word would be sent to the driver of the truck they had ridden in on to pick them up in a new location.

They were dropped at an abandoned building that sat about 200 yards off the main paved road for the area. Noah posted Marco and Dave on watch, with Jim keeping the suppressor-equipped pistol aimed at Song's head, while the rest of them sat down against the walls and tried to get some sleep.

Three hours later, Noah woke and relieved Jim, then woke Neil and Jenny to take over guard duty. The sun was just beginning to create a glow over the eastern horizon by that time, and a few of the others were stirring.

Dale came and sat beside Noah, holding out a small radio receiver. "Snagged this from Soo Mi's gear, and I've been following what's going on back in Pyongyang," she said. "The Ministry of State Security is all over this thing, and they're screaming like mad over Colonel Song being missing. They've got roadblocks set up all over the place this morning, so I don't know what's going to happen. We may never get out of here."

"Don't give up hope," Noah said. "Any idea when the truck is supposed to pick us up?"

"Because she called it in the way she did, it set off an emergency extraction program. The truck should pick us up here at a little after eight, about an hour from now. After that, we should meet the sub at about ten-thirty, so that leaves plenty of time for us to get there. The only question is whether State Security is gonna be stopping trucks out on the farms."

"That's why I brought the weapons," Noah said. "It's very important we get all of you people back to American soil."

The truck showed up on schedule and they climbed into it quickly. As soon as the side door was closed, it moved out again. It stopped several times on its journey, and each time Noah and the others prepared themselves for a gunfight, but each time the truck moved on again without the doors being opened.

The ride was slow and long, taking almost two hours. The abandoned building had been quite some distance off the normal route of the truck, but the drivers would be able to claim the roadblocks had caused their tardiness. It was just after ten when it stopped once more, and the side door popped open.

"Hurry, hurry, out," the driver's helper said, and they rushed out of the truck and over the bank. They were right back where they had been dropped the morning before, and settled in to wait for the last leg of the trip.

An hour later, there had been no sign of the submarine. Dale's radio had not indicated that it had run into any problems, but when it didn't show up by noon, Noah began to consider other options.

"How far are we up the coast?" he asked.

"About eight miles," Dale said, "but if you're thinking of trying to hike out, you better think again. The closer you get to the border, the more intense the patrols will become. Up till now, there hasn't been any sign that the government here is aware of our little submarine, but that's because it swings out so wide. If we tried to operate it anywhere near the border, we'd have been found out long ago."

"I'm beginning to wonder if it hasn't been," Noah said. "It's well over an hour late…"

Neil, who was sitting beside him, suddenly tapped him on the shoulder and pointed out to sea. Noah turned and looked, and saw what looked like a dark bump on the surface of the water, and the hatch popped open as he watched. He turned back to Dale and shrugged. "Okay, so maybe the traffic was bad."

Nobody laughed.

THIRTEEN

Five days, Sarah thought as she rolled out of bed. *How much longer before Chung's superiors decide he's not doing his job? Oh, God, Noah, where are you?* She looked out the window that was beside the bed, and noticed the guard standing a dozen feet away. The sun was just rising. There was always a guard there, no matter what time of day or night she looked out; there was always one guard on duty on each side of the house.

She went into the bathroom and took a quick shower, then put on a pair of jeans and a long sleeved shirt. The air had been a little cool the night before, and it wasn't feeling much warmer even with the sun up and shining. She slid her feet into the sandals and sat down in the chair that faced the TV, then used the remote to turn it on.

She had tried watching the news channels at first, but there was nothing going on that she thought was connected to her situation. She'd never been one to watch a lot of regular television, but she'd come across a BBC channel full of old variety shows, and found them entertaining. The one that was on at the moment was an old Benny Hill show, and she managed a few chuckles at some of his ribald jokes.

The knock she was waiting for came just a few minutes later, and she turned off the TV as she got up and went to open the door. Chung stood there, dressed more casually than he had been the day before.

"Are you ready for breakfast?" he asked, and she automatically put her hand in the elbow he extended. They walked together to the dining room, and she was surprised to see a more American-style breakfast this time. Scrambled eggs, bacon and waffles were waiting as Chung held her chair for her to sit, and she smiled when she saw a bottle of genuine maple syrup. "I thought you might like a taste of home," Chung said.

"I'm delighted," she said. "Is all this stuff readily available in China?"

Chung laughed, and it was an infectious sound that put a smile on Sarah's face. "I confess that I had to do some searching to find the syrup, but everything else was easy to locate. In China, waffles are usually topped by fruit, but I tried them the American way once and found it not unpalatable."

Sarah chuckled at that, and put a big scoop of eggs onto her plate, then took several strips of bacon. She bit into one and moaned with pleasure. "That is some good bacon," she said. "If you ever decide you want a girlfriend, be sure to feed her some of this bacon."

"Perhaps I'm already trying that technique," he said, winking at her. "From the look on your face, it might be working."

Sarah rolled her eyes, but the smile remained in place. "Sorry, Chung, you already know I'm taken. You'll have to try your ploy on some other unsuspecting girl."

Chung's flirtations, she had concluded, were all part of his methodology. He was trying to win her trust, trying to break through her loyalty to the organization so that she might consider the possibility of betraying them. She had little doubt that he would happily become her lover, but it would last only as long as it took to get the last bit of information out of her. She wasn't about to risk letting him get that close.

Sarah wasn't particularly what someone might consider a patriot. She did feel a loyalty to her country; it was simply overshadowed by her loyalty to Noah and Allison. Allison had given her a new life when her old one was about to become even worse than it had already been, and Noah had given her a reason to live. Between the two, she had everything she thought she could need, and wasn't willing to risk losing either.

"How would you feel," Chung asked her, "about taking a trip into the city today? We would of course be under guard the whole time, but I thought you might enjoy seeing Hong Kong, perhaps even doing some shopping while we're there."

Sarah looked at him for a moment, her smile fading slightly. "Do we have to? Look, we both know this isn't going to last long, and someone is going to start using some pretty unpleasant tricks to try to get information out of me. Right now, I can put a lot of that out of my mind, but if we start doing things like taking trips into the city, things that are supposed to wear down my resistance and make me think about switching loyalties, then it's all going to go sour in a hurry."

For a brief second, Sarah thought she saw coldness in his expression, but then he smiled sadly. "We don't have to go," he said. "It was merely something I thought you might enjoy. Believe me when I tell you that I have no problem simply enjoying your company here."

"Good," Sarah said, letting her smile return. "We can keep playing twenty questions, as long as you remember that I may refuse to answer some of them. It was actually sort of fun, yesterday."

"As it was for me. I learned very little, I confess, but the tiny details I was able to glean made me smile. For instance," he said, leaning back in his chair, "you told me very little about your childhood, but I was able to—how do you say it? I could read between the lines, yes—and so I learned that you were raised by your father, whom you love but do not necessarily like. Am I correct?"

Sarah narrowed her eyes and looked at him. "Pretty much," she said. "I don't remember even mentioning my father. How could you have gotten all that?"

"Ah, but you did. Twice, you said, 'me and my dad,' which implies that your mother was not present. There was also a small expression of displeasure that appeared on your face when you said it, even though there was fondness in your voice. Therefore your father raised you, and even though you love him, there is some resentment."

Damn, Sarah thought, *I've got to be more careful what I let slip. He can learn as much from the things I don't say as from the things I do.*

"That's pretty amazing," she said aloud. "What else did you learn yesterday?"

"Not as much as I had hoped," he said with a laugh. "Let me see; I learned that the unpleasantness in your life as you were growing up helped you to accept the opportunity to do what you do now. You are not personally a killer, but you accept the role your employer plays in the world because it helps to keep your country safe, and in some way makes the world a better place."

Sarah shoved another bite of eggs into her mouth. "Okay," she said after she swallowed, "I'll concede both of those points. But do you know what that tells me?"

"It tells you that you hope to be more careful in the future," Chung said, chuckling. "And yet it was you who suggested we play twenty questions again today."

"Oh, we can play," Sarah said, chuckling. "But I think I'm going to start throwing some false information into my answers. Think you can spot when I'm fibbing?"

Chung smiled, showing his teeth, and a chill went down Sarah's spine. "Oh, I believe so," he said.

They finished breakfast and walked out into the courtyard. The air was cool, but the sun felt good on Sarah's face. She let him lead her to the bench they had sat on before.

"Well, I guess we might as well get started," she said. "First question?"

Chung looked at her for a moment, a half-smile on his face. "Sarah," he said, "I have not been entirely truthful with you. Please understand that if I mislead you, it is only because it is part of my job."

She gave him a humorous sneer. "What, you thought I didn't know that? I'm not that dumb."

He let his smile grow a bit. "Very well. I had told you that my government was trying to confirm the existence of the organization you work for, E & E. In truth, we have known about that agency for some time, but there are some details that have eluded us. One of those details involves the particular assassin that you work with.

The one who was given the code name of Camelot."

"Who? Camel pot? Don't know who you mean."

Chung burst out laughing. "Oh, my goodness," he said, "you are so entertaining. As I told you before, I have heard a recording that was made in which you warned one of your captors that he should be afraid of Camelot. We already know that you are his driver, but perhaps I should tell you why we are so interested in him. Will you listen?"

"I'll listen to anything you got to say," Sarah said politely, "but that doesn't mean I'll tell you anything."

Chung bowed his head in acknowledgment. "There was a time, not long ago, when certain important people in my government were being manipulated, forced to cooperate with foreign agents under threat of having an embarrassing or threatening bit of information revealed."

"Blackmail," Sarah said. "Okay, go on."

"Yes, blackmail, as you say. This was the work of a single individual, one of the most evil men of whom I have ever heard. He was a former Russian agent, named…"

"Nicolaich Andropov," Sarah said. Her face had gone blank, but her eyes held something that caused Chung to look at her differently for a moment.

"Indeed," he said. "Andropov was manipulating high-ranking officials in many countries, and we believe his goal was to completely disrupt international relations between the East and the West. My government and others had spent massive amounts of money and resources trying to eliminate this man, but he always seemed untouchable."

"He thought he was," Sarah said. She looked into Chung's eyes but said nothing more.

"A year and a half ago, Andropov was disavowed by the Russian government. This was because of a situation that arose involving the kidnapping and rescue of the daughter of the Mauritanian president. We were able to learn that Andropov's plans were thwarted by an American assassin who killed a number of Russian officials who were also involved in criminal operations. These killings, we were told, were part of a plan to draw Andropov out, because he had abducted a young woman who worked with that assassin."

Sarah continued to stare into his eyes, but did not speak.

"There was a confrontation between Andropov and the assassin, but it apparently went badly. Andropov escaped, and this led to a gun battle in the streets of Moscow. After that, Andropov was not seen again, but it came to the attention of certain sources we have in Russia that the assassin who confronted him was known only as Camelot. Because this Camelot had done a great deal of damage to the Russian government in his quest to recover that young woman, we became concerned about whether he might be deployed against any of our own officials. Locating and identifying Camelot became a priority of Chinese intelligence operations, and it was because of those efforts that we learned of the death of Nicolaich Andropov sometime later, in the United States." He cocked his head to the right and looked closely at Sarah's eyes. "Sarah, we know that Andropov had taken you hostage, and I can only imagine what tortures you must have suffered while in his grasp. Under most circumstances, your government would have considered you lost, and no attempt would be made to rescue an agent in that position."

Silently, Sarah turned her eyes toward his. There was

something in his expression that spoke of compassion, perhaps even of admiration and respect. "There are a few legends in the intelligence community. Mata Hari, Sidney Riley, Nancy Wake, so many others—and yet, there is one that stands out even though his identity still remains a mystery. While you were captured, while you were actually used as bait to set a trap for Camelot, he chose to walk unarmed into that trap in order to bring you out safely. This makes Camelot an enigma, and this is why my government is so fascinated by him. It appears that he follows no rules other than those he sets for himself, and that frightens many people."

Chung leaned his head down so that he was looking up at her eyes slightly, then grinned. "The thing that fascinated me the most about that report, however, was not his courage or devotion. It was a final footnote at the bottom of the report. You see, Sarah, according to our intelligence, it was not Camelot, but you who delivered the final, fatal blow that ended Andropov's life."

Sarah continued to look him in the eye, but a single tear began to trace its way down her left cheek. She said nothing, as Chung watched her.

After a moment, he sat straight again. "Sarah, as you can see, we already know a great deal. Our concern is that, with our current trade policies being challenged by your leaders and political tensions beginning to reach levels not seen since the Cold War, this Camelot may become a serious threat to our own governmental officials. The entire purpose of our bringing you to China is to try to ascertain just how great that risk might be. If you will tell me about Camelot, then it is possible that we can stand down our efforts, and feel secure that he will not be employed against us."

Sarah continued to stare at him, but after a moment he saw her lick her lips.

"Sarah? I need this information."

"And I'm not going to give it to you," she said.

For a split-second, Sarah saw a flash of anger in his face, but it vanished as quickly as it had appeared. His calm smile returned and he leaned slightly forward again.

"Sarah, we must not play games. As you have pointed out, any failure on my part to learn what I must learn will result in more extreme measures being taken to secure that information. I do not wish to see you tortured, Sarah."

Sarah blinked a couple of times, and another tear made its way down her right cheek. She shrugged her shoulders with a slight grin, but shook her head. "I'm sorry," she said, "but I will not answer."

Chung sighed deeply and lowered his eyes to the ground. He started to speak, but she cut him off.

"I'd like to go back to my room," she said. "I'm afraid we have nothing more to talk about."

FOURTEEN

The submarine ride had been much longer than before, and its pilot explained that they were having to go farther out to avoid patrols. It was after seven in the evening by the time they arrived back at Incheon Island, and Noah was surprised to see a bus waiting for them. A chubby, dark-haired American woman was standing beside it as they climbed out of the inflatable boat that had barely managed to carry them all to the shoreline, and Noah went straight to her.

"Camelot? I'm Anna Harris. I work with South Korea's Tourism Bureau, but I'm also CIA. We got a coded message telling us that you were able to retrieve our people alive, and I want to personally thank you for that. If you'll get everyone into the bus, we have a Gulfstream 550 waiting for you. You'll be in the air in fifteen minutes."

"At this moment, what I need is a phone capable of calling my HQ securely. Can I use my encrypted cell phone from here?"

Anna's eyes went wide. "Good Lord, no," she said. "I don't care how good the encryption is, every cell signal in this area is picked up by both North Korea and China. If it can be cracked, they'll crack it." She looked upset for a moment, and frowned at him. "Is it something that simply cannot wait? You'll be in San Francisco in less than ten hours."

"It can't wait. Delay the flight if you have to, but I absolutely must call in."

The woman rolled her eyes. "Okay, fine, get on the bus. When we get to the hangar I'll get you a line you can use."

Noah got everyone onto the bus, with Jenny enjoying the position of escort for Colonel Song this time. Anna climbed on with them, and the driver took them directly into a hangar that looked like it had seen much better days. A beautiful Gulfstream airplane sat inside it, its door open and a flight of stairs pushed up to it.

Noah told Jenny to get everyone onto the plane, while he followed Anna into a small office in the hangar. She picked up the handset of a landline phone and dialed a number, then held it to her ear. "Kenny? It's Anna. Listen, one of my tour group out here says he has to call the home office immediately. Can you patch him through? Great, just a second and I'll put him on the line." She scowled at Noah, but handed over the phone.

"Hello?" Noah said.

"Hello, sir," said a voice. "This is Kenny Johnson at Republic Tours. Have you got a number?"

Noah rattled off the number for E & E headquarters, and Kenny told him to wait just a moment. There were a series of beeps, some of them pretty loud, and then the voicemail message came on the line. Noah punched in the code that bypassed it and the after-hours operator came on.

"This is Camelot," he said. "Patch me through to the Dragon

Lady."

He was on hold for less than sixty seconds, and then Allison's sleepy voice came on the line. "Camelot? Report."

"I'll make this quick," he said. "In the course of the mission, I was personally captured by the same people who had the targets, and locked in with them. While there, I learned that their organization's management has a very serious security leak, a mole. Were you aware that CIA has picked up chatter indicating the Chinese have been looking for a way to identify me?"

"Hell, no," Allison said, suddenly wide-awake despite the fact it was 4:30 in the morning for her. "Where did you get this information?"

"My targets had heard about it. Under the circumstances, I chose not to terminate the targets but to bring them out. There is a mole in the CIA, selling information to China, and some of that information is what got them arrested. It appears that North Korea only picked them up for the Chinese, they didn't even seem to know what they'd been doing. Their local station chief was also involved, and was the one who actually handed them over. She has been terminated. However, we then learned that the mole has even turned some of our own people, and this led to a new hypothesis which has proven to be true. Somehow, the mole found out that Team Camelot was involved in the Bangkok operation and that our female operative was part of the team. Knowing that China is after me, they would give just about anything to get their hands on one of my team members, so the mole contacted Randy Mitchell on Jenny's team, while they were still in Hanoi. Randy was instructed to notify one of the *Nay Thas* bosses about Sarah being in the prison undercover and who she really was. That man arranged the abductions, and undoubtedly made contact with China to arrange for transportation there."

"Damn!" Allison yelled in his ear. "I can't argue with your logic, it makes too much sense. I'm calling our liaison at Langley and reaming some ass, but that isn't going to help the situation. I'll call in every possible favor and see if we can find out just where in China she might be held. Meanwhile, we need to get those agents back to the states. It might be that they can help figure out just who that mole could be."

"They are already on the plane, and I'm sending Cinderella back, as well. She will be bringing Randy to you, and he might be able to help identify the mole. I want to take my team back to Thailand. I know who Randy contacted, and I believe I can track him down and make them talk. At the moment, I'm only a couple of hours from there by air. If we can get any kind of location, I can get to China in pretty short order. If Sarah hasn't been broken yet, we may still have the chance to get her out alive."

Allison hesitated. "Noah? You're right about being close, but are you really thinking this through?"

"I believe I am," Noah said. "Sarah is extremely valuable, and while she may not know enough to do any serious damage to national security, she'll still be facing treason charges if she gives up any information at all. If I can get her out, I want to; if not, I think she'd rather be terminated than betray our country."

"And could you pull the trigger?" Allison asked harshly. "Could you actually terminate her if it came down to it?"

"Yes," Noah said. Allison waited, but he didn't add anything else.

"All right, then," she said at last. "Send the others back with Cinderella, and I'll instruct our liaison there to provide anything you may need. I will authorize you to go to Thailand and to stay there for three days, and hopefully you can find out where she's being held by then. If you do, I want you to do everything possible to bring her back alive, but if you cannot do that then I expect you to eliminate her."

"Yes, Ma'am," Noah said. He handed the phone to Anna and indicated that she should put it to her ear.

"Hello? Yes, Ma'am. I can do that, Ma'am, but I'll need authorization from—yes Ma'am, no problem." She hung up the phone and turned wide eyes to Noah. "Seems I have to put you up for a little while," she said. "Get the people you're keeping with you off the plane. I need to get it in the air."

Noah went into the aircraft and told Marco and Neil to come back down. He glanced at Colonel Song, who was belted into a seat with Dave and his pistol facing him, then quickly explained to Jenny what was going on.

"You did what? Where's that phone? I'm not leaving you to handle this all by yourself, let me call…"

"Jenny, stop it," Noah said. "You have your orders, just as I do. I appreciate all you've done, but this one is all on me."

Jenny scowled at him, but there was a hint of a smile on her face. "Fine! But next time we're both in Kirtland, let's get together and hang out. Just make sure you got Sarah back by then, or I'll kick your ass myself!" She flopped hard into her seat and started buckling her seatbelt.

Noah carried his duffel off the plane and collected Neil and Marco, then followed Anna Harris out of the hangar. A Kia Sorento was waiting beside the building, and she motioned for them to get in. Neil and Marco got into the back, while Noah took the front passenger seat.

"Do you have ID kits?" Anna asked. "Passport, anything?"

"Yes," Noah said. "We've got the basics, and we each know our back story. I'm Ross Duncan, and if I'm checked out you'll find I live in Taos, New Mexico, and make my living as an investment analyst."

"Well, good, that saves me a little bit of a headache, at least. We'll run through customs; there's a special desk we use for private flights, so it'll only take a few minutes. I'll put you up at the Hyatt, here at the airport. That'll cover everything. It has restaurants inside, a casino…Everything will be charged to your room, and we'll pick up the tab."

She stopped at a small building that sat outside the terminal and took them into it. This was the customs inspection desk for private aircraft passengers, and she was right; it took only a few minutes to get them legally into the country.

When they got back into the car, she fumbled in a pocket for a moment and passed Noah a business card. "That's my office number. If you need anything else, call me there with a landline. If you need to call in again, call that number and say, 'hot relay.' Whoever is on the switchboard will transfer you to my secure line, and the operator there will ask for the number you want to call. Do not use a cell phone for anything that might be even remotely sensitive. If you run into any kind of problems, make sure you call me first. I know the lawyers, the cops, even the judges around here. I'll get you a plane arranged tomorrow to take you to Thailand, so don't get too comfortable here. You're not staying that long."

It seemed to take only a few minutes to get to the hotel, and Anna walked inside with them. She spoke briefly with the desk clerk, who seemed to speak perfect English, and then Noah, Neil and Marco produced their identification. Within minutes they were booked into separate rooms that were side-by-side on the fourth floor. Anna said she'd check with them the following day, and all three of them headed for the elevator.

Noah called in immediately, using the "hot relay" through Anna's switchboard, but only left a message with the hotel and room number. As soon as that was finished, he stripped out of his clothes and took a long, hot shower. One of the best luxuries to be found in a luxury hotel, he decided, was a nearly endless supply of hot water.

When he came out of the shower, Noah opened the duffel and spread its contents on the bed. The clothes he had been provided were all dark, suitable for a mission that might have to be carried out stealthily. He stepped into a pair of briefs and sat down to put on his socks, then chose a pair of gray slacks and a matching polo. Once he was dressed, he stepped out into the hallway and tapped lightly on Neil's door across the hall.

Neil had obviously showered as well, and Marco's hair was also wet when he responded to the knock. "Time to eat," Noah said.

Neil scoffed. "It's been time to eat for the last twelve hours. I'm ready."

They went to the West Tower, where a buffet was available twenty-four hours a day. All three of them loaded their plates with steak, vegetables and fruits, and all three went back twice for more. The food was delicious and hot, and went a long way toward restoring them.

"So what are we doing, boss?" Marco asked.

"Well, we know that the CIA has a mole," Noah said. "For some reason, they didn't bother to let the Dragon lady know that little fact, nor did they mention that the Chinese are trying to track down a particular agent of the government who is known as

Camelot. It seems the mole has been doing a lot of business with China, feeding them information for money. Those people we just rescued were doing a job for Uncle Sam that the Chinese have interest in, and it appears that they were arrested for the purpose of handing them over to China. Our hostess back there, Soo Mi, handed them and me over to the DPRK State Security on his orders, so that got me to thinking; the mole would undoubtedly be aware of China's interest in Camelot, and the CIA helped set up the Bangkok prison rescue, but instead of sending their own people in to find Miss Ingersoll, a request came in to have E & E do it. My gut feeling is that the mole got wind of the fact the job was handed to us, and would have known that the girl who got sent into the prison to make contact was one of us. One quick message relayed through Randy Mitchell, and China sets up an operation to have her snatched and handed over."

Neil was still eating, but he was listening intently. Marco looked at Noah for a moment and then nodded.

"Shame about Randy," Marco said. "If the mole was really threatening his family, you think there's any hope for him to come out of this?"

"That'll be up to Allison," Noah said. "I'm sure he'll never be trusted on a team again, and it's possible she'll even order him executed. I just don't know."

"Okay. Then what's our next move? Sarah's been in somebody's hands for close to a week now. She's a tough little gal, but that's a long time to be under interrogation."

"I agree. Allison is going to try to find out what she can from CIA, and call in every other favor she has coming to her, from NSA, Homeland Security, whoever. The idea is to try to find out where they'd be most likely to take Sarah, and if she gets any leads at all, she'll let me know. Meanwhile, we're leaving sometime tomorrow for Thailand again. We're going back to Pattaya; Randy's contact was a guy named Lom who works for Pak, the promoter. We're going to start with him, and find out who he passed her off to. Sooner or later, we'll find out where she was taken."

Neil chased the last few peas around his plate with a fork and shoved them into his mouth. "Noah," he said, "do you really think there's any hope we'll find her? That we'll get her back?"

"If we can get to her in the next forty-eight hours, I think we have a chance. She would have been in transit for the first couple of days, so she's probably only been under interrogation for the last three. Most interrogators don't go straight to torture unless something is time sensitive; I'm hoping she hasn't been hurt too badly, but I figure it won't be more than two more days before her captors will do whatever it takes to break her. She'll fight, she'll try her best not to tell them anything they can use against us, but nobody can hold out against some of the things they will do."

"Then why are we sitting on our asses? We're in South Korea, it's not that far back to Thailand. Let's go see that asshole now, tonight, and just beat it out of him, find out where she is."

Marco glanced at Neil, then cut his eyes back to Noah. "I get the feeling the kid is pretty worried," he said. "Thing is, he's actually got himself a point. Pak or his boy could maybe tell us where he sent her, and that might save a lot of time in getting to whoever's got her now."

"You're absolutely right," Noah said, "and that's going to be the next move, but we're not going until tomorrow morning."

"Morning might be too late," Neil said. "We should be on the way now!"

"Not one of us has had more than a few hours sleep out of the last forty-eight," Noah shot back. "We're going to go back upstairs to our rooms and rest for tonight. I'll check in with Allison in the morning, and shortly after that, we'll be getting on a plane and headed back to Pattaya. We need to rest, Neil, or we won't be in any shape to help her when we get there."

Neil slammed his fork down onto his plate, and it bounced off the table and onto the floor. "I know, I know, you're right," he said. "I just can't stand the thought of what she might be going through over there. Scares the hell out of me, you know?"

Marco leaned close to him. "Let you in on a secret," he said softly. "Scares the hell out of me, too."

"You barely even know her," Neil said, the anger evident in his voice and face. "If Moose was here…"

"Moose is gone," Noah said. "Marco is part of the team, now, Neil. I'm sure he can imagine what she's going through, just as well as you can. None of us want her to suffer, so we're going to do everything we can to get her back. Understood?"

Neil glared at him for a second, but then he lowered his eyes and nodded. "Understood," he said. "Sorry, Marco."

"Ain't nothin'," Marco said. "We good."

FIFTEEN

Noah was already awake when the phone in his room rang at just after six AM. "Hello?"

"It's Allison," he heard. "I've been on this all day, and I'm making a little bit of headway. I got through to Alex Kuiper, he's my top liaison with CIA, and I reamed him a new asshole over this. He confirmed that they do have a security leak, and that there is an ongoing internal investigation. He swears up and down he hadn't heard about any Chinese interest in you before this, but after listening to me scream at him for half an hour, he managed to find it. It looks like somebody high up in Langley was trying to keep it under wraps until they could get more information, but it's been confirmed. China has been trying to track you down for over a year, so you're right, that would have made Sarah an attractive opportunity for the mole."

"Of course," Noah said. "Do they have anything on her? Where she would've been taken, anything?"

"Nothing definite, I'm afraid. However, I turned him loose on the whole situation that went down in Pattaya, and it turns out your friend Mr. Pak has some pretty deep connections with the

Chinese. The *Nay Thas* are really just an arm of the Chinese black societies, organized crime groups who run a lot of the Asian sex trade, so it's a pretty safe bet that China pulls his strings. He doesn't make contact with them himself, though, he's got a man working for him who handles his dealings with China. That man is called Lom, and everything I've been able to learn says he is ruthless and dangerous. He's a former *Muay Thai* street champion, and unsubstantiated rumors claim that he has killed more than a dozen people without ever picking up a weapon."

"That's the guy Randy was told to contact. I get the impression he's the one who handles Pak's dealings with China," Noah said, "so he's probably the one who arranged to hand Sarah over to them. If anyone would know where she is, it would probably be him. Permission to go back to Pattaya and question him?"

"Permission, hell, those are your orders! Your cover identities are still intact, just have our liaison there make the arrangements. Our station chief in Pattaya will provide everything you need on that end. Go get her, Camelot, and bring her back safe."

"What about Randy? Any idea yet what you're going to do with him?"

"We haven't even had the chance to question him, yet. Do you have a suggestion in mind?"

Noah actually hesitated for a moment. "If he was telling the truth, the threat against his sisters was probably more coercion than he could resist. Jenny would cut his throat in a heartbeat; she killed the Korean girl who sold out the CIA people without even finding out what sort of leverage the mole had on her. I doubt he could ever be trusted in the field again, but if his story turns out true, it's possible he could be useful somewhere else. That isn't so much a suggestion as an observation."

"Understood," Allison said. "I'll take it under advisement."

The line went dead as it always did when Allison was done talking. Noah picked up Anna's business card from where he had laid it beside the phone the night before and started to dial the number, but then remembered that it was still early. He pulled on his slacks and stepped out the door, knocked loudly on Neil's and then Marco's, and left his door open as he went back into his own room. He was dressed and ready when they came into his room ten minutes later, and he filled them in quickly.

"I talked with Allison this morning," he said, "and her liaison and CIA agree that it was most likely the mole at Langley that burned Sarah, using Randy as his messenger boy. The problem is that we don't have any clue where she's being held, but it looks like Pak is tightly connected to the Chinese. He has this guy Lom who probably handles all his dealings with them, so we're leaving ASAP for Pattaya. Mr. Lom and I are going to talk, and I intend to find out whatever he knows."

"It's about damn time," Neil said. "At least we're doing something."

They went down to breakfast and ate quickly, then returned to Noah's room. He called Anna's office and found that she was already in.

"I've already gotten the call from your boss," she said when she came on the line. "We're putting together your flight right now, but, frankly, she says this is top priority and could lead anywhere, so I'm setting you up with a private charter jet. A car will pick you up in front of your hotel in twenty minutes, and you'll be going to the same hangar we left last night. There is a Gulfstream 4 being fueled and ready for you, with a double flight crew so you can be ready to go at a moment's notice, but here's a heads up: the flight crews are not, I repeat not, field agents. They'll fly you wherever you want to go, but they are not cleared for classified information. You'll take off in about an hour, and land in Pattaya two hours later. Someone from your outfit will meet your plane, so then you're out of my hair."

"I appreciate it," Noah said. "And I apologize if we've created any headaches for you."

"Hey, I'm just being grumpy. I really do appreciate you bringing those folks home safe. I hope you have a great trip, and get what you're going after."

The car arrived on schedule and everything seemed to go smoothly. The airplane was smaller than the one that had brought them from San Francisco, but the flight crew welcomed them aboard and the plane was in the air fifteen minutes ahead of schedule. A flight attendant gave them each a large cup of coffee and passed around a box of donuts, keeping Neil happy all the way.

The plane landed, and Noah saw Maggie Lightner, the E & E station chief for Pattaya, standing on the tarmac when the aircraft came to a stop. The flight attendant opened the door and the three men walked down the short steps and straight to Maggie and the car she was standing beside. She had the trunk open so they tossed their bags inside it.

"Good to see you again," Maggie said with a smile. "I was a little surprised when I got the call this morning that you were coming back. I'm supposed to see to it you get anything you want while you're here, so just name it." They climbed into the car, with Neil having to twist sideways because of a lack of legroom in the backseat.

"Weapons, for one thing," Noah said. "I'm going after someone who may know what happened to Sarah, where she was taken. How are you fixed for backup if I need it?"

Maggie glanced at him, and her eyes were wide. "You mean armed? Honey, I've got three other girls and one guy in my office, basically just overpaid secretaries, but we all went through training at Neverland. You say the word, we'll gun up and do our best."

Noah looked at her for a moment, then turned his eyes back to the road in front of them. "It's just a thought, at the moment. If everything goes according to plan, I won't need it." He looked back over at her again. "I need a car, too."

"Okay, first things first. As far as weapons go, my little office here has a nice selection of handguns, as long as all you want is a nine-millimeter Beretta or a Colt forty-five. I got one rifle, an old M-16, and zero automatic weapons. If you need anything other than those, I'll need to call Bangkok and get somebody on the way down here."

"Marco and I can handle the .45's, and let's give Neil a Beretta. What about a vehicle?"

"Okay, now you have some choices. You can take this Civic, or I've got a Toyota Camry. Your call."

"I think this will do. How long till we get to your office?"

"About fifteen more minutes. Do you need somewhere to stay while you're in the city?"

"I don't know yet," Noah said. "If everything goes well, we may be heading out for China later today."

"Okay," Maggie replied. "Let me know, though, so I can make any necessary arrangements for you. Any idea where in China?"

"Not yet," Noah said, and Neil piped up with, "That's what we're here to find out."

Maggie stopped the car at the terminal, and took them inside to go through customs. Because of her diplomatic credentials—she was officially assigned as a researcher for the US State Department —she was able to get them through in a matter of minutes. The passports stamped, they got back into the car and Maggie drove out of the airport complex.

She pointed out a few interesting landmarks as they rode, finally pulling into an alleyway and tucking the car in behind the building that housed her office. All three of the men followed her in, and Marco blushed slightly when Julie, the girl who had joined them on the yacht a week before, looked up and gave him a finger wave and a wink.

Maggie called out to another woman toward the back of the room. "Trudy, I need two of the .45's and one of the nines. Give me three magazines for each, loaded, and a box of extra bullets for each one."

"You got it, babe," Trudy yelled back. She got up and disappeared into another room, but was back only five minutes later with a box in her hands. She set it on a table beside Noah, then reached in and handed each of the men a gun. She instinctively gave the Beretta to Neil, then passed out the extra magazines and boxes of cartridges.

Noah handed the boxes back. "If we run into a situation that requires more than three magazines, we're probably not going to be in any position to reload, anyway. That would just be extra weight to carry, so you might as well keep it here."

Maggie nodded to Noah with a smile. "Like I said before," she said, "if there's anything in the world more that we can do…"

Noah nodded back once and shook her hand. "I appreciate it, Maggie," he said. "But we've got to get going." He turned around immediately and walked back out the door. They climbed into the

Honda, with Marco letting Neil take the front seat so that he could slide it back, and they were off again.

Noah punched Champions' Arena, the name of the gym that Pak owned and operated, into his GPS and followed the directions it gave him. According to the app, they were only twenty minutes away. Noah managed to cut it down to seventeen.

He parked on one of the residential streets a block away, and the three of them got out and started walking. They had to go around the block to get to the front entrance, but even though it was still early in the day for a *Muay Thai* gym, it was standing open when they arrived.

"We're going in," Noah said, "but don't show your weapon unless it's absolutely necessary. They'll know we're carrying them, but as long as we don't draw, we should be able to keep this on a conversational level."

"Boss," Marco said, "some of the guys in there can beat a man to death with their toes."

"Yeah," Neil said. "What do we do if they decide to attack?"

"Well," Noah said with a shrug, "in that case, I guess you can shoot somebody." He stepped through the front door and a dozen pairs of eyes turned to look at him. One man, the same one who had taken them to see Mr. Pak the last time they were there, walked slowly toward Noah.

"Mr. Pak, he is not here," he said. "He be back tomorrow."

Noah put a smile on his face. "That's okay," he said. "I'm looking for Mr. Lom."

The man cocked his head to one side and his eyes narrowed. "Mr. Lom? Why you want to see Mr. Lom?"

"Because I understand he helped take care of the funeral

arrangements for my girlfriend last week," Noah said, trying to sound sad. "I wanted to thank him, but I also have a few questions about how the funeral was conducted. I'm afraid I don't know that much about your customs, here."

The man looked into his eyes for a couple of seconds, then turned and motioned for them to follow.

He took them through a door in the back wall, the same one that led to the offices where they had met Pak before. This time, however, he turned to the right and knocked on another door. A voice from inside called out in the local language, and he opened the door and stepped inside, closing it quickly behind him.

A moment later he reappeared, and held the door open wide. Noah, Marco and Neil walked into the room and saw a thin, wiry man sitting at a desk that was facing the back wall. He had turned his chair toward them and looked calmly into Noah's eyes.

"I am Lom," he said. "How may I help you?"

Noah glanced at the man who had brought them in, and Lom smiled. He dismissed him with a wave of his hand, and the door closed behind the fellow as he left.

"He is gone," Lom said. "We need not bother with pretenses. I know who you are, and I am quite certain that I know why you're here."

"Do you?" Noah asked. "And why do you think that might be?"

"You do not believe the girl is dead. You have come because you wish to ask where she was sent."

"You're half right," Noah said. "I don't believe she's dead, but I didn't come to ask anything. I know that you are the one who handles Pak's dealings with China, and I'm pretty sure that's where she's gone. What I want to know is how to find her, and I'm prepared to do whatever it takes to get that information from you."

Lom smiled. "And you believe you can wrest that knowledge from me? Perhaps from my dead body, since I see that you are all carrying firearms?"

Noah stared into his eyes and shrugged. "I don't care if I have to skin you alive. I intend to find out what I want to know. We can do it any way you wish."

Lom had been holding a pen, and he slowly turned and set it on the desk before he looked back at Noah. "Any way I wish?" he asked. "Then, may I suggest a simple wager?"

Noah's eyes narrowed. "What kind of wager?"

"You are young, and have the build of a man who keeps himself fit. You have the muscle definition of one who has been trained in different fighting techniques. I, on the other hand, am well past my fiftieth year. Because of my age, I have great difficulty finding men who will spar honestly with me in the ring. I do not know if you have ever been competitive, but it becomes a form of addiction. I often find myself trying to think of ways to get back into the ring, where I once felt alive."

"You want to fight?" Noah asked him. "And if I win, you'll tell me what I want to know?"

"I shall tell you," Lom said, "simply for stepping into the ring with me. The wager I propose is that you will not do so."

"And what will the other men in the gym have to say about this?"

"The reward I offer in exchange for your compliance is only between you and me. They will know nothing of it, and I can assure you that they have honor. They will not interfere in the fight, nor in any way seek to trouble your men."

"Do you plan to kill me in the ring? The information won't do me any good if I'm dead."

"I never seek to take a life in the ring," Lom said. "That is not honorable. I cannot be certain that you will be completely unharmed, but I will make no effort to kill you." He rose to his feet, and looked Noah in the eye.

Noah nodded once, and turned to open the door. Lom smiled and followed him out, with Neil and Marco bringing up the rear.

SIXTEEN

Sarah spent the rest of the day in her room, even refusing to come out for lunch or dinner. At lunch time, Chung pleaded with her to come and eat, but finally left her door without her. When dinner came, however, he knocked on the door and was holding a tray when she opened it.

"Still trying to be Mr. Nice Guy, huh?" she asked. "I'm afraid it's not gonna do you any good."

"Not entirely," Chung said. "Regardless of whether I gain your cooperation, I am responsible for your well-being while you are in my custody. I cannot let it be said that I allowed you to go hungry."

Sarah's eyes flicked down to the tray in his hands. "How do I know it's not drugged? If you're not getting the results you want the easy way, how do I know you won't resort to something a little more drastic?"

Chung actually looked pained. "Would you like me to taste the food for you? I will do so, if you wish. I do not use drugs, Sarah, for I find them as distasteful as torture."

She stood there a moment longer, then reached out and took

the tray from him. She carried it to the small table in her room and set it down, then pulled out the chair and sat down to eat. When she took the cover off the tray, she couldn't hold back a grin. On the plate before her was a generous serving of lasagna, which she had accidentally confessed was her favorite food.

Chung stood in the doorway for a moment, then cleared his throat. "May I come in?"

Sarah shrugged noncommittally. Chung stepped into the room and pulled out a second chair. He sat down and watched her eat, but didn't speak.

After a couple of minutes, it became annoying. "If you're gonna sit there, at least have the decency to offer conversation. No questions, though, I'm done answering questions."

Chung looked at her for a moment, and the corner of his mouth lifted slightly. "It is lovely weather, isn't it?"

A giggle escaped her. "Oh, you're such a charmer," she said. "Too bad we're enemies. I could actually get to like you, if we met under other circumstances."

Chung's slight grin grew a bit. "Perhaps I should defect to the West," he said. "The affections of a beautiful woman could be a powerful inducement."

The fork stopped halfway to her mouth. "I said I could like you," she said, glaring at him. "Don't read more into it than is there."

"Oh, of course," Chung said. "There is the fiancé. I will confess that I wish I knew more about him, but I won't ask. Having come to know you these past few days, I believe he must be an incredible man. Almost a Superman, perhaps."

Sarah couldn't catch herself in time; her eyes went wide and suddenly turned to search his own. The crinkle that came into them as she watched told her that he'd learned exactly what he wanted to know.

"On second thought," she said, "I don't need any company. You can go."

Chung let out a remorseful sigh, but he stood immediately and turned to walk out the door. He stopped in the doorway, looked at her for a moment and almost said something, but then he simply closed the door and walked away.

I gave it away, dammit, she thought bitterly. *That son of a bitch knows damn well who my fiancé is. He may not know his name, but he's absolutely certain the man I love is Camelot. Thank God I didn't tell him more.*

Disgusted, she dropped the fork onto the tray and turned away from the table. She sat down in the armchair and turned on the TV, but even the antics of British comics couldn't take away the feeling that she had made a serious mistake.

She wasn't disturbed the rest of the day, and finished off the lasagna an hour later, after it had gotten cold. Even cold lasagna was better than no lasagna, she thought, eating it while she watched old reruns of Monty Python.

Out of boredom, she turned back to the news. There was only one story of interest, about four Americans who had been illegally detained in North Korea, but who had managed to escape and even captured the man who had detained them. According to the story, they were able to overpower a couple of guards and take their weapons, then managed to walk almost 100 miles through hostile territory until they reached the border with South Korea. At that point, they managed to steal a boat and make it across, and then contact the US Embassy there.

A couple of years before, she might have believed it. She'd learned a few things since then, however; in particular, she learned that when certain agencies pull off rescues and daring missions, they never get credit. Instead, some partially credible story of personal heroism is released, and the news media even acts like they believe it.

There was nothing else exciting, and she couldn't even find a movie she wanted to watch, so she finally turned it off and went to bed. It wasn't very late, but Sarah was beginning to feel depressed. Whenever she got depressed, she sought solace in sleep.

Morning came, and Chung knocked on her door. "Sarah," he called through it. "Won't you come down to breakfast? There is something important I need to discuss with you, and it doesn't even involve asking you any questions."

She was already up and dressed, but had been lying on the bed. She rolled her eyes and let out a deep breath, then forced herself to get up and open the door.

"What's for breakfast?" she asked as she stepped out. Chung extended his elbow, but she made a point of not taking it.

"We are having steamed buns," he said, "stuffed with lamb. It is a local delicacy, and very good here in the Hong Kong region. I believe you will like it."

Sarah said nothing more until they reached the dining room, then allowed him to pull her chair out for her. She sat while the servers put two of the steamed buns on a plate in front of her, and then did the same for Chung.

"Okay, I'm here," Sarah said. "What's so important?"

He sat across the table and looked at her sadly. "I have been given until the end of today to see results in questioning you," he said. "If I cannot report that I'm making progress by this evening, I shall be removed. Another interrogator will come, one who is notorious for his excruciating methods. His name is Xiao, and his philosophy is that it is possible to cause terrible pain without truly damaging any part of the body." He looked down at the plate in front of him. "Sarah, I do not wish to see him inflicting his skills upon you."

"Well, you can tell yourself it's not your fault. And really, it isn't your fault. I'm the one who's refusing to talk, right? You tried, I'll give you that, but I'm not going to give up any information if I can avoid it. It's just not going to happen."

Won't you? she heard a voice inside herself say. *How can you be so certain? You've never been tortured, but think about what it might be like. Needles up under your fingernails? Beatings on the soles of your feet? How long can you hold out before you beg them to stop, before you're willing to say or do anything to bring it to an end? And sooner or later, you're going to cave in and you know it. Sooner or later, you're going to tell them anything they want to know, because the pain will reach a point where you're willing to do or say anything, just so you can beg them to let you die.*

"Sarah, please reconsider," Chung said. "You can give me little things, things that are not important, but they will tell those above me that I am making progress."

"Stop it," Sarah said. "Do you think I haven't figured you out? Every little thing I tell you, you find out three other things from it. I'm not giving you anything. Now, shall we eat breakfast together, or shall I just go back to my room?"

Chung stared at her for another moment, then began eating. When breakfast was finished, he walked her back to her room and stood there as she closed the door in his face.

* * * * *

Neil hurried around the smaller man and rushed to Noah.

"Noah? Are you nuts?"

"I don't think so," Noah said. He stopped beside the ring and carefully handed his gun to Marco, then stripped off his shirt and took off his shoes. He sat down on the edge of the ring to remove his socks, leaving him in only his slacks.

Lom stepped out of the loose pants and shirt he was wearing to reveal that he was wearing boxing trunks underneath, and spoke rapidly in Thai. The two men who were sparring in the ring stared at him for a moment, then looked at Noah. They both wore expressions of humor as they climbed out of the ring and began taking off their sparring gear.

Two men hurried toward them, and Noah held out his hands to be wrapped and gloved while Lom did the same. The process took a couple of minutes, and then the pair stepped away. Lom climbed into the ring, and Noah did likewise.

"A single round is three minutes," Lom said, "and the match consists of five rounds. Between rounds, we must rest for two minutes before we continue. Do you understand?"

"I do," Noah said. "And you've lost the wager. Where is she?"

Lom smiled, as the two who had wrapped them climbed into the ring and offered them each a mouthpiece. "Shall we sweeten the wager? I will tell you now that she is near Hong Kong, but—should you manage to stay on your feet for all five rounds, or even beat me—I will reward you with the precise location."

Noah looked him in the eye for a moment, then nodded slowly. "Just tell me one thing," he said. "Isn't this going to cause you trouble with Pak?"

"Mr. Pak is a businessman. As such, he has many who work for him to handle those things which he finds distasteful or mundane. I am one such, and there are others. Because he has placed certain matters under my care and left me to my own devices, he would not be able to continue those matters should anything happen to me."

"But won't the Chinese be displeased with you? For giving me this information?"

"No. They will be displeased with Mr. Pak. They have never met me, and so they believe that they have been conducting their business with him all along."

Noah nodded. "You are a shrewd man, Mr. Lom," Noah said. "With one move, you're giving me a reason not to kill you and setting your employer up to be eliminated. I'm guessing you'll be able to take over his operation?"

Lom smiled at him, and put the mouthpiece between his teeth. Noah did likewise, and they each went to a corner.

A bell was struck with a small hammer, and the two moved toward each other. Lom danced lightly on his feet, while Noah stood firmly on his and stared into the man's eyes.

The first strike came without warning, a vicious kick by Lom, aimed at Noah's head. The grin on the older man's face betrayed his confidence, but Noah merely leaned back, thrusting his knees forward to maintain his balance. The foot passed an inch in front of his face, and Lom had to dance a little more to keep from losing his own balance.

The other men in the gym began cheering for Lom, and some of them were making derisive noises at Noah, but he ignored them. Lom occupied all of his attention, and he knew that, even if Lom wouldn't kill, he could easily injure Noah severely.

At that moment, Noah closed in. Two sharp jabs to Lom's ribs threw the man even further off kilter, but he recovered almost instantly. Noah hopped backward, as Lom spun around to face him once more.

Another kick was aimed at Noah's groin, but he blocked it with his knee and then followed instantly with a kick of his own. Noah was fast, but Lom was faster; the foot that should have caught the man in the belly only flew by, and Lom landed a solid punch into Noah's thigh.

The cramp that began at that moment was one of the worst Noah had ever known, but he forced himself to ignore it and bounced back out of reach before Lom could strike again. He began bouncing on the balls of his feet, trying to stay in motion so that he would make a harder target.

Suddenly, Lom leapt forward and upward, his right foot spiking high into the air as he rose, then suddenly slashing down like an ax. It made contact with Noah's left shoulder, and the impact was enough to send a shock to his entire body. He spun away as quickly as he could, and narrowly missed another kick that was aimed at his head.

With great determination, Noah shook off the shock and thrust himself forward. Before Lom could react, he had closed the distance between them and spun, tucking his fists against his chest and extending his elbows straight out. One of them caught Lom on the chin, and the wiry little man went down.

He was only there for a second, and then flipped back onto his feet. The smile on his face was distorted by the mouthpiece, but Noah could see the excitement in his eyes, as well. They began to circle one another again, and Lom was just about to make another move when the bell rang, and the cheering and shouting began to die down a bit.

Instantly he stepped back and raised his hands, then turned and went to his corner. Noah did likewise, and found Marco there with a towel, wiping the sweat off his face.

"That was a pretty neat trick," Marco said, "with the elbows, there. Where did you learn that?"

Noah split the mouthpiece out into his gloved hand. "Right then and there," he said, breathing heavily. "I just thought about what I had that could do the most possible damage, and used it." Neil popped up on the side of the ring with a bottle of water, and held it for Noah to take a big drink.

"You caught him off guard," Neil said. "I don't think he'll let you do that again. Better watch out, I think he's really pissed."

"No he's not," Noah said, shaking his head. "He's having more fun than he's had in years." He fumbled the mouthpiece back into his mouth and sat there until the bell rang again, then was on his feet and back in the center of the ring in a moment. The cheering began again in earnest.

Lom came close, and suddenly he bowed. Noah resisted the temptation to try to kick him at that moment, and instead focused on being ready for whatever Lom would do next. He didn't have to wait long, as the smaller man suddenly leapt straight at him, his fists pistoning into Noah's rib cage. In the span of only a couple of seconds, Lom managed to land a dozen hard blows, and Noah had to fall back.

Lom fell back as well, giving Noah a moment to recover. When he stepped forward again, Lom tried to go for the same move once more, but Noah had anticipated and thrown himself into a spinning back kick. His left ankle caught Lom by the neck, and the man was flipped off his feet and onto his back. Noah completed the spin and threw himself downward, his right fist aimed for Lom's chin, but the man rolled and Noah punched the floor of the ring. Lom's eyes were wide at the sound of the impact, for he knew that it could easily have broken his jaw.

Noah bounced back to his feet and kept moving, making himself as difficult a target as possible. He didn't have any delusions about winning the fight, but he was determined to make it through all five rounds.

The second round ended, and they went to their corners. Once more Marco wiped his face, while Neil held a water bottle for him. Noah didn't bother talking, he was too busy trying to breathe in as much air as he could during the respite. When the bell rang, he already had the mouthpiece back in and sprang to his feet.

Lom ran at him, and Noah spun aside to avoid him, but then he realized his mistake. Lom had not been trying to strike, but merely to get behind him and he suddenly sensed the man behind and slightly above. Something, he knew, was coming down at his head, but there was no time to duck so he threw both arms up to make an X above his neck.

The downward jumping elbow is one of the most dangerous blows in *Muay Thai*, and Noah felt the impact as the elbow slashed down into his crossed wrists. Instinctively, he twisted his hands and clasped them together, catching Lom's arm between them. The move was unexpected, and when he pulled forward and bent at the waist, Lom suddenly found himself flying through the air. He slammed onto the mat on his back, the breath knocked out of him for a moment, but before he could recover Noah bent his own elbow and dropped. The point of his elbow contacted Lom's solar plexus, and the fight was over.

The shouting men had suddenly fallen silent, staring in shock at the *farang*—foreigner—who had beaten one of the greatest fighters *Muay Thai* had ever known. Lom was a legend in the sport, even though he had never held a major championship; he had instead traveled around Southeast Asia, amassing a small fortune in the officially illegal street fights. Had he ever chosen to, he could probably have won a national or even world championship, but he was content to keep his fame contained while building his wealth. A number of helpers had placed bets on him in every fight, and each took a share of what he won. He was a legend throughout Southeast Asia, and Noah realized he was lucky to be walking away unscathed.

SEVENTEEN

The shock of seeing him beaten by a *farang* delayed the bell for several seconds, but finally it rang when Lom waved a hand in the air. It was a sign of surrender, and acknowledgment that he was beaten. He lay on the mat for a moment longer, looking up at Noah, and then reached a hand up to him. Noah grasped it between both of his hands, because of the gloves, and helped the smaller man to his feet.

Lom spat out the mouthpiece and looked at Noah with eyes full of wonder. "Should you ever choose to enter the world of *Muay Thai*," he said, "I beg of you to let me be your teacher." He took hold of Noah's right hand and raised it in the air, then dropped it and walked to the ropes. Noah followed him, and a couple of men began stripping the gloves off of them and unwrapping their hands.

When they were finished, and both Lom and Noah were dressed again, Lom motioned for them to follow him back into his office. He closed the door behind them and then sat down in his chair once more, motioning for them to take seats in the other chairs in the room.

"You are very strong," he began, "and possess the ability to analyze the moves of your opponent far more quickly than most men. I confess that I underestimated you, and I do not make that mistake often. As agreed, I will now give you the precise location of the young woman, but I must also warn you that it will be heavily guarded. I must also warn you that there is no assurance that she will be unhurt."

"I understand that," Noah said.

He turned to his desk and opened a laptop computer, waited for it to power up, and then called up a browser. A moment later, they were looking at a map of the Hong Kong area, and Lom motioned for Noah to come closer, pointing to the screen.

"Hong Kong is a special administrative region, SAR," he said, "which enjoys considerable autonomy compared to the rest of China. A large part of it is situated on Hong Kong Island, much of which is not accessible by automobile. There are large areas that are considered to be parks, especially in the mountainous regions, where automobiles are often prohibited. Here"—he indicated a particular point off Shek O Road, in the southeast corner of the island—"fifty feet off Shek O Road on this path that leads to Hong Kong Trail, Section 7, there is a gate. The path is wide enough at that point for a vehicle, but narrows after it passes the gate. If you go through that gate, you will be on a private drive that leads to the Tung Li Estate. That estate once belonged to Tung Li, who served as a liaison between Hong Kong and China while Hong Kong was under British rule. He passed away in 1989, and his estate was later purchased by the Chinese government. It is considered to be a place of military or government activity, and even its existence is known only to a limited number of people."

"So, anything I do there," Noah said, "could be considered a military action?"

"Yes. If you are captured or killed there, you run the risk of creating an international incident." He turned from the computer and looked at Noah. "There is one large house on the estate, completely hidden by trees from any view. It is used primarily as a safe house, but also as a place for the detention of foreign agents who are being interrogated. There are many reasons for this, but the simplest one is the most obvious. If the foreign agent were to die, disposal of the body takes place in Hong Kong rather than in Beijing, the seat of government for China."

"What else can you tell me about the place?" Noah asked.

"It is maintained by the Army of the People's Republic of China. Besides housing more than two-dozen soldiers in barracks rooms in the basement, there are military managers, cooks and orderlies to take care of the house and its occupants. The estate covers thirty hectares, most of which is wooded, and the guards patrol its perimeter and interior. Its only vulnerability is from the south, where the terrain is steep and rocky. The guards are not as diligent there, because some few of them have fallen prey to tigers that roam the area."

"Tigers?" Neil asked. "You're talking about South China Tigers? I thought they were extinct in the wild."

Lom smiled. "That is the official statement, yes," he said. "However, since 1995, there have been more than fifty sightings of tigers on Hong Kong Island, all of them in this particular area. This is probably because of an abundance of prey for them, but it seems to be true that once a tiger has tasted human flesh, it wants more. Game wardens in that area believe the few attacks on humans, including the Chinese soldiers, are the work of only one or two of the Tigers on the island."

Noah was leaning forward, studying the map on the screen in front of him. "Mr. Lom," he said, "I appreciate the information." He started to rise, but Lom put out a hand and motioned for him to sit once more.

"Will you perhaps satisfy an old man's curiosity?" he asked.

Noah looked at him, his face blank. "In what way?"

"Pak was ordered to use any means necessary to procure this young woman," he said, "because the Ministry of State Security received information indicating that she is an agent of an organization from the United States that specializes in assassination. They have been trying for some time to identify one particular agent of that organization, a man known only as Camelot." Lom looked directly into Noah's eyes, and there was a sense of calm conviction about him. "Are you that man?"

Noah stared into his eyes for a long moment, then cocked his head slightly to the right. "I could answer your question," he said, "but then I would be forced to kill you."

Behind him, he heard Neil gasp and then say, "Oh, geez! Could you be any more corny?"

Noah glanced at him, confused. Despite the fact that the line was often used sarcastically, Noah had been quite serious.

Lom understood, and smiled. "I can accept that answer. However, I suspect the day will come when you and I shall meet again, in your official capacity. Would it be possible that, on that day, you might grant a last request?"

"Why would you expect me to visit you again?" Noah asked. "You've actually been most cooperative, and I truly appreciate it."

"As I told you, I believe that Mr. Pak will shortly cease to be. At that time, I will ascend to take over all of his business interests.

Since you are now aware that those interests include the transfer of intelligence and—other items—to China and others, I am forced to believe that I might one day see your face again."

Noah shrugged. "It's possible," he said. "What would be the last request?"

Lom smiled and spread his hands. "A rematch, of course," he said softly. "As I told you, I underestimated you. I would not make that mistake again, because you are undoubtedly a worthy opponent. If you come to kill me, I would consider it an honor to die at your hands in a rematch."

"Mr. Lom," Noah said, "should that day arrive, I would be under orders to carry out my mission by the most efficient means possible. That doesn't allow me to offer a sporting chance. However, should the opportunity arise in the near future for me to return to Thailand, I will make a point of coming to see you. We can have that rematch, but not to the death. Is that acceptable?"

Lom stood and bowed. "Indeed it is," he said.

Noah stood, and Neil and Marco joined him. He extended a hand to Lom, who shook it firmly, then turned and walked out into the gym.

There had been about a dozen men in the gym when they had entered, and a few more had drifted in by the time he and Lom had entered the ring. Now, though, as they were preparing to leave, there were more than thirty men, and they were standing in a group between Noah and the door. Several of them turned to look at him, and Noah stopped and let out a deep sigh.

They began to spread out, and Noah saw them picking up different items around the gym. Some of them had small wooden cudgels, some were holding bottles, and others held the iron discs from the barbell.

"This isn't necessary," Noah said.

The man who had first spoken to them cast an angry look his way. "We cannot let a *farang* beat our teacher," he said. "We cannot let you leave here."

Noah shook his head and turned to Marco, and suddenly there was a pistol in his hand. He spun back around and aimed it at the forehead of the man who had spoken. "Clear a path," he said calmly, "or you will be the first to die. Mr. Lom has conducted himself with honor. Would you dishonor him now in this way?"

"*Chao!*" Lom shouted suddenly. "This is unacceptable. All of you, stand aside." He repeated the command in Thai.

Slowly, the group spread apart and began dropping the items they had picked up. Noah and the others began walking slowly toward the door, keeping their eyes on the men around them. When they reached the door without further incident, Noah shoved the gun back into his waistband and pulled his shirt over it, and the other two did likewise. He looked at Lom, who was standing just inside the room, and bowed to him. Lom returned the compliment, and Team Camelot left the building.

"Oh, geez, geez," Neil muttered. "Are they gonna come after us?"

"Not with Lom standing there," Marco said. "I've got a feeling they're about to get their asses chewed and spit out."

They returned to the car, and headed back toward the E & E office. Noah simply retraced the route he had taken to reach the gym and found it with no problem. He parked the car where Maggie had, and the three of them walked inside.

Maggie was sitting at a desk, and looked up at them as they entered. "Hey, guys," she said cheerily. "Everything go okay?"

It took an hour to explain to Maggie all that had taken place, and that they needed to be in Hong Kong as soon as possible. The plane, they knew, was still waiting for them at the airport, so all Maggie had to do was file the appropriate paperwork for a private flight into Hong Kong's semi-sovereign airspace.

"E & E has a station in Hong Kong," she told Noah. "The chief there is Peter McDermott, and from everything I know, he's a pretty good guy. I sent him an encrypted email, letting him know that you are on the way and will need a vehicle and equipment. I also included a copy of the orders I received from HQ, which contains the AA code. That means you get anything you want, no matter what it takes or what it costs."

"I appreciate it," Noah said. They had turned in the guns when they got back, because there was a strong possibility the plane might be boarded when it landed in Hong Kong. According to the documents Maggie filed, they were visiting Hong Kong to look at some property that a client of Noah's was considering purchasing as an investment, but it was not uncommon for China's State Security Ministry to board and search private aircraft before allowing the passengers to disembark. Carrying weapons into the region was strictly prohibited for any foreigners.

As soon as she was done, Maggie turned and looked at Noah and the men. "Okay, so I know you've been going like mad since early this morning. How about some lunch before you guys leave? Care to join us?"

Neil sat forward quickly, and Noah glanced at him, then nodded. "Probably a good idea," he said. "Could be a while before we get the chance again."

Trudy, one of the women in the office, was chosen to stay and watch the place while they were gone, but everyone else headed out the back door. Noah, Neil and Marco climbed into the Honda with Maggie, while the others got into the Toyota. Maggie pulled out first, and drove them to a steakhouse that was on the way to the airport.

"I figured we'd eat here, so we can go straight back to the plane when you're done. You guys all eat meat, right? No vegetarians?"

All three of them assured her that they were carnivorous, and then followed her inside. The others from her office had been right behind them, so they were able to get a large round table that seated them all.

The food was excellent, and Maggie explained that most of the beef in Thailand actually came from Australia. It was part of the trade agreement the country had made under the last king, and Neil proclaimed it to be the smartest thing the king had ever done. By the time they left an hour later, he had managed to put down a pair of porterhouse steaks and about half a pound of rice and other vegetables.

"Oh my God," Maggie whispered to Noah, "where does he put it all?"

Marco overheard and came to Noah's rescue. "You've heard of somebody having a hollow leg? Well, Neil is hollow all the way from the neck down. We figure he must be, the way he shoves food in and never gains any weight."

Maggie and Julie looked at each other, and the third woman, Carol, said what they were thinking. "If only I could catch whatever it is he's got that lets him do that. All I've gotta do is look at a steak wrong and I gain five pounds."

EIGHTEEN

Chung brought lunch up to her, and she accepted it without a word. She left the door open as she carried it to the table, and he took it as an invitation to come inside. Sarah paid him no attention as he pulled out a chair and sat down, but she only concentrated on eating the noodle soup.

"I received a telephone call," Chung said. "Xiao will arrive here this evening, before dark. He wishes to meet with you as soon as he arrives, but his interrogation will begin in the morning."

Sarah glanced at him and realized that he truly did look sad, but she couldn't allow herself to feel any sympathy. He was still the enemy, no matter how concerned he might seem to be for her health and well-being.

"Sarah, you can stop him. If you would only tell me something, something I can use to stall him off…"

"Give it up, Chung," she said. "I'm not going to cooperate, not with you, not with him, not with anybody. He'll have to do his worst."

Chung lowered his eyes to the floor for a moment, then looked back up at her. "That is exactly what I fear."

He got up and left the room, and Sarah continued eating. With no idea what might be coming, she felt that she needed to keep up her strength the best she could. Noodle soup might not be the most delicious meal she'd ever eaten, but it was definitely filling. She could only hope that dinner would be more appetizing, and more plentiful.

She spent the afternoon watching television, trying desperately to keep her thoughts away from Xiao and the things he might do. Chung had said that he was known for inflicting pain without doing harm, but Sarah didn't know enough about torture to understand how that might work. The problem with a lack of knowledge was that it tended to let loose the imagination, and hers just happened to be a vivid one.

Dinner was brought to her by one of the servers from the dining room, and she wondered if Chung had decided to avoid her so that he wouldn't be so upset when the torture began. It crossed her mind that Noah would say he was being logical, but that only made her even more depressed. She had been a prisoner for a week, now, and a part of her had given up hoping that he would come for her.

No! I can't think like that. He'll come, he always does.

The only question that remained was whether she would be alive and intact when he did, but she had reached the point of considering suicide as an alternative to torture. She thought about jumping from the window, but she was pretty sure it wasn't high enough to do more than break a few bones, and that would not be enough. She considered trying to hang herself with a bedsheet, but there was nothing on the ceiling or walls that she could find to hang from. She hadn't been provided a razor, and the flatware they used was only plastic, so cutting her wrists or throat was out, as well.

Her only hope, she had concluded, was to attack one of the guards and pray that he killed her in self-defense. She had begun watching out the window several times a day, paying close attention to the lone guard who always worked her side of the house. Every so often, the path he walked would bring him to just under her window. She began to think about jumping out onto one of them. If she could make enough of an impact, surely the man would turn and shoot her before he could think.

The server returned and took the tray away, but there was another knock on the door a moment later. She opened it to find Chung standing there with another man, a man who was considerably older and wore the look of someone who was accustomed to being obeyed.

"Sarah, this is Xiao," Chung said. The look on his face was one of resignation.

Xiao stepped into the room and looked her over, walking all the way around her as he examined her from head to toe. Sarah steeled herself against the feeling that she was being undressed in his mind, and force herself to put on a smile.

"Mr. Xiao," she said. "I've heard so many wonderful things about you."

Xiao looked up at her, his eyes suddenly wide. "Go and sit down," he said, pointing at the chair she used when she was eating. She looked at him for a moment, then went and sat down in the chair. Mr. Xiao followed her and sat in the other chair, just as Chung had been doing.

"So you are the driver for Camelot," he said, more of a statement than a question. "Tell me about him."

Sarah stared into his face, but said nothing. Xiao looked from her to Chung and back.

"I have no interest in you, young woman," Xiao said. "I wish to know about Camelot. You will tell me what you know of him, now."

Sarah raised her chin. "No," she said, "I will not."

Xiao struck so quickly that she didn't even see him move, but his hand came across her cheek so hard that it threw her and the chair to the floor. Her head was reeling and she saw stars, and it took her a moment to realize what had happened. Blinking back tears, she rolled off of the chair and onto her back.

When she looked up, Xiao was looking down at her. "I will tell you this again," he said. "You will tell me what you know of Camelot, and you will tell me now."

Slowly, Sarah got onto her hands and knees, then pushed the chair back upright. She leaned on it, still somewhat dizzy from the blow, and got to her feet before sitting in the chair again. She looked at Xiao and steeled herself for whatever might come next.

"I will not," she said.

Xiao stared into her eyes for a moment, then leaned forward. He reached a hand toward her, and she flinched backward, but he moved slowly until his hand rested on the side of her face, just where he had struck her. He gently caressed her face for a moment, but then, with the speed of a striking snake, he twisted his hand and drove his two middle fingers down into the flesh between her shoulder and her neck, digging in behind her collarbone.

She screamed. The pain was absolutely incredible—she never would have believed that anything could be like that. He dug in even deeper, and she wondered if he was going to rip her collarbone completely out. She reached up and grabbed his wrist, trying to push his hand away, but the man was incredibly strong.

It ended suddenly. He yanked his hand back and leaned back in his chair to watch her face. Sarah was crying, sobbing aloud at the agony she had just felt, but she forced herself to sit up straight and look him in the eye again.

"Young woman," Xiao said, "you have been shown great patience until now. It is unfortunate for you, however, that my superiors insist that you tell me what we need to know. The simple tests I just used show me that you do not have sufficient tolerance for pain to resist me for long. Tomorrow, if you still refuse to answer my questions, I will show you pain a thousand times greater that what you have felt tonight. Think of this, as you try to sleep tonight."

He rose from the chair and turned away, walking directly out the door. Chung was standing just inside it, simply looking at Sarah, and she could see the tears trying to overflow from his eyes.

The forbidden sympathy came without warning. She looked up at him and forced a smile onto her face. "It isn't your fault, Chung," she said. "Go on, now. I need to try to relax for a while, and I can't do that with you watching me."

He stood there for another minute, then turned and walked away. He pulled the door closed behind him.

There was no way she would be able to resist Xiao's tactics, she knew. If he managed to begin his tortures, she would be broken within hours, at most. The thought of betraying Noah and Allison was simply abhorrent to her, and so she decided it was time to take action.

She got up from the chair and walked over to look out the window. As always, the single guard was pacing along the side of the house, and she waited until he had made it all the way to one end before she raised the window as quietly as she could. It wasn't large, but fortunately she wasn't either. When the guard turned and started walking back the other way, she stood back just enough to keep from drawing his attention to the window and waited until he would be just underneath.

She lunged headfirst, and her timing was perfect. She landed on the guard's back and instinctively wrapped an arm around his throat, letting her weight drag them both to the ground. Her momentum, however, was still angular as she fell, and her body swung around as if his neck was a pivot pole. The grisly *snap* came as they hit the ground, and the rattle of exhalation shocked her as she realized that she had broken his neck.

The man was dead, and for at least a moment, no one was aware that she was outside. She grabbed the AK-74 he had been caring and quickly made sure that its selector was set to auto, then threw her back against the house.

There were additional single guards on each side of the house, and she didn't even entertain the notion of trying to fight her way out. She had picked up the rifle instinctively, but had no intention of deliberately engaging any of the guards; all suicidal thoughts had gone out of her mind at the moment she realized the guard was dead. The tree line was less than 100 feet away, and she sprinted forward immediately.

Just before she reached it, there was a shout from behind her. The burst of adrenaline that hit her at that moment thrust her forward even faster, and when shots rang out a moment later, she could hear them thudding into the trees behind and around her.

She'd been seen, which meant the rest of the guards would be coming for her. Her chances of escape had dropped to almost zero, she knew, but she wasn't going to give up without a fight. She dropped into a small ravine and turned to face back the way she had come, the rifle steadied on the bank as she watched for the guards to enter the trees searching for her.

One of them came running in, charging like an enraged bull elephant, and her squeeze of the trigger sent three rounds into the center of his chest. He was dead before he hit the ground, and the next man to come running into the woods suddenly slowed, but not quite soon enough. Sarah got her sight lined up on him and squeezed off another three round burst. Two of those rounds missed him completely, but the third entered his right eye and blew most of his brain out the back of his skull.

Through the gaps in the trees, she could see that there were quite a few more soldiers approaching the tree line, but they were staying low and she couldn't draw a bead on one of them. There was no real hope that she could escape, she knew, and suddenly the terrible weight of impending torture and the fear of her own betrayal of those she cared about was too much for her.

She slid down into the natural ditch of the ravine and put the butt of the rifle on the ground between her feet, while she leaned her forehead against its muzzle. She had her thumb resting on the trigger as she whispered a silent goodbye to Noah, to Neil and to her father, who didn't even know she was alive.

She steeled herself to press the trigger, and everything went dark.

* * * * *

Hong Kong International Airport is on a small offshoot of Lantau Island, a neighbor to Hong Kong Island. The mainland is reached by a highway that spans more than a dozen miles, and hops two other islands on the way. There is no direct bridge to Hong

Kong Island, so it is necessary to drive almost 20 miles around and through the mainland in order to reach that portion of the city.

Team Camelot arrived at Hong Kong International at just after seven PM local time. The concern about being boarded turned out to be baseless, and they were able to leave the plane and walk into the customs line of the terminal with no problem. That line, however, turned out to be quite long because there was no special lane for private flights and two jumbo jets had landed just before they did. It was well after eight by the time they made it to the declaration desk.

When they finally got done with customs, Neil spotted a man holding a sign that said "Ross Duncan," and pointed him out to Noah. The man smiled as they approached, held out a hand and said, "Mr. Duncan? I'm Peter McDermott. Welcome to Hong Kong."

"Thanks, it's great to be here," Noah replied. "Got someplace lined up for us?"

"Yeah, and I hope you don't mind," McDermott said, "I'm putting you at the Island Resort, over on Hong Kong Island." He was leading them out of the terminal as he spoke, but the walk to his car took almost fifteen minutes, itself. Once they were inside, he turned to Noah and became more official.

"Camelot," he said, "it's an honor to meet you. Heard an awful lot about you over the last year or so. I understand your situation, and I'm ready to provide anything you need, up to and including combat personnel."

"Really? How is that?"

"It's part of my cover. Officially, I'm the owner and manager of McDermott Corporate Security Company. We provide security to quite a few American-based businesses that have big offices over here. Most of my people are regular security guards, but I've got about two dozen that I don't keep assigned to any one job, and every one of them was special forces before I got 'em. They're all cleared, and I'd trust any one of them with my life or my wife."

Noah nodded. "That's good," he said. "You were briefed on where I'm headed? The Tung Li Estate?"

"Yep. I don't know the place personally, but I've heard of it. The resort where I'm stashing you is only about four miles away, but it'll take eight miles of crooked road to get you there."

"Okay, what about weapons and vehicles? I want to get out there tonight and do a full recon."

"Well, if you want to go in stealthy, I've got just the thing for you. Ever heard of the Zero Motorcycle?"

"Electric motorcycles," Neil said from the backseat. "Pretty awesome, from what I've read."

"They are indeed," McDermott said. "And I've got eight of them. We use them occasionally for patrolling construction sites, but they're all free at the moment, and fully charged. Mine are the DS models, good for riding on the road, or off the road, and the nice thing about them is that they are just about silent. That sound like it would work for you?"

"Yes," Noah said, nodding. "I'll need three of them."

"You got it," McDermott said. He took out a cell phone and placed a call, telling someone to load three of the motorcycles into a truck and deliver them to the resort along with "that care package I put together." When he got off the phone, he turned to Noah. "The care package you heard me mention is some weapons and equipment that we have on hand, stuff I think you might need. I got you set up with three Glock forties, couple extra mags for each and spare ammunition, plus three China South QCW-05 submachine guns. Don't let the fact that they're made in China throw you, these are some dandy little weapons. Fifty-round box magazine, sound-suppressed so it barely makes any noise at all, and accurate up to fifty meters with the silencer in place. If there's a better gun for a nighttime stealth assault, I've never seen it."

"Sounds good so far," Noah said. "What about surveillance gear? How are you fixed for that?"

"In the care package," McDermott said. "Three Armasight PVS7 goggles. Pure starlight vision, crystal-clear. Put them on in a pitch-black room and it suddenly looks like daylight, only green."

Noah glanced over his shoulder at Marco, who grinned. He turned back to McDermott. "Peter, it sounds like you've got us pretty well set up. Let's get to the resort, and we'll do our recon tonight. By morning, I should be able to have a plan in place."

"Sounds like a winner to me," McDermott said. "My guys will be delighted if you can figure a way to include them in this thing. We've got an old factory building on the mainland that we use for training and practice, but they've been itching for some actual action for a long time, now." He looked over at Noah and winked. "These boys are some of the best I've ever seen at what they do, and I used to train guys like them, back in the day. What I would've given for a class made up of these guys!"

"Then make sure they're ready," Noah said. "When I go in, it's going to be fast and hard, and I'll take all the help I can get."

NINETEEN

Dear God, my head hurts, Sarah thought, and then it dawned on her that she shouldn't be thinking anything at all. She carefully opened her eyes and saw that she was back in her room, and a quick but gentle hand on her head revealed a knot the size of a small egg.

"So you're awake," she heard, and looked to her right to see Chung sitting on a chair beside the bed. "You managed to give me quite a fright, Sarah. Mr. Xiao was impressed that you got so far, and even more so that you were actually attempting to end your life when he found you. The knot on your head was a gift from him, but at least it kept you alive."

"I should've done it sooner," Sarah mumbled. "For just a moment, I thought I could escape, but I should've known better. I should've shot myself as soon as I got the gun."

"Considering Xiao's anger," Chung said softly, "I could almost wish you had, but there is that part of me that is glad you did not. I do not want you to die."

"Do you think I give a damn what you want?" Sarah asked angrily. "Chung, for all your trying to be Mr. Nice Guy, you're still

185

the enemy. Do you honestly think I could ever forget that? You're keeping me a prisoner, and while I admit that I find you charming, had I gotten you in my sights when I had that gun, you'd be dead. Do you understand that?"

"Of course I do," he replied. "That is your duty as a captive, and as an enemy combatant. If you can escape, you must do so, and with no concern for the lives of those who might stand in your way. However, it should be obvious now that you cannot escape, nor will you be permitted the avenue of suicide. Xiao will begin his interrogation in the morning, and there is no doubt that you will eventually give him all of the information he wants."

He leaned forward and gently put a hand on Sarah's arm. "I am going to tell you something, and I hope you can understand it. I have asked for and received permission to keep you in my custody once he is done with you. There will be no more interrogations after that, and I will do everything in my power to see that you're comfortable. You will have the best medical care and—"

Sarah yanked her arm away from his touch and glared at him. "What, you think you're going to keep me as a pet? Don't you get it? If he breaks me, I don't want to live! I wouldn't want to live here with you, or anywhere else!" Tears began streaming down her face, but they were tears of rage rather than grief. "You know, when I was first captured, I thought I was being sold into the sex trade. If I manage to survive what your Grand Inquisitor is going to do to me, then staying here with you would be no different than that. I'd be broken, and you'd be able to do anything you wanted with me. Dear God, I'd probably end up thinking I was in love with you."

"Would that be such a bad thing? Your own life is over; there will be no going back once Xiao is done with you. Would it be so bad to be my lover, in that case?"

Sarah shook her head, amazed that he could be so stupid. "And I actually thought you were a likable guy," she said. "You want the truth? That would be a fate worse than death. Now, do me one last favor and get out of my sight."

She rolled over and closed her eyes, but it was almost a minute before she heard him rise and walk out the door. When she was sure he was gone, she got up off the bed and changed into the nightgown, then crawled in under the covers.

I tried, she thought. *I really tried, but at least I took a few of the bastards out along the way.*

* * * * *

The rest of the drive was almost like a tour, with McDermott pointing out different landmarks and features of the city. By the time they crossed the last bridge onto Hong Kong Island, Neil was looking out the window and making occasional whispered comments about McDermott's talkativeness. Marco elbowed him in the ribs a couple of times, but even he was rolling his eyes periodically.

When they got to the resort, McDermott took them inside and got them checked in, then waited while they carried their bags up to their room. When they came back down, he drove them down the street a short distance to where a Mercedes delivery van was waiting for them, with McDermott Corporate Security on the side. The logo for the company showed a car, a helicopter and a small airplane all emblazoned onto a shield.

The driver had already unloaded the motorcycles, and the weapons and other gear were packed into saddlebags mounted on them. The two men showed them how to control the night vision gear, gave them a quick explanation of the little machine guns, and then drove away.

Each of the motorcycles had a helmet sitting on it, and Noah said it was time to find out if Sarah was actually present at the estate. They put on the helmets and climbed onto the motorcycles, turned the keys, and cranked the throttles.

With 70 horsepower and 116 foot-pounds of torque, the bikes moved out smoothly and quickly. Neil, who had only ridden a motorcycle a few times when he was younger, let out a squeal of delight as he gave it power to catch up to Noah and Marco. They were so quiet that even with the helmets on, they could talk to one another as they rode.

Noah had programmed in the coordinates of the estate to the GPS on his iPhone, and it was talking to him through the Bluetooth earpiece. It took almost 15 minutes to reach Shek O Road, but then only another ten minutes until they found the section of Hong Kong Trail that led to the estate's driveway. Noah rode past the trail for a short distance, then turned off the road into the forest. It only took a couple of minutes to find a good spot to hide the motorcycles, and then they opened the saddlebags.

With the night vision goggles strapped onto their heads, the darkness in the forest became a bright green world, and the built-in infrared caused even the smallest rodent to show up vividly. With the handguns tucked into their belts and the machine guns hanging on their straps, they began walking toward the estate.

Because the forest was so thick and the terrain was so rough, it took almost an hour to reach a point where they could actually see the house. Moving as quietly as they could, they got to within 500 feet undetected, though they had seen three different soldiers who were apparently on guard duty. Two of them had been lounging in the woods against trees, smoking cigarettes and paying little attention to anything around them. Team Camelot had passed completely undetected within thirty feet of one of them.

The third one was standing watch close to the house, and seemed to be a bit more attentive. Rather than simply staring into the darkness, he was keeping his eyes moving, using his peripheral vision to try to see as much as he possibly could.

Using hand signals, Noah told the others that they were going to move laterally. He turned off to the left and they followed, slowly working their way completely around the house while staying within the forest. It took the better part of an hour to get around to the other side of the estate, and they had seen one guard on duty on each side of the house itself.

Suddenly, Noah held up a hand to halt them. Using two fingers on his left hand, he pointed at his goggles and then at the house, telling the other two to look closely.

There was a light on in a second-floor room, and the flickering indicated that a television might be playing. They froze where they were and watched for several minutes, and it paid off. The flickering suddenly stopped as the television was turned off, and they caught a glimpse of Sarah, with her short blonde hair, as she walked across the room past the window.

"That's her," Neil whispered. "That was Sarah, she's alive."

"Yes," Noah said. "She's alive."

Marco shrugged his shoulders. "She's alive," he said just as softly, "watching TV in what looks like a pretty nice little room. Do you reckon they already broke her? Kinda looks like she's being pampered just a bit, doesn't it?"

Noah shook his head. "I don't think so," he said. "I know Sarah, and I know her type of person. If she had broken and given up, she wouldn't be watching television. I suspect they've been trying the friendly approach. Sometimes they put you in a halfway-comfortable position, and they bring in somebody they think can charm you into cooperation. This looks like that kind of setting, to me."

"It doesn't matter," Neil whispered furiously. "We know she's there, let's go get her!"

Noah shook his head. "There's only three of us, against we don't know how many of them. We'll be back tomorrow night, after we've gotten some rest and a little more intel, and worked out a plan to get her out of here safely."

Neil shook his head. "Damn, this sucks! How do we know she'll still be here tomorrow night?"

"Did you see how relaxed the guards were? They're not anticipating any kind of rescue attempt, they don't expect anyone on our end to even know she's alive. As far as they are concerned, they have her and they've got all the time in the world. There's no reason to move her anywhere else, so they'll keep her here. Until they're done with her, anyway, and I'm pretty sure they're not."

They continued their circuit around the house, and then made their way back to the motorcycles. They repacked their gear into the saddlebags, pushed the bikes out onto the road and turned them on. Thirty minutes later they were back at the resort, and trying to figure out how to carry the weapons and goggles up into their room.

"Hey, check this out," Marco said. He stuck a hand down between the saddlebag and the frame, and suddenly the saddlebag lifted off. "I noticed that the lids have a handle on them. Wouldn't be no point in that if they don't come off, right? There's a little spring hook down inside there, you just push it and then lift."

Noah and Neil did as he instructed, and then the three of them walked into the resort carrying their saddlebags and helmets. Fortunately, there were enough motorcycles on the road around Hong Kong that no one paid them a lot of attention as they stepped into the elevator. Noah managed to punch the button for the fourth floor, and the doors closed.

When they opened again, the three of them made their way down the hall to their room. Noah had to set one of the saddlebags down to get the keycard out of his pocket, but then the door was open and they carried everything inside. When the door closed behind them, Noah took out his iPhone and tapped the icon that would call the headquarters number.

"Brigadoon Investments, how can I direct your call?"

"I like to speak to Mrs. Peabody, please," Noah said.

"Just one moment, please." He was put on hold and listened to the generic music for a moment, and then Allison came on the line.

"This is Mrs. Peabody," she said, sounding like a much older lady. "Can I help you?"

"Is that a buzzing noise I hear?" Noah asked. That was the code to tell Allison to call him back on the encrypted lines. The system used 2,048-bit encryption, and the iPhone was equipped to unscramble it. All Allison had to do was use another encrypted phone that was kept in her office. He was fully aware that the call would probably be monitored by the Chinese government, but he was counting on the encryption being strong enough to keep them from hearing anything they could use or cracking it long enough for him to accomplish what he was out to do. The way he understood it, all a monitoring station would hear would be noises that sounded like computerized data transmission. It just wouldn't make any sense if they tried to decode it as data, and if they started running decryption algorithms on it, it should take weeks or months to break the actual code itself. Noah didn't plan on being in China more than another thirty-six hours, at most.

"Oh, yes, it sounds terrible, doesn't it? Let me try calling you back, okay?"

Noah ended the call and simply sat on the bed and waited. A moment later, the phone rang and he answered.

"Camelot," he said.

"Report, Camelot," Allison said. "We are secure."

"The three of us went out for a surveillance run tonight, and I can confirm that Sarah is present at the estate. I'm planning to go back tomorrow night and get her out, but I'd like to know anything else you can find for me about that location. Considering what it's used for, it surely has to have shown up in our intelligence files at some point."

"I'll call Alex, see if he can find anything on it. How did the situation look to you?"

"The estate is fairly large, probably about sixty-five or seventy acres, and most of it is densely wooded. With night vision gear, we were able to see and bypass the patrols in the forest, but there are also guards at the house itself. According to Mr. Lom, the total cadre of the place is probably about 30 to 35 people, all of them Chinese Army. Two dozen of them serve as the guards, but I'm sure the rest are capable soldiers, as well."

"They would be if it was one of our operations," Allison said. "Safer to assume they know how to behave like soldiers than not. What time is it there?"

"Almost midnight, here. We're going to hit the beds and get some sleep, then get up in the morning and try to plan this out."

"All right, good. You get some rest, and I'll rattle the trees. I'll call you again in six hours, to let you know what I find out."

The phone was dead. Noah dug out his charger and plugged it in, then stripped quickly to his underwear and crawled into one of the three queen-size beds. Neil was already asleep, lying atop the covers on his bed, and Marco was sitting on the third one taking off his boots and socks. By the time he peeled off his shirt, Noah was sound asleep.

Noah awoke three minutes before his phone rang and snatched it up on the first. He saw the icon indicating the encrypted line, and said, "Camelot."

"It's me," Allison said. "Okay, according to Alex Kuiper, the Tung Li Estate is considered to be one of the weakest safe houses in China. You're right about the Army, but it turns out CIA has been inside the place on three separate occasions. I'm going to email you a simple layout of the inside, but he warned me that it's three years old. There may have been a few changes, so take that into consideration."

"No problem," Noah said. "What else?"

"There isn't much else. The place is almost completely hidden from any vantage point, so you have to get into the forest in order to even get a good look at it. Have you talked to Peter McDermott yet?"

"Yes, he picked us up at the airport and brought us to the hotel. He supplied us with some electric motorcycles that we used to get out to the place, along with weapons and night vision gear. He also offered to lend us some backup, a squad or so of former special forces that work for him. I'm planning to take him up on that."

"Good. I want Sarah back, but I don't want to lose you in the process. McDermott's no fool, he'll know to put them under your command."

"That's going to be the plan, then," Noah said. "We'll go in tonight, probably around ten. It'll be plenty dark enough, and we should be able to hit them hard and fast."

"All right. I'll be in the office, that's tomorrow for me. I want your report as soon as you've got her and gotten safely away from that place."

"You'll get it," he said, and then the line went dead. Noah looked around at the other two men, saw that they were still sleeping and pulled the covers back up over himself. He had learned long ago to always take the opportunity to rest whenever it was available.

TWENTY

Sarah hadn't expected to be able to sleep, but between her depression and the knowledge that whatever was coming was inevitable, she had finally drifted off around two in the morning. Her sleep was fitful, as she dreamed over and over about being tied down to a table while an ugly man cut pieces of her away.

Suddenly, the dream seemed even more vivid, as hands grabbed her arms and legs, but then her eyes came open and she realized that she wasn't dreaming anymore. Three soldiers had hold of her, and she was being carried out of her room.

"Hey! Hey, put me down, I can freaking walk!" Her protests did no good, as the men continued carrying her along, taking her down the stairs to the main floor, then further down into the basement. She was carried into the same room Chung had removed her from and thrown onto the mat.

The soldiers filed out and the door was shut behind them. She sat up on the mat, tucked her knees up to her chest, and wrapped her arms around them. Her heart was racing, partly from the nightmare and partly from the shock of being dragged physically out of bed, and it was all she could do to force herself to relax.

The room had only one dim light, and she hadn't noticed whether the sun was up yet. There was no way to know if it was morning or still nighttime, but she decided it didn't matter. The point of dragging her there that way was probably to disorient her, and she wasn't going to give Xiao the satisfaction of realizing that it worked.

She lay down on the mat and curled up, putting an arm under her head for a pillow, and tried to go back to sleep, but it wouldn't come. She tried counting seconds to estimate how long she was there, but she kept losing track. After what seemed like a couple of hours, she sat up again and just leaned back against the wall.

She been sitting there for quite some time, trying to imagine what she would be doing if she were back home, when she heard the bolts slide back on the door and it opened. Xiao stood there looking at her, and then he stepped into the room.

"I thought perhaps you could think better down here," he said, "with fewer distractions. Have you considered the wisdom of cooperation?"

"Screw you," Sarah said. "I told you, I'm not going to give you anything."

"Oh, but you certainly will. Your friend Mr. Chung had tried to prevent you from suffering my particular ministrations, but when he was unable to get the answers we want, our superiors decided it was time to let me take over. You see, little Sarah, I have never failed to extract information from the subject. There were some few who held out longer than I expected, but none have ever been able to withstand my talents for long. You simply do not have the pain tolerance capability that you would need, so I do not expect it to be long before you willingly tell me anything I want to know."

Sarah looked up at him, and tried desperately to force herself to stop trembling. For the first time, she admitted to herself that she was terrified, but she was determined not to let this monster see it.

"I guess we'll see," she said, and she mentally cursed herself when she heard her voice crack. *Oh, give yourself a break,* she thought. *After all, they didn't train you in how to resist torture. They probably never figured a driver would ever be in this position.* "Of course, you didn't think I could manage to kill one of your guards with my bare hands, steal his gun and take out a couple more of them, either, did you? I'll guarantee you, I have a lot more surprises in store for you than that."

"Yes, we shall see," Xiao said. He turned and stepped out the door, motioning to someone who was out of sight. Two soldiers came in and took hold of her by the arms, lifted her to her feet and walked her out the door. They turned her to the right and followed Xiao down the hallway to another room. He opened the door, and they marched her inside.

Sarah had heard of torture chambers before, but she had never imagined she would ever see one. There was a table in its center, very much like the one in her dream, and it only took a couple of moments for the soldiers to lift her onto it and begin strapping her down. She tried to fight, but they were simply too strong.

Her wrists were strapped down at her sides, her ankles to the end of the table, and then another strap went around her waist while one more went around her forehead. She could manage to wiggle just the tiniest bit, but other than that she was completely immobile. Xiao stepped up beside the table and looked down at her, and it almost looked like he had an expression of pity on his face.

"I will give you one more chance," he said. "Tell me everything you know about Camelot, and I will release you from these restraints."

"Go to hell," Sarah said through clenched teeth. "I'm not telling you shit!"

"If there is one, I most certainly will." He leaned over her, looking closely into her eyes, then straightened again and turned away for a moment. When he faced her again, he was holding what looked like a scalpel in his hand, and Sarah's nightmare came back in full force. Her eyes flew wide open and her mouth opened for a scream, but her sheer terror kept her from even making a sound.

Xiao reached toward her with the blade and she closed her eyes, waiting for the pain to begin, but all she felt was a tugging sensation. The cotton nightgown she had put on after regaining consciousness the night before was all she was wearing, but it was the work of only a few seconds with the scalpel for him to slice it down the center. He had to pull it up a bit through the strap around her belly, but then he pulled it back down to complete the cut. Two more quick slices at her shoulders, and he was able to pull it completely out from under her.

Sarah lay naked, except for the straps. Xiao looked her over appraisingly, then reached toward her once more. His fingers probed her belly, the way a doctor might do when searching for a mass, and then he suddenly pressed two fingers into her lower abdomen as hard as he could.

Sarah's eyes flew open, and she felt as if he had stabbed her. The pressure of those two fingers at that point on her abdomen felt like—it felt for all the world like when she had ruptured her appendix as a child. The pain was unbearable, and she couldn't keep herself from screaming. It went on and on, and he kept twisting the fingers, digging in deeper and deeper, until she began to sob and retch.

Suddenly it stopped, though the pain went on for several minutes more. Sarah was crying harder than she could ever remember having cried, and it took everything within her to try to get it under control. Even so, she was still trembling with suppressed sobs several minutes later.

"Tell me everything you know about Camelot," Xiao said. Sarah looked at him briefly, then closed her eyes and tried once more to slow her breathing.

She waited, knowing that more pain was coming, but all she felt was his fingers gently stroking her. There was nothing sensual in his touch, even when he let his fingers slide down and over her breast, and they continued down her belly, across the strap and then down the outside of her thigh to her knee.

Then suddenly she was on fire, as he dug his thumb into the tendons just above her kneecap. Somehow, he had struck a nerve so perfectly that it was telling her brain that her lower leg was being ripped away, and the sensation was so intense that she felt a massive wave of nausea. She began to retch again, and he yanked his hand back, but the pain continued. It took almost two minutes for it to subside to the point that she could breathe again, and a part of her mind began trying to tell her that she simply couldn't take anymore.

"Tell me all that you know about Camelot," he said again, and part of her wanted to speak, wanted to tell him that the most important thing he could know about Camelot was that he was Death incarnate. Her mouth tried to open, but she clamped it shut and closed her eyes, refusing to speak.

Once more she felt the fingers trailing along her body, this time moving upward. He was dragging them up her inner thigh, and she expected him to touch her most private place, but he pulled his fingers away and ran them along her side again. They came up onto her belly and up between her breasts, and then one finger was thrust into the hollow of her throat.

This time, it wasn't so much the pain as the fear. The pressure on her windpipe was so great that she began to fear it would collapse, and she had heard stories about people dying in agony with a crushed larynx. The pressure grew, intensified, and she suddenly heard herself begging him to stop.

He released the pressure instantly then gently touched her face. She opened her eyes, blinking furiously to get rid of the tears that had built up behind the lids, and then looked into his face. "Please," she croaked out, "please stop…"

"Of course, of course," he said. "I will stop, and all you have to do is tell me about Camelot."

Sarah's mouth was working, but no sound was coming out. A part of her wanted to answer him, tell him anything he wanted to know if it would make this ordeal come to an end, but another part of her thought of Noah. The Chinese, she had read, could be ruthless. If they ever learned who he was for sure, they would undoubtedly send their own assassins after him. They were afraid of him, that was obvious, and people who would torture like this would do anything to get rid of something they feared.

She clamped her mouth shut and closed her eyes again.

There was no gentle caress, this time. She felt his fingers close on her nipples, and he dug his thumbnails into them until she screamed again. He squeezed and squeezed and continued to squeeze, letting minutes pass by as she screamed and wept, but finally he let go. Ironically, the blood rushing back into them hurt even worse than what he had been doing, and she screamed anew.

He waited, then, until the sobbing died down and she started to get her breath under control, and then he peeled back her eyelids and looked into her eyes. "If you tell me now about Camelot, I can stop. If you do not, you should be aware that it is only ten o'clock in the morning. We have many, many hours left in the day, and I will continue until it is time for me to sleep."

She looked up at him and started to cry again, trying to shake her head from side to side but unable to do so because it was strapped down. "Please…"

"The choice is yours," he said. She closed her eyes again and sobbed, waiting for whatever he would do next. She heard him turn away and couldn't resist peeking, but then she wished she had kept her eyes closed. When he turned back to her, he held what looked like bottle caps in his hand, and he laid a dozen or more of them onto her belly. He held one up for her to see, and she realized that they were small candles, not even a quarter of an inch high inside the metal caps, and then he pulled out a lighter. He lit the first candle, the one he had showed her, and set it on her breastbone. She couldn't see it, but she could smell the burning wick and the wax, as he lit all of the others and set them back onto her skin.

She could guess what was coming. The flame on the wick would melt the wax, and it would get hot. The little metal caps would also grow hot, and that heat would make it to her skin.

She was right. It was only a few minutes later that it began to feel like the flame was directly on her flesh, though she knew it wasn't. She wanted to try to shake them off, but the thought of the hot, molten wax splashing onto her skin forced her to hold still. The heat built up and built up until it was unbearable, and then she screamed again. It wasn't as loud as before, because her voice was giving out.

It took nearly 20 minutes for the little candles to burn out, and she could imagine the burns and blisters on her skin. She had never felt such pain in her life, and even wondered how she had managed not to die of shock while they burned. When they finally went out, she watched him as he picked them up, one at a time, and dropped them into a metal cup.

He looked into her eyes once again. "Tell me everything you know about Camelot," he said.

Sarah closed her eyes and waited for the next agony to come. She didn't wait long; each time he asked the question, an entirely new kind of pain would assault her only moments later.

He picked up something from the shelf behind him, and held it up for her to see. It was a plastic envelope, and it was full of large needles that appeared to be several inches long. Each one had a small pearlescent knob on one end, and she watched as he pulled one out and lowered it toward her body. She couldn't see where he was going with it, but suddenly she felt it. The tip of the needle touched her skin just over her solar plexus, and he began applying pressure slowly. It was just a sting, she thought, not that bad, but then she felt a pop as it broke through the skin and the underlying tissue. The needle's tip touched the nerves of her solar plexus, and her body went into what could only be considered a seizure.

Sarah couldn't feel anything for a moment or two, but then all the sensations came back. He had another needle in his hand, and he jabbed it suddenly into the center of her left nipple. Another went into the right nipple, and then she felt needles being driven into her belly, between her ribs, everywhere he could think to put one. There were at least two dozen of them, and if she rolled her eyes downward she could see many of the little pearl heads. She could feel each and every one, a stinging agony that was multiplied over and over, but then he reached out his hand and brushed along the tops of them all, and it felt like she had 100 tiny chainsaws cutting away just under her skin.

She blacked out, then, and when she regained consciousness, he had removed all of the needles. He was simply standing there, looking down at her face, and then he saw that her eyes were open.

"Tell me all that you know about the man known as Camelot," he said.

"I will," she managed to whisper. "I will..."

Xiao smiled at her and leaned closer to her face. "Tell me about him," he said again.

Sarah tried to nod, but her head was still strapped down. She looked up into his eyes and said, "Camelot—Camelot—he's the most dangerous man alive..."

Xiao scowled at her. "Tell me who he is," he said, "or I will continue."

"Okay, okay," she whispered. "I'll—I'll tell you—he's—he's the man who is going to kill you..." Her voice began to grow louder, more shrill, as all the pain and rage she had felt so far boiled up out of her into the most devastating curse she could imagine. "Camelot—you want to know about Camelot—Camelot is Death, he is Death incarnate, and he—is—coming—for—you!"

Xiao's face contorted for a moment, and she actually hoped that she had pushed him over the edge, that he would simply kill her now and be done with it, but she saw him force himself back under control. He leaned back away from her and looked her over again, then turned around and picked something up. She couldn't see what it was, but he moved down the table toward her feet, and it was all she could do to wait. Her breath was ragged, her heart was racing, and then suddenly there was a white hot fire across the souls of both feet. A second later it came again, and then again, and then it was coming so fast that it seemed like they were being beaten by a machine. The thin metal rod he was using was thick enough not to cut the skin, and stiff enough to bruise the muscles underneath.

Sarah screamed.

TWENTY-ONE

Noah awoke again at just after nine, and looked out the window. The sky was heavily overcast, and there was a heavy feeling in the air. He didn't normally pay a lot of attention to the weather, but something about the darkness, almost like night trying to encroach upon the day, made him want to get up and do something.

"Hey," he said loudly, "wake up. It's morning, though you might not believe it."

Neil, who was still in his clothes from the night before, sat up and looked at him. "Sorry," he said. "Guess I needed the sleep."

"We all did," Marco rumbled. He tossed off his blanket and rolled himself up to a sitting position, then took a look out the window. "Damn, is it an eclipse?"

"No, just clouds." Noah looked around and picked up the remote for the television, turned it on, and found a channel showing a weather report. The weatherman was speaking Chinese, but it was captioned in English, as he explained that the clouds were expected to linger throughout the day, resulting in a thunderstorm in the late afternoon.

Noah looked out the window again, then reached for his phone. He dialed the number McDermott had given him and waited. When it was answered, he asked to speak to McDermott himself, and the man came on the line a moment later.

"Ross Duncan," Noah said. "I'm thinking about stepping up my timetable. You said you had some helpers I could use?"

"Sure do," McDermott said. "How soon you want them?"

"We'll be ready in an hour. Can you have them meet me out front?"

"No problem," came the reply. "Look for our delivery van, the same one we brought the motorcycles in last night."

"Sounds good," Noah said, and then he ended the call. He looked around at Neil and Marco. "Get yourselves awake," he said. "We're going after Sarah this morning."

Marco looked at him, and seemed confused. "In broad daylight?"

"That doesn't look like broad daylight to me," Noah said. "Something about that sky makes me want to get her out of there. I don't want to wait until tonight."

Marco made a sleepy grimace. "You're the boss," he said. "If you want to move that quick, I'm not even gonna worry about a shower. Just going to get all sweaty, anyway, might as well wait till later."

"What about breakfast?" Neil asked.

"There's a McDonald's downstairs," Noah said. "I'm sure they've got something you can eat."

Noah and Marco each hit the bathroom, then got dressed while Neil took his turn. Ten minutes later they walked out the door of the room, saddlebags and helmets in hand. They rode down the elevator and went directly into the McDonald's that was just outside the front door, and Marco watched all their gear while Noah and Neil went to pick up their food.

By the time they finished eating, the truck had arrived and was parked just outside. Noah walked up to it and saw that McDermott himself was driving.

"You sure you want to be in on this?" Noah asked.

"Standard procedure on this type of thing," McDermott said. "I'll drive, and man the truck while y'all do your thing. I took a look at a satellite map this morning, and I got a good idea where to park this rig while I wait. You want to ride with us?"

Noah glanced at the motorcycles, then looked up at the sky again. "I think we should," he said. The three of them walked around to the back door and it swung open, and they climbed inside to find eight men dressed in combat gear and carrying the same submachine guns McDermott had given them.

The door closed, and the truck moved out. Noah walked up to the front and leaned into the cab.

"How close is your parking spot to where the trail crosses the road?"

"Quarter-mile," McDermott said. "The way I got it figured, you'll be able to jump out the back of the truck and move into the woods, then it should be about another half-mile to the estate. By the way, lean back in there and holler for Jonesy."

Noah pulled back and looked around. "Who is Jonesy?"

A young black man sitting just behind the cab raised his hand. "That's me," he said. Noah suddenly noticed that he was wearing a vest with a lot of pockets.

Noah looked back at McDermott. "Jonesy," McDermott said,

"is a very talented young man. All that extra gear he's carrying is to make sure nobody inside can call for help. There's no landline phone into the place, but it has a satellite uplink and there are two cell towers within range, so Jonesy is going to put them out of commission. He's got the neatest little gadgets that will send a signal full of pure rubbish to any cell phone or satellite receiver within half a mile. All he's got to do is hang 'em on a tree and turn them on."

"Glad you brought him along," Noah said. "The last thing we need is for them to get reinforcements."

The ride took about forty minutes, simply because the truck couldn't take all the curves the way the motorcycles could, but finally they pulled up and parked at the spot McDermott had chosen. He and Noah watched in the mirrors and out the windshield for a moment to be sure there was no other traffic coming, and then all of them spilled out the back doors and hurried across the road into the forest. They went far enough in to be out of sight from the road, then stopped.

"Who's your unit commander?" Noah asked, and one of the men stepped forward.

"Davidson," he said. "I run the squad. You tell me what you want us to do, and we'll do it."

Noah reached out and shook his hand. "We're going wide," he said. "There are a few men likely to be scattered around in the forest, and we want to neutralize them as quickly as possible. When we get to the house, you will find one soldier on guard on each side, but there are more inside the building. I want to hit them hard and fast." He pointed at Marco. "He and I will be going inside as soon as possible. The tall skinny kid needs to cover our six when we do, but I wouldn't mind if a couple of your boys follow us in."

Davidson looked around at his men. "Morgan, Lewis," he called out. "You guys shadow these two," he said, indicating Noah and Marco. He looked at Neil. "Do you know how to handle that weapon?" he asked.

Neil looked at the gun in his hands, then looked up. "It's a little different from what I'm used to, but they all work pretty much the same."

Davidson nodded. "Okay, but I get the feeling your boss wants you out of the line of fire as much as possible. When he gets ready to make his move, why don't you hang back with us?"

Neil looked at him and nodded, and they all started moving. Davidson sent four men to move around the front of the property, while he and the rest followed Noah. Noah took them along the same general route he and Marco and Neil had used the night before, and they hadn't gone 200 yards before they spotted the first of the patrol guards.

The man was about 100 yards away, walking nonchalantly through the woods as if there were no possibility of anyone being within a mile of him. Davidson pointed to one of his men, then swept his hand around to point at the guard. The man he had indicated stepped forward silently, dropped to one knee and raised his weapon. The gun made a coughing sound, and the guard dropped like a stone.

They moved up quietly to where the soldier had fallen, and Noah saw that the shot had blown out the back of his skull. The man had died instantly, and hadn't even made a sound. They checked him over and found a radio, a simple walkie-talkie style. Davidson took it and shoved it into a pocket.

"I speak Mandarin," he whispered. "If they call this guy and he doesn't answer, things could get nasty in a hurry."

Noah nodded, and they moved out again. Ten minutes later they found another man on patrol, and he met the same fate as his compatriot. His radio was taken and shoved into another of Davidson's pockets, and they moved on.

Thirty minutes later, they encountered the other group coming toward them. They had also taken out two of the guards, but had not seen any others.

"Maybe they didn't feel the need for so many men on patrol during the day," Noah said. "Now we've got the four men up close to the house to deal with, but we're not going to be able to get that close to them. Jonesy, you got your toys set up yet?"

Jonesy grinned. "Try making a phone call," he said.

"Okay. Then let's get ourselves into position around the building. If we can put a couple of men on each side, hidden in the trees, then we can hit all four of them at once. As soon as they are down—"

Davidson interrupted him. "How about this? Your idea is going to alert whoever's inside, and we don't want to do that until the last possible moment." He turned and motioned for one man to come toward him, a short, thin fellow. "This is Wendell Liu, about as Chinese as anybody they got here except he grew up in Chicago. Those guys aren't dressed much different than we are, so how about if Wendell takes himself a stroll right up to the man we can see from here and puts him down? That'll give you guys a clear field to the house, and then we can move around it and take out one of them at a time. Nice and quiet, nobody the wiser."

"I like it," Noah said.

Davidson reached into a pocket and pulled out one of the

radios, then handed it to Wendell. "Wave it like it's not working," he said. Wendell took it, then moved off to the left a dozen yards before standing up straight and walking toward the house.

The guard by the wall spotted him almost instantly, and Wendell held up the radio and shook it. The guard kept his weapon pointed downward as Wendell approached, but just as Wendell got close enough to be out of sight from either end of the house, the guard appeared to become suspicious. He took a couple of steps toward Wendell and started to raise the muzzle of his weapon, but Wendell was quicker. There was a burst of smoke from his silencer, and the guard fell flat.

Noah, Marco and their two shadows broke into a low run and hurried to the house. Noah and Marco went toward the front, while Wendell and the other two started around the back. Wendell stepped around the corner and fired once, then took off at a jog. The other two men followed him, while Noah leaned out to look around the corner at the front of the house. There was one guard on duty there, as well, and Noah flipped the selector on his gun to single-fire and squeezed the trigger once. The guard dropped, and Noah and Marco stayed close to the wall as they hurried toward the front door.

A moment later, Wendell and the other two men came from the other side and flanked the door. Noah and Marco stood and started up the steps, and that's when they heard the scream. Noah took two more steps and kicked the door, and it flew open. A dozen feet down the hall, two men turned to see what was going on, and Noah's gun coughed twice more. Both of them went down, and then Noah and Marco rushed inside, followed by the other two. Wendell stayed just outside the front door, ready to cover them from the rear if they had missed anyone.

The two men Noah had shot had fallen just in front of an open doorway, and there was sudden shouting from inside that room. Marco hurried past Noah and looked into the room, then fired a couple of quick bursts. The shouting stopped, but there was more noise coming from deeper inside the house. Noah and Marco pushed forward and had almost reached the stairwell leading down when three men suddenly boiled up out of it carrying assault rifles.

Noah and Marco instinctively dropped to their knees and began firing, while the two men behind them fired over their heads. All three of the guards fell instantly, and Marco hurried forward and threw himself flat at the head of the stairs, with his gun aimed down them.

Morgan, one of Davidson's men, ran up the stairs to look for anyone who might have been hiding there, while Lewis stayed with Noah. At that moment, another scream rang out, and this time they could tell that it was coming from the basement. Noah went right over the top of Marco, descending the stairs three at a time. As he got to the bottom, he saw four soldiers come running out of the room where they had apparently been sleeping, because they were holding their rifles by the barrels and still trying to get their shirts on. He flipped the selector to auto and sprayed them with lead. They fell, all of them dead but one, and Noah quickly put him out of his misery.

A man suddenly stepped out of another room, his hands high and empty. Noah raised his weapon but didn't fire, and the man looked him in the eye.

"She's in that room," he said, pointing at a door just behind where he stood. He dropped to his knees and put his hands on his head, as Noah hurried past him. Marco pushed the man down flat on the floor, as three more soldiers ran out of the bunk room. They looked at their comrades lying dead on the floor, looked up at Marco and the two men behind him, and dropped their weapons.

Lewis looked into the bunk room and declared it clear, just as Noah reached the door behind which Sarah was still screaming. He reached out and tried the knob, but it was locked, so he stepped out and kicked it as hard as he could.

The door frame shattered, and the door flew open to reveal Sarah strapped naked to a table. For a brief second, that was all Noah saw, but then a man spun out from behind the door with a pistol in his hand. The gun was aimed directly at Noah's face, the end of the barrel less than four inches from his nose, and the look in the man's eyes was one of glee.

Noah expected the shot to come, but the man simply held the gun pointed at him and stared into his eyes. Noah stood frozen, slowly lowering the muzzle of his gun, keeping his own eyes on those of the man in front of him. He let the submachine gun fall free, hanging from his shoulder by its strap, as he slowly raised his hands.

The man was still looking him directly in the eye, and then he spoke. "You," he said softly. "You are Camelot."

And Sarah screamed again. This time, it wasn't the scream of someone in pain, but a scream of pure rage, a scream of hate and anger and fury, and it was so loud and so shrill that Mr. Xiao instinctively turned his head to look back at her, and that's when Noah swept the gun away from his face with his left hand. The pistol went off, but the bullet sailed past Noah's ear and thudded into the wall behind him. His right hand struck Xiao's elbow and he snatched away the pistol, spinning it instantly to point it back into its owner's face.

Noah grabbed Xiao by his throat and pushed him into the

room, looking at Sarah lying there immobile and exposed, and realized instantly that he was holding the man who was torturing her. Sarah was still screaming, but her eyes were going from his face to Xiao's, and Noah understood instantly. He yanked Xiao around so that Sarah could see him clearly, then looked the man in the eye again.

"Yes," he said. "I am Camelot." He pushed the barrel of the pistol against Xiao's forehead, then, and squeezed the trigger.

TWENTY-TWO

Noah dropped Xiao's lifeless body and hurried to Sarah. It took him only seconds to release all the straps, and then she was sitting up in his arms. She clung to him as she wept, ignoring her own nakedness and the torment she had been going through for over three hours, just holding on to the one rock that was always solid in her world.

Marco looked into the room, then pulled the door shut. He looked down at the man who had surrendered to them and considered putting a bullet through his head, but he had heard what this man had said. He had told Noah precisely where to find Sarah, but whether he thought he was helping or trying to send Noah into a trap, Marco wasn't sure. He'd leave that for Noah to decide.

A moment later, the door opened and Noah stepped out. He was bare to the waist, while Sarah was wearing his shirt. She was having trouble standing, so Noah was supporting her with his left arm while holding his gun with his right.

And then she saw Marco. Days of speculation that he had betrayed her suddenly rushed to the forefront of her mind, and she leapt at him with her fingers curled into claws. Marco's eyes flew wide as he stumbled back from her, and Noah wrapped an arm around her to hold her off him.

"Easy, easy," Noah said. "It wasn't him, Sarah, it wasn't him! I'll tell you all about it later, but it wasn't Marco, he's been risking his life right beside me every day since you were taken, helping me track you down so we could get you back."

Sarah continued to growl and gasp for a few moments, but finally Noah's words got through to her, and she turned to look at him. "You're sure?"

"Yes," he said, "absolutely certain. Marco is part of the team."

Sarah looked at Marco for a moment, then nodded. A second later, she pointed down at the man on the floor. "Is he hurt?" she asked.

"Nope," Marco said.

"He told me where you were," Noah said. He looked at Marco and motioned with his chin for Marco to pull the man to his feet.

"It's Chung," Sarah said. "He tried—he tried to keep me from being tortured…"

Noah looked at Chung, and the Chinaman met his eyes.

"I am Chung," he said. "I was sent here to interrogate Sarah, but I prefer less—egregious methods than others do. I did all I could to prevent this, but it was beyond my control."

"For what it's worth," Noah said, "I appreciate that. Unfortunately, you leave me with a dilemma. This is an unsanctioned mission, so I cannot leave witnesses."

Chung nodded sadly. "I completely understand," he said. "I am only glad that I was able to see you come for her. About the only thing I was able to learn from her about you is that she loves you,

Mr. Camelot. She loves you more than she loves her own life. I have been monitoring what was happening to her, and I can tell you that she endured everything Xiao could do to her, and never revealed anything. Neither of us could break her, by any method."

Noah looked at Chung, and then at Sarah. There were tears in her eyes as she looked at the man who had tried to protect her, because she understood what Noah had said. An unsanctioned mission could be considered an act of war, so witnesses could not be allowed to testify.

Noah turned back to him. "Run," he said.

Chung looked at him in confusion for a moment, then smiled and shook his head. "I would prefer to die as a man," he said. "I will not run from you."

Noah nodded. "That's exactly what I thought you would say," he said. "I have a problem. I can't leave witnesses to testify that Americans did all this, but I don't want to kill you. Any ideas?"

Chung blinked a couple of times, glanced once at Sarah and then stared at Noah. "Ideas? I—I don't know what to say."

"Defect," Sarah said suddenly. "Maybe you'll meet that beautiful woman who can make it worthwhile."

Chung looked at her for a moment, then began to chuckle. He turned back to Noah. "Can you arrange asylum?" he asked. "I hold the rank of Captain in the Ministry of State Security."

Noah looked into his eyes for another few seconds, then said, "Come with me." He half-carried Sarah up the stairs, and was starting toward the front door when Davidson entered.

"Everything under control in here?" the soldier asked.

"Yes," Noah said. He turned and pointed at Chung. "This man is a captain with State Security. He wishes to defect. You guys

217

know how to handle that?"

Davidson looked at Chung and his eyes went wide in recognition. He laughed. "Captain Chung Ho-seng? Hell, yeah, I know how to handle it," he said. "We'll just dump his ass at the embassy. Trust me, they are going to be thrilled to get their hands on him."

"Good, I'll leave it to you," Noah said. He started forward again, but Davidson stopped him.

"You want me to send somebody to get McDermott and the truck to come up here? Doesn't look like this girl can walk very far."

"I can do better than that," Noah said. He handed his gun to Davidson and turned his back to Sarah, crouching down. She looked at him in confusion for a moment, but then she realized what he was doing and put her arms around his neck. He reached back and hooked his hands around her legs, and lifted her up so she was on him piggyback, his long shirt hanging just low enough to cover her.

They moved quickly across the estate and through the trees, and reached McDermott after about twenty minutes. Noah let Sarah slide off him into the truck, then climbed in beside her. The rest of the men piled in, and Neil, who had brought up the rear, squeezed in on the other side of Sarah.

"Hey, little brother," Sarah said to him, her voice rough and hoarse. "You came too?"

Neil rolled his eyes at her. "Do you think I would've let him come without me? We're Team Camelot, remember? We don't leave anybody behind."

McDermott drove directly to the US Embassy, and both he

and Noah escorted Chung inside to ask for asylum. The embassy's intelligence officer, a lieutenant named Darnell, got one look at him and nearly fainted. It seemed that Captain Chung had long been on the list of Chinese officers the CIA wanted to get their hands on.

McDermott shook Noah's hand, then, and drove away from the embassy quickly. It wasn't uncommon for American businessmen to visit the embassy from time to time, and McDermott even had a security contract on the building, but he didn't really want Chinese Intelligence noticing that he had visited it less than an hour after the Tung Li Estate was raided. Thankfully, the overcast sky was getting even darker, so it wasn't likely too many people were paying attention to the traffic in the streets at that moment.

The embassy had a small medical clinic, and Sarah was taken into it to be examined and treated. She was shocked when it turned out that she had no burns. When she told the doctor what Xiao had done with the little candles, he explained that the sensation of burning pain was simply her subconscious expectation, magnifying the heat she was actually feeling into something agonizing.

The needle punctures and the beatings on her feet, however, were very real. Since there was no way to know if the needles had been sterile, the doctor gave her a shot of powerful antibiotics, but her feet would simply need time to recover.

Between McDermott and Darnell, hasty arrangements were made for a passport and other documents for Sarah. They were printed up in a little room in the basement of the embassy, and one of the secretaries found some clothes that would fit her. They came from a suitcase that had been accidentally left behind by a tourist and never been claimed, and it was given to Sarah as well so that she would have luggage. Even with a private plane, there was little doubt that someone would be watching when they boarded; seeing a young woman climb onto the plane with no luggage might set off alarm bells, especially after the massacre at the Tung Li Estate was discovered.

An embassy car drove them back to the resort, where Marco and Neil went up to the room to collect their things. Noah used the time to call the pilot of the plane and tell him to file a flight plan for the Kirtland airfield in Colorado. The flight would require a fueling stop in San Francisco, the pilot told him, but they'd be back home within fourteen hours after taking off.

And then Noah called Allison. The night operator took the message asking for Mrs. Peabody to call him at her earliest convenience, and his phone rang less than two minutes later.

"Camelot," Noah said as he answered the encrypted line. "I've got her."

"About damn time," Allison replied. "Do me a favor, will you? Don't let that girl out of your sight anymore. Give her a hug for me and tell her I'll see her as soon as you guys get home. I'm going back to sleep."

Noah put the phone back into his pocket and looked at Sarah, then turned her face toward his and kissed her gently on the lips. She smiled at him.

"I knew you'd come," she said softly. "I knew you'd find me."

"Yes," he said. "My world isn't right if you're not in it." He reached down and took her hand into his, then glanced at it. It was her left hand, where he had recently put an engagement ring, but she had left it behind when they had departed for the mission in Thailand. "I almost forgot," he said. "I've got something for you." He reached into his pants pocket and fumbled for a moment, then pulled his hand out. He held onto hers as he did so, and then slid the ring onto her finger.

Sarah looked down at it, and tears began to flow down her cheeks. She looked up at him, blinking.

"Allison was keeping it for you, remember? She caught me before I left to come look for you, and told me to put it back on your finger as soon as I could."

Sarah looked back at the ring, then leaned close to Noah and held onto him. The tears that fell needed no words to explain them.

Neil and Marco came back with their bags, and the driver took off for the airport. They had only gone a few blocks when it suddenly became apparent that something was going on. Several intersections were blocked by police and soldiers, and it was only the diplomatic license plates and markings on the car that allowed them to pass through.

The driver called in to the embassy and explained what he was seeing. A moment later, the partition between the driver's compartment and the passenger section slid downward.

"Mr. Duncan?"

"Yes," Noah said.

"I was just informed, Sir, that an army barricade has been erected around your airplane. It seems the Army is looking for some foreign agents, and they are blocking all private aircraft from being boarded. It's been suggested that I bring you back to the embassy immediately."

Noah looked out the window for a moment, staring at one of the roadblocks as they passed it. "If we go back to the embassy," he said, "what avenues are there for getting us out of the country?"

"Not many, I'm afraid," the driver said. "Unfortunately, our embassy doesn't get many large packages. Trying to smuggle all of you out would be just about impossible."

"Then going back to the embassy would be a very bad idea. Just drive around the city for a bit, while I try to figure out what to do."

Sarah was looking up at him, and Noah could see the fear she was holding back. To have gone through all of this only to be trapped in China? Even if they tried to remain in the embassy, sooner or later Chinese sharpshooters would be assigned to try to take them out.

Noah took out his phone and called McDermott. It took a moment for him to come to the phone, and Noah could hear the concern in his voice when he answered.

"Duncan? Bit of a mess, isn't it? I hear tell they've got your plane surrounded. What are you going to do?"

"That's what I'm working on," Noah said. "Listen, I noticed on your logo that you have a helicopter and an airplane on it. Do you actually use aircraft?"

"Well, yeah," McDermott said, "but mostly just for aerial surveillance. Construction sites, stuff like that, we fly over periodically just to make sure nobody's messing with anything. I don't have anything like your Gulfstream."

"What do you have? I'm speaking of an airplane, not a helicopter."

"Not much. I've got a Piper Cub and an old Cessna 195. Ain't neither one of them much good. What have you got in mind?"

"Stealing your Cessna. Where do you keep it?"

"Shek Kong airfield," McDermott said. "It's fueled up and

ready to fly, but you may have trouble getting there. You in the embassy car still?"

"Yes, at the moment. Any suggestions?"

"Hell, yeah! Tell the driver to take you toward the airfield, but to be sure to go through the Tai Lam Tunnel. When he gets into the tunnel, keep his speed down to around eighty KPH, then keep your eyes peeled for my truck. I'll see you there."

The phone went dead, and Noah relayed the instructions to the driver.

TWENTY-THREE

The embassy driver hadn't even made it off Hong Kong Island before the roadblocks began to appear, so it was going to take a little while to make it to the tunnel. Twice, police officers at roadblocks had pretended not to see the diplomatic markings on the car, but the driver was no fool. Whenever they tried to reach for the door handle, he simply stepped on the gas and shot the car forward. No one was going to fire any shots at the car, he knew, because it would create an international incident. The Chinese were great ones for avoiding international incidents.

"Boss," Neil said after a couple of minutes, "any chance you're going to let us in on what you got in mind?"

"I have in mind getting us the hell out of China," Noah said. "They've got us blocked from getting to our regular plane, so we need to find another way out of the country. If we can get into McDermott's Cessna, I'm willing to bet I can fly it under the radar all the way into Vietnam. I'm going to have the Gulfstream take off without us, then divert to Hanoi. The Cessna should have enough range to get us there, and then we can fly on home."

Neil and Marco looked at each other, and Marco shrugged.

Neil turned back to Noah. "Boss? Can you fly a plane?"

Noah nodded his head. "Yep," he said. "My grandfather taught me when I was a kid."

Neil's eyes went wide, but he only nodded. "Oh. Good. That settles that, then."

"Relax, Neil," Noah said. "It's like driving a car, it isn't something you forget. And considering the alternative is being stuck in China for the rest of our lives, which wouldn't be very long, I think it's the best chance we've got." He had his phone in his hand, and held up a finger to tell Neil to wait while he dialed a number. The call was to the pilot of the Gulfstream, and was very short.

"This is Ross Duncan," Noah said. "Under the circumstances, it looks like I'm going to be finding another way home. I think you should go ahead and take off on your flight plan, but if you happen to stop by Hanoi, you might run into some old friends."

"I've always wanted to visit Hanoi," the pilot said. "I suppose it would be okay if I made a short stop over there?"

"That would be absolutely fine," Noah said. "Have a nice flight."

He ended the call and put the phone back into his pocket. "Okay, that part is all set. Now, if McDermott can get us to the plane…"

Marco, who was sitting beside Neil in the rear-facing middle seat, suddenly grinned. "You mean that McDermott?" He pointed out the back window, and Noah turned in his seat to look.

Sure enough, McDermott's truck was right behind the embassy limo. He gave a short wave when he saw Noah looking out the back, then pointed ahead. Noah turned and looked forward, and saw that they were about to enter the two-and-a-half mile long tunnel.

As soon as they were inside the tunnel, McDermott gave the truck its throttle and whipped out to the right, pulling alongside the limo. As soon as it was beside the rear passenger door, a sliding door in the box of the truck opened and Davidson stood there motioning for them to transfer.

"Here we go," Noah said. He opened the passenger door and swung it wide, and Davidson leaned out of the truck and grabbed hold of it to keep the wind from blowing it shut. He looked at Noah, who was climbing out and holding onto the door.

"Fancy meeting you here," he yelled over the echoing sound of vehicles in the tunnel. "This is as close as we can get. Send one of the men over first, to help the girl."

Noah nodded and pointed at Marco, who immediately got to his feet and started climbing out the door. He managed to keep one foot on the doorsill of the limousine while stretching the other leg out to the truck, then grabbed the side of the truck and pulled himself in. As soon as he had done so, he turned and leaned out again.

Noah motioned for Sarah, and she nervously stood and held onto him while reaching out for the hand Marco was extending. She let out a squeal when Noah lifted her free of the car, passing her bodily to Marco, who wrapped an arm around her waist and hauled her inside. He set her on the floor, then leaned back out and yelled for Neil.

Neil, whose legs were the longest part of his body, simply stepped from one vehicle to the other. It took very little assistance from Marco to get him into the truck, and then it was only Noah still on the car. He reached out and grabbed Marco's arm with both hands and kicked off at the same time, leaping from the car into the truck. Davidson slammed the passenger door shut on the car, then closed the door on the truck.

"That's what we do for fun around here," he said with a grin. "Mac says things might get a little lively at the airfield, so we brought you some toys to play with." He pointed at a box on the floor of the truck, and Noah saw three of the little silenced submachine guns.

"Weapons?" Noah asked. "Are we likely to need them?"

"It's possible," Davidson replied. "Shek Kong is used as a military airfield during the week, and not too many people have permission to fly out of it other than on weekends. Because of our security work, we can get away with it, but if their security or any of the soldiers were to see you, things are going to get pretty nasty in a hurry. We operate on the philosophy that it's better to have a gun and not need it than to need it and not have it."

"Yeah," Marco said, "I operate on the same philosophy. Gimme one of those!"

Neil had grabbed the box, and passed one to Marco, then started to hand one to Noah, but he shook his head. "Give it to Sarah," he said. "I've got to get into the plane and get it started, or we'll stand a snowball's chance of getting out of here alive. Speaking of which, do you have the key to the plane?"

Davidson chuckled. "You're talking about an airplane that belongs to a security company, parked at an airport maintained by the Chinese military and patrolled by Hong Kong police. The key is in the ignition switch. Trust me, nobody would bother trying to steal that airplane."

Noah looked at him. "That's exactly what I'm about to do," he said. "How close can you get us?"

"We planned this out," Davidson said. "I'm gonna climb up in the cab with Mac, and when we get to the airfield, he'll pull right up to the plane. We'll get out and move the wheel chocks and unstrap it like we always do, and then Mac will actually start it up. Once you hear the engine running, you wait two minutes and then come out fast. We'll try to have the truck blocking anybody's view, so hopefully you can get into the plane without being seen, but be ready just in case. While you're getting into the plane, Mac will hide in the truck. If the three of you keep your heads down, you look enough like Mac from a distance that nobody will pay much attention as you taxi toward the runway. The tower speaks English, so you shouldn't have any trouble there, just remember to identify the plane as niner-niner-Charlie-Zulu. As soon as you are in the air, I'll climb back in the truck like I always do and drive away. Sometime tomorrow, we'll notice that somebody stole our plane and make a report."

Noah nodded his head again. "That sounds like an excellent plan," he said. "How long before we get there?"

"About five more minutes," Davidson said. "The road into the airport is rough, by the way, so you might want to sit down. I'm going up front now."

He opened a small sliding door and squeeze through into the cab of the truck, then closed it behind him. A couple of minutes later, the ride did indeed become very rough. It lasted another minute or so, and then the truck came to a stop.

It was almost 15 minutes later when they heard the Cessna engine, a seven-cylinder radial, thunder into life. It sputtered and backfired for nearly 30 seconds before it finally settled into a smooth idle. Noah was counting seconds in his head, and when he hit 120, he snatched open the side door and bounded out of the truck.

McDermott smiled as they passed one another, and Noah held the aircraft door open while Sarah, Neil and Marco hurried inside, then climbed in himself and took the right front seat. A headset with microphone was hanging on the control yoke and he put it on. A moment later, Davidson banged on the side of the airplane and waved, then sauntered over to the truck and climbed in behind the wheel.

Noah keyed the microphone. "Tower, this is Cessna niner-niner-Charlie-Zulu, requesting permission for takeoff."

There was a moment of staticky silence, and then a voice came through the headphones. "Niner-niner-Charlie-Zulu, permission granted. You are number three for takeoff, you may taxi to position."

"Niner-niner-Charlie-Zulu, Roger," Noah said. He grasped the throttle and eased it forward slowly, and the airplane began to roll. Using the tail wheel that was connected to the rudder, he steered the airplane across the tarmac and lined it up behind an army airplane and one that belonged to the Hong Kong Aviation Club. The military plane suddenly powered up and started rolling forward, and the club aircraft moved into the next takeoff position.

As soon as the military plane was in the air, the club plane powered up. Noah gave the Cessna throttle again, and swung the plane around to face into the wind on the runway.

"Niner-niner-Charlie-Zulu," came a voice through the headset, "takeoff clearance is denied. Return to parking and shut down your engine."

Noah glanced quickly over to where he had left McDermott, Davidson and the truck, and saw that the truck was no longer there. There was, however, an army vehicle driving quickly toward the runway, and he knew he had only a second in which to make a decision. He glanced at Sarah in the seat beside him, hunched down so that she couldn't be seen through the windows, and then looked forward to the windscreen.

He shoved the throttle all the way forward and the big Jacobs engine suddenly sounded like a locomotive. He released the brakes and the plane began rolling instantly, then leaned back and yelled, "Unpleasant company coming!"

Neil was sitting right behind him, and he popped up to look through the window. The Army truck coming toward them had several soldiers in it, and some of them were pointing guns toward the airplane. Neil shoved the window open and stuck his gun's muzzle out through it, flipped the switch to auto, and squeezed the trigger.

The only thing he managed to hit was the front grill of the truck, but the radiator obliged him by blowing the hood open on the vehicle. The cloud of steam made it impossible for the driver to see, and most of the soldiers fell off when he slammed on the brakes.

"*YAHOO!*" Neil yelled, and Marco echoed him. Sarah only looked back and stared as the tail of the airplane lifted off first, and then Noah pulled back on the yoke a few seconds later and they were in the air. The airfield was surrounded by trees, and Noah leveled the plane off just a few feet over the tallest ones, then made a slow turn toward the southwest.

"You can sit up now," he said. "All we've got to do is stay low and hope the sky stays overcast. The clouds are dark and low, so as long as I stay under radar, we should be able to make it." He took out his phone and told Siri to show him how to get to Hanoi, then adjusted his course by the compass enough to be pointed in the general direction.

The Cessna 195 was one of the legendary workhorses of aviation. Built between 1947 and 1954, it was still considered a classic and one of the most reliable airplanes ever designed. It could cruise at 170 miles per hour easily, and had a range of 800 miles. With room for a pilot and four passengers, Noah could not have asked for a better aircraft for the purpose he had in mind.

From Hong Kong to Hanoi was about 550 miles, most of it over rugged, mountainous terrain. Noah kept his eyes on the altimeter and the horizon, but the darkening skies made it very difficult to be sure he was going to clear the trees and ridges ahead. Finally, he decided to keep the altimeter at 1800 feet, and watch as closely as he could for anything looming toward them out of the darkness.

"I can't believe we haven't been shot down," Sarah said after they'd flown for a couple of hours in silence. "They've got to figure our stealing this plane is related to what happened out at that safe house. Wouldn't they have military planes out looking for us?"

"I'm sure they do," Noah said. "I'm hoping that thunderstorm just over our heads is going to make it difficult for them to find us, but I'm still trying to stay under any ground-based radar. If one of their military planes gets a lock on us, however, there's probably not much chance we're going to get away. This thing just isn't fast enough or maneuverable enough to outrun bullets or missiles."

Sarah grinned at him. "You don't have to sugarcoat it, Babe," she said. "I'm a big girl, I can take the truth."

Noah shrugged. "Just telling it like it is," he said. "We've got about another hour to the Vietnamese border, and after that we might not have to worry so much. I don't think China wants to start any border wars at the moment."

231

Noah felt her fingers brush his cheek. "Thank you," she said. "I didn't think to say thank you before now, but thank you for coming for me."

Noah looked at her. "My world isn't right without you," he said again.

TWENTY-FOUR

A loud roaring noise suddenly burst onto their senses, and a few seconds later something big and fast flew over their heads. A Russian Sukhoi fighter jet banked to the right, and Noah knew instinctively that it was coming around for the kill.

"They found us," he said, his mind racing. "Okay, listen, we got one shot, and it's got to be a good one. Marco, Neil, get your guns out the windows. When he comes around, he's going to be trying to line up for a kill shot, and I'm going to be doing everything I can to keep him from it. I don't have any way to know when he gets a radar lock, so the minute I think he's lined up on us I'm going to roll this baby over and throw it into a diving reverse. That'll give you a few seconds to fire, and all I want you to do is put as many bullets as possible in front of his plane. Don't try to hit him, just let him fly into them. And if this doesn't work, then I want you to know that I've never felt closer to anyone that I do to you guys."

Sarah and Marco were watching the jet through the left-side windows as it circled wide and came around behind them. "He's coming up behind," Marco said. "Say when, boss, we're ready!"

"Sarah, watch him the best you can and tell me when it looks like he's coming right in behind us."

"He's close," she said, holding onto Noah's seat as he threw the plane into a series of dips and wiggles. "There, I think he's right behind us."

Noah wrenched the yoke to the right and then yanked back on it all at the same time, causing the plane to stand on its right wing tip, and he caught a glimpse of tracer rounds flying past as he did so. "Now!" he shouted, and both Neil and Marco squeezed the triggers on their guns and prayed that their aim was true. They emptied both fifty-round magazines, and then Noah cut the yoke to the left and hauled back again. This time he eased the yoke back to the right, and they saw the jet fly past them once more.

There was a difference, though, as its right engine was trailing black smoke. As they watched, that engine seemed to explode, and then the plane was spiraling toward the ground. Noah followed it just far enough to be sure that it crashed, then checked his compass reading and got back on course for Hanoi.

"Geez, we hit him!" Neil said, his voice full of surprise.

"Maybe," Noah said. "I think it's more likely a few of your bullets got into the path of his induction fans and got sucked in. His left engine did a pretty good job of blowing itself to bits. That's the kind of thing that happens when little pieces of metal end up in places where they're not supposed to be."

"Don't spoil it," Neil said, "we got him! That's the important part, right?"

"Absolutely. In the history books that will unfortunately never be written," he said, "there would be an interesting paragraph about Marco Turin and Neil Blessing, the only men ever to shoot down a supersonic fighter jet with slightly overpowered handguns from inside an antique piston-powered airplane. Remind me to make sure that's included in my report, so you guys can each get a copy of it."

"Why do we need a copy?" Neil asked. "Hell, we know we did it!"

"Exactly," Noah said, "and you're not going to be able to resist telling people, but do you really think anyone's ever going to believe you without documentation?"

There was silence from the backseat for a moment, and then Neil slowly leaned forward and looked closely at Noah. "Boss? I think you just—I think you just made a funny."

Noah blinked and looked at him. "I did?" he asked. "I actually thought I was being pretty serious."

"Whatever," Marco said. "I'm having enough trouble getting my heart to slow back down. If another one of them shows up, we're dead, you know that, right?"

"Forty more minutes to the border," Noah said. "Personally, I'd be saying whatever prayers you can think of."

"I already am," Sarah said. "Our father who art in heaven…"

"Hallowed be thy name," Neil and Marco joined in.

They flew on, with Noah straining his eyes to see anything that might be ahead of them, but it seemed everything that might've gotten in the way was at least low enough to let him fly under his 1800-foot ceiling. He kept glancing at his phone, checking the time, and then Siri startled them all by announcing, "Welcome to the Socialist Republic of Vietnam."

They looked around, but there was no sign of further air pursuit. Sarah leaned over and kissed Noah on the cheek, and Marco grabbed Neil into a hug, then rubbed noogies on his head.

"Ow!" Neil yelled, and he elbowed Marco in the ribs to make him let go. "Stop that, dammit, I don't like that!"

Siri guided Noah to the airport at Hanoi, and he was able to raise a tower operator on radio.

"Hanoi Tower, this is niner-niner-Charlie-Zulu out of Hong Kong," he said. "We've had instrument malfunctions and have gotten lost, we're just lucky we found you. I'm getting low on fuel and request permission to land."

The confused operator came back a moment later. "You get lost in Hong Kong, end up in Hanoi?"

"Yeah, something like that," Noah said. "Look, I really need to put it down. All I want to do is get my compass fixed and buy some fuel, then I can go back home, okay?"

There was another hesitation, but then the operator replied again. "Okay, niner-niner-Charlie-Zulu, you land now. You no leave airport, you buy gas, you take off. Okay?"

"Okay," Noah said, "niner-niner-Charlie-Zulu, Roger that. Turning for final approach now."

Noah lined the airplane up on the runway, and lowered his flaps as he reduced throttle. He came in a little fast, not being sure what the actual stall speed was on the old Cessna, but the runway was long and he had no trouble easing its speed down until the tail wheel settled onto the runway. He turned the plane around and taxied toward the terminal, but then they spotted the Gulfstream sitting off by itself.

Noah punched the speed dial button for the pilot and he answered on the first ring. "This is Duncan," Noah said. "See the little Cessna coming at you? How soon can you get that baby started and ready to fly?"

"Engines are idling," the pilot replied, "and I can be in the air two minutes after you get aboard. Door's open and stairs are down."

Noah shoved the throttle in again and the plane gained a little speed, taking off across the grassy field between the runway and the parking space where the Gulfstream waited for them. The ride was rough and bouncy, and Noah slid the plane to a stop a moment later. The door flew open and Sarah was the first out, followed by Neil, Marco and then Noah, and they all ran for the jet.

A siren started going off, but Noah didn't bother to look behind him. As soon as the others were in the plane, he dived through the hatch and landed on its floor as one of the flight crew pulled the hatch closed and latched it in place.

"Get into a seat and buckle in," he yelled as he ran for the cockpit. Noah clambered into a seat beside Sarah and helped her get buckled before he bothered to fasten his own seatbelt, and then the plane was moving.

"Ladies and gentlemen," came a voice over the loudspeaker, "this is your captain speaking and it looks like we are about to annoy some people. Everyone please hold on, I want to get the hell out of Dodge!"

The plane bumped across the grass onto the runway, and then the engines began to scream their loudest. It seemed like only a few seconds later that the wings bit into the air, and the rumble of the wheels came to an end. They were in the air, and fifteen minutes later the pilot announced that they were over international waters.

According to Noah's iPhone, it was just a little past eight o'clock. He thought over the events of the day and was amazed that so much could happen in such a short time. He glanced around the plane at his team, looking first at Marco, who was staring out the window at the endless sea of clouds below. Neil had leaned his seat back and had his feet propped on the seat facing him, snoring loudly.

He turned and looked at Sarah beside him. She was awake, and watching his face, and smiled when she saw him turn to face her.

"Am I dreaming?" she asked. "I'm afraid I'm going to suddenly wake up and find out that this is all a dream, that I'm still strapped to that table."

Noah looked at her for a moment, then reached over and pulled her face toward him. He kissed her lips gently, then pulled back and looked into her eyes. "Did that feel like a dream?"

"Mmmm, no," she said. "That felt wonderful." She raised her hand to touch his face, and saw the engagement ring on her finger once again. She held it out in front of them and looked at it, then turned her gaze back to him. "Do you regret this?" she asked, wiggling her hand to indicate the ring. "Is it really what you want to do, or are you just trying to give me what you think I need?"

Noah continued to stare into her eyes for a moment, and then he leaned forward and kissed her again. "I asked you to marry me because it's what I want," he said. "I don't want to be without you, and I'm uncomfortable at the thought of you being with some other man. I find that I want to see you smile, and I want to be one of the reasons that you smile. I want to lay beside you when I go to bed, and I want you with me when I just feel like relaxing. If I have to face the world, I want you at my back, and I want you to know that I will always be at yours."

Her eyes were wide, and her breathing was a little bit ragged. Their eyes were locked onto each other, and after a moment, Noah blinked.

"The last few days," he said, "I've been—impatient, I guess, impatient to get you back, impatient to find out whether you were all right, impatient to get my hands on whoever did this to you. I've had to stay busy because I didn't want to be overwhelmed by my own thoughts, but there were a few times when there was nothing else to do but think, so I thought about what I was apparently feeling and the only conclusion I can come to is that I love you. I don't know if it's the same thing you feel, when you say those words, but I know that it fits the only definition of love that I understand, that love exists when the happiness and well-being of one person is essential to the happiness and well-being of another. Well, your happiness, your well-being, they are essential to my own."

Sarah was breathing rapidly now, and Noah put an arm around her and pulled her close to him, kissing her again. "I love you, Sarah," he said.

* * * * *

The plane landed for refueling in San Francisco, and was back in the air in less than an hour, finally touching down at Kirtland at just after one o'clock in the morning. Noah and Sarah held hands as they came down the steps and walked to the Corvette. Marco took charge of their bags, so Noah just fired up the car and headed for home. When they got there, he parked the car and walked around it to open Sarah's door, then surprised her by sweeping her up into his arms and carrying her to the front door.

And then he found that he couldn't unlock the door while holding her, so she took the keys out of his hand and managed to get the door open, laughing happily the whole time. He carried her straight through the living room and into their bedroom, then into the bathroom. When she started to undress, he pushed her hands away and unbuttoned her, then lifted the dress over her head and removed her underclothes, then turned and started water running in the big bathtub.

He tried to pick her up and put her in the bath, but Sarah drew the line at that point. She climbed in and lay back in the hot water, ready to soak all of the pain and horror of the day before away, but Noah wasn't finished. He picked up her favorite bath soap and dipped it in the water, then lathered his hands and began to wash her. She had to sit up a few times to cooperate, and even stand for a moment, but the pure, nonsexual pleasure of letting him wash her body was almost heavenly.

She slid down under the water to get her hair wet, and Noah squirted a tiny bit of shampoo into his hand and worked it in. With her hair so short, it didn't take much, and when he reached for the conditioner she told him not to bother. She opened the drain with her toe and got to her feet in the tub, while Noah wrapped her in one of their big bath towels and rubbed her head down with a smaller one.

And then he picked her up again, ignoring her protests, and carried her to the bed. He took the towel away and laid her down, pulled the covers up over her and kissed her. "I'll be right back," he said, and started stripping his own clothes as he headed back toward the bathroom and a shower.

The shower took Noah only a few moments, and it was less than ten minutes later that he came back to her and slid into bed beside her. Sarah was wide awake, smiling at him as he slid close to her, then put her head on his chest.

"When I was in that house, before things got bad," she said, "Chung tried every way he could to get me to talk about you. I always refused, and so he would change the subject. He asked me things about myself, things I thought were perfectly safe, so we would just chat like that. He tried to flirt with me, but I told him I was engaged and that my fiancé was an absolutely wonderful man who didn't know anything about the kind of work I did, and other silly, girlish things that every girl wants to be able to say about the man she loves."

She rolled over so that she could look up toward his face. "Do you know that he figured me out? I'm not sure how I gave it away, but the day before Xiao got there, he told me that he knew that my fiancé was you. That was the kind of information that could have gotten him a reward of some kind, it would have meant that he could keep control over the situation, but he had stupidly made me a promise that he wouldn't reveal anything I told him about my personal life, and he kept his word. He never told Xiao, and I believe he never told anyone else."

Noah looked at her, his face relaxed. "There was something about him," Noah said. "I think it's that he had a sense of honor, and so that promise was something he simply couldn't break. Sooner or later, he knew that Xiao would figure it out for himself, but he kept his word to you." He stroked her face gently. "I'm glad I didn't kill him."

"Me, too," Sarah said.

She stopped thinking about Chung and her ordeal, then, and reached out to pull herself closer to Noah. She kissed him, and the passion that flared in her was too hot to control.

EPILOGUE

Noah's phone rang a few minutes after eight AM, and he answered it on the second ring. "Hello?"

"It's Allison," she said, even though he knew it from the caller ID. "Hate to wake you so early, but I need you and your team for debriefing at ten. That ought to give you enough time to find some breakfast somewhere."

"Yes, Ma'am," he said, but the line was already dead.

"If that was Allison," Sarah mumbled, "tell her I died."

"She wouldn't care," he said. "She'd bring in a voodoo doctor to turn you into a zombie and put you back in the field. Get up, we've got time for breakfast on the way to debriefing."

She grumbled, but stumbled her way into the bathroom while Noah called Neil and Marco and told them about the debriefing. Neither of them complained, and they all agreed to meet at The Restaurant, the one that was in the area new recruits were brought to and where Noah had eaten his first meal in Neverland, for breakfast.

The food there was always good, and Noah found the place fascinating because of all the excited, curious expressions on new faces. A lot of the people who worked for E & E, even outside the actual assassination teams, were recruited out of prisons, jails and other situations they wanted to put behind them, and Noah found that he could spot them easily in that part of town. They were the ones with the eager expressions, the look of hope that getting a second chance at life can give you.

When breakfast was finished, they drove downtown and into the underground garage of the main office, then rode the elevator up together. Allison's secretary simply waved at them as they walked by, and they found her waiting in the conference room where they expected her.

She wasn't alone, however. Jenny and her team were there, as well, including Randy Mitchell. Randy was sitting in a chair off by himself, his eyes on the floor as Noah, Sarah, Neil and Marco came into the room. The three men froze, but Sarah had never met Randy, and didn't realize that she was looking at the man who had sold her out.

Jenny leapt to her feet and ran to Sarah, throwing her arms around the girl and pulling her into a hug. They had only met a couple of times before, and hadn't really ever spoken, but Noah and the guys had told Sarah on the plane how Jenny had worked with them to try to help get her back. She was happy to return the hug.

"Girl," Jenny said, "you and me have got to go do something together. I have to put up with all these men all the time, and I don't have any real girlfriends to hang out with, or go shopping with or whatever, and I bet you find yourself feeling the same way, am I right?"

Sarah burst out laughing, and agreed. "That sounds like fun," she said, "as long as you promise not to torture any of the salespeople. I heard what you did to those guys in Thailand, that was—um, yeah."

"Oh, don't worry," Jenny said. "I only torture people on the job, not when I'm out having fun. I promise, no bloodshed when we're out having girl time, okay?"

"That sounds great," Sarah said, but then Allison cleared her throat loudly.

"Girls? We have to get down to business, if that's okay with you?"

Jenny returned to her seat while Noah and his team settled in, and then Allison turned to Donald Jefferson.

"Now that Sarah is safely back with us," he began, "we can start to put together the incredible jigsaw puzzle that you two teams have uncovered. We've taken all of the information that you gathered, including statements from the agents you rescued in North Korea, from Randy, here"—he pointed at Mitchell—"as well as pulling in a lot of things from station chiefs and their staffs around the world, and we handed it all to some of our top analytical people. One of them managed to make some sense out of it all." He pushed a button on the desk beside him, and a side door opened.

Molly Hansen, Noah's childhood friend who happened to be a super genius, walked in. She had learned about Noah almost a year earlier, when he had been forced to reveal that he was still alive in order to keep her safe from someone who wanted to use her as leverage against him. She had been working for a government think tank at the time, but Allison had recruited her for the analysis division of E & E, and she was very happy in her new job.

"Molly?" Jefferson said. "Would you care to tell them what you figured out?"

"Sure. Okay, well, it turns out that there definitely is a mole in the CIA, but after analyzing all of the bits and pieces of information we've been able to collect, it's become obvious that he or she seems to have access to information that should be so compartmentalized that it would be nearly impossible to correlate it. For instance, whoever it is managed to get into sealed files at NSA, which is the only place where E & E operatives' past lives are recorded. He got deep enough in to find Randy Mitchell's file, and has been using Randy as a messenger off and on, whenever he's out of the country on a mission. Now, theoretically, the CIA has no way of knowing when one of our operatives is in country or out of country, but this person always seems to know. What this has to mean is that the mole either holds an extremely high rank in the Company, or has somehow managed to tap into sources of information that we can't even identify."

"So," Jefferson went on, "we are taking an extreme step. After carefully interviewing Mr. Mitchell and wringing him dry, Allison, Doctor Parker and I all agree that he was acting under extreme duress. Now, this doesn't mean all is forgiven; there are still a number of things he's going to have to answer for, but right now we desperately need him to continue doing exactly what he's been doing. As far as we can tell, the mole has no idea that Randy has been exposed as one of his puppets, so we are keeping him on active status. Jenny and her boys can handle him, but we felt that Team Camelot needed to be aware of this, just in case one of you runs into him around town. He's now under constant monitoring, and absolutely everything he says or does is being recorded on a micro recorder one of Wally's people came up with. It's actually under the skin behind his left ear, and everything it records is downloaded through a cell phone several times a day."

"So he can't give it away that we are using him to find the mole," Allison said. "What we've got to do is come up with a situation that requires the mole to meet Randy face-to-face. At the moment, we don't have any idea what kind of situation that might be, but we'll be ready to take him into custody the moment it happens."

Sarah had turned her head and was staring at Randy. "So it was you?" she asked. "You're the one who sold me out?"

Randy swallowed, his eyes flicking up to hers for just a second before going back to the floor. "He had my sisters," he said softly. "I'm sorry, I know that doesn't excuse anything, but…"

Sarah stared at him for a moment after he trailed off, her expression cold. "When I was recruited," she said slowly, "I made a vow that I would never let any threat to my father be used against me. We've all had to make that same vow, I know that. That means you had to make it, too." She looked at him in silence for a few more seconds before speaking again. "That doesn't mean I can't understand the pressure you must've been under. I'll be honest and tell you that I hate your guts right now, and if I could've gotten my hands on you a couple of days ago, I would've killed you myself. But now, after hearing all this, I just feel sorry for you. No matter what happens next with you, you have to live with this."

She looked at Alison. "Sorry," she said. "Didn't mean to interrupt, but I had to say that."

Allison only nodded. "Now, as for you," she said. "I know you've been through a horrible ordeal, and I'm ordering Team Camelot to stand down for the next three months. You're going to be seeing Doctor Parker every weekday for a while, for some intense therapy that will help you put this behind you. And just for the record, I can tell you that it works. How do you think I managed to get back in the saddle so quickly after the Andropov raid?"

Sarah started to grimace at the thought of seeing the psychiatrist, but suddenly her face froze. "Andropov," she said. "That's what started this whole mess. When Chung was trying to get me to talk, he told me that the reason they were so concerned about Camelot is because of Nicolaich Andropov. He had so much dirt on so many Chinese officials that he was just about running them like a puppet show, and no matter how they tried, they couldn't get rid of him. When they heard that an American assassin, code-named Camelot, had destroyed his entire operation and got him disavowed by the Russians, then walked right into two different traps to get me back, they figured he must be some kind of Superman. They're scared to death he's going to be coming after some of their people, and that's why they want to know everything they can about him."

Allison slowly began to nod, but then Molly gasped and everyone turned to her.

"That's it," Molly said. "We need to find something that would make the mole willing to risk exposure? She just handed it to us. From what she just said, I can tell you that the most valuable piece of information in the intelligence world today would be a copy of Noah's file. If Mitchell had a copy of it, but refused to turn it over to anyone else, I don't care how security conscious this mole is, that would be a bait he couldn't possibly resist. Let alone what it would be worth in terms of selling it to the Chinese or any other potential enemy of the United States, this is a man or woman who deals in power, and what greater power could there possibly be than to know how to manipulate and use Camelot himself? I'm telling you, this is it."

"I'm not doubting you for a second, young lady," Allison said, "but there is no way in hell I'm giving anyone a copy of Noah's file. My God, do you know how many laws we had to break just to create Noah Wolf? Let alone the fact that that file contains after-action reports on every mission he's undertaken."

"Of course not," Molly said. "You'd never give up the real file, because it contains the genuine, truly damaging information, like about his condition. Heaven help us if that ever got out, but give me a couple of weeks, and I can put together a genuine-looking file that will describe an entirely different person than the Noah Wolf we all know and love. We give that file to Mitchell, and he carries it to the mole." She shook her head, as if having an epiphany. "Oh, it's so perfect! The mole doesn't even have to expose himself directly; he'll do it indirectly the moment he tries to use that information to compromise Noah. I'll build in a way he can contact Noah that will seem undetectable, but it'll actually be a trap that will trace right back to the origin of the contact." She spun around and looked at Neil. "You! Computer boy! I need your help, you game?"

"Yeah," Neil said, his eyes wide. "Of course."

Allison looked at Molly, then turned to Donald Jefferson. "Donald? Opinion?"

"Ms. Hansen has impressed me since we brought her on board," Jefferson said. "I have to say this sounds like the best idea I can imagine any of us coming up with. The question in my mind is whether we dare to let it out of this room. If we even tell one person at the CIA, there's a pretty good chance our target is going to know about it before it ever gets off the ground."

"And that's why we're not telling anyone," Allison said. "That's an order, people. This idea stays completely within this room, which means it doesn't get discussed anywhere else, or with anyone who isn't here right now. Neil, if you're willing to help Molly, I'll let the two of you work out the details. Jenny, you keep an eye on Randy, and Noah—tell you what, we'll start Sarah seeing Doctor Parker week after next. Noah, why don't you take that girl on a vacation somewhere."

Noah looked at her for a moment, then turned and whispered something to Sarah. Sarah's eyes went wide and she sat back suddenly, but then a smile spread across her face and she nodded vigorously.

"How about this," Noah said. "I'm going to run down to the courthouse and get a marriage license. Allison, do you happen to know a JP or a preacher who might be willing to drop whatever he's doing to perform a wedding?" He grinned at Sarah. "I think I'd really prefer to take her on our honeymoon, rather than just a vacation."

GET EXCLUSIVE NOAH WOLF CONTENT

Building a relationship with my readers is the very best thing about writing. I occasionally send newsletters with details on new releases, special offers and other bits of news relating to the John Milton series.

And if you sign up to the mailing list I'll send you all this free stuff:

A copy of the prequel to the Noah Wolf thrillers, The Way of the Wolf. Learn and walk through Noah's horrific childhood, shady upbringing, and what exactly happened to mold him into the cold blooded killer he is today.

A copy of the opening novel in my bestselling Sam Prichard series, The Grave Man. If you liked Noah Wolf, then you'll love Sam!

Just for fun, I'll also throw in the *second* novel in the Sam Prichard series as well, Death Sung Softly. That's a quarter of series absolutely yours and ready to read for free.

Finally, you'll be eligible to enter exclusive giveaways I have for only my readers. The odds of winning are great since only subscribers on my mailing list are eligible to enter. Prizes include Kindles, Amazon gift-cards, Bestselling paperback and ebooks, and much more!

You can get the three novels, eligibility to the giveaways, and exclusive Noah Wolf content, for free, by signing up at

www.davidarcherbooks.com/vip

WHAT'D YOU THINK?

Thank you for reading Black Sheep. I had a blast writing it, and I hope you had fun reading it.

If you enjoyed the book, please consider telling your friends, or posting a short review. Word of mouth is an author's best friend and is much appreciated.

All the best,

David Archer

WANT MORE?

Check out ALL of David Archer's books on his website:
www.davidarcherbooks.com

You can connect with David on Facebook at
www.facebook.com/authordavidarcher